RAGGED MAN

BY

JACK PRIEST

A BOOTLEG BOOK

A BOOTLEG BOOK
Published by
Bootleg Press
2431 NE Halsey, Suite A
Portland, Oregon 97232

Bootleg Books may be purchased for educational, business, or sales promotional use. For information please e-mail, Kelly Irish at: kellyirish@bootlegpress.com.

Second Bootleg Press Trade Paperback Edition.

September 2005

10 9 7 6 5 4 3 2

ISBN: 0974524603

Cover by Compass Graphics

Printed in the United States of America

I knew the Bootleggers.
They were men and a woman
With a different kind of moral code.
Not better, not worse, different.

Though the names in my tale have been changed
And the story is complete fiction,
The Bootleggers were real
And it is to them that I dedicated this book.

So to:
DUB, KEN, DAVE, PETER, JOHN, MIKE, MALCOLM,
STAN, FERRY, MAX, GREG, ROB, GUY, GARY AND ANDREA

And to:
RICARDO and CHARLIE who are no longer with us

This story is for you. I have nothing but
Admiration for you all.

RAGGED MAN

CHAPTER

ONE

RICK GORDON SPUN AROUND THE TURN, saw the problem ahead. He fought the wheel, made a hard left to avoid hitting the overturned Jeep. Then he was into the slide. He cranked the wheel more to the left, into the direction of it. Too far, he felt the rear wheels slide right, spinning the wheel back, he regained control as he hit the dust. Downshifting, gently riding the accelerator, the Toyota Land Cruiser hydroplaned over six inches of fine red bull dust, like driving over baby powder.

He turned back to the right, red dust flying from all four tires, losing traction again, correcting, driving blind, then back on the track, shooting out of the cloud. He made it around the Jeep. Shifting down into third, hitting the brakes, then second, he stopped the car, turned to look back at the Jeep that would race no more.

"I'm okay, get going!" the driver yelled.

Rick flashed a smile, waved, shoved in the clutch, shifted into first and was off.

The track went straight out for the next ten kilometers. Sometimes barely wide enough to give the Toyota room between the desert growth. Sometimes through sharp rocks that ripped into the tires when traveling at speed. Sometimes no road or track at all, nothing but fine red sand till vision's end.

Looking ahead, afraid to blink, he tried to go faster than he knew he should, the thrill of speed overcoming the fear. He floored the Toyota, shifting through the gears a hair before redline. They were sailing, determined to make it one more day.

"Gully coming up, half a click, double caution!" Ann called out, reading from the rally instructions. A click was a kilometer and an explanation mark on the instructions meant caution, two, double caution, meaning that the terrain was even more dangerous, and three of those vertical black lines with periods under them meant extreme caution.

He downshifted into fourth, tapping the brakes as he went into third, standing hard on them for the briefest time as he went into second, left foot flying between clutch and brake pedal, the right keeping the accelerator on the floor. He took his foot off the brakes inches before the front tires hit the gully and the Toyota floated over the depression in the earth. Then he punched the clutch, shifting again into third, then fourth and, as they picked up speed again, fifth.

"Another double, quarter click!" Ann shouted.

"Here we go again!" Rick shouted back as he did it all again, downshifting, braking, releasing, clearing the gully and back up through the gears.

"Perfect, two in a row and both perfect!" Her voice cracked above the roar of the engine. "But you have to do it again in half a click and it's a double."

For the third time in as many minutes Rick found himself downshifting, preparing to glide over another of the many depressions nature had made in the dry desert earth. Minutes ago they were sliding in fine dust six inches deep and now they were traversing dry caked ground, jumping gullies made by long dead waterways and up ahead, more dust.

Double clutching, he slammed the Toyota into second, but he misjudged his timing and jumped on the brakes a fraction of a second late. The front tires hit air as he released the pedal.

"Oh shit, hang on!"

Despite his error in judgment, the front tires cleared the gully, but the rear wheels hit hard, knocking Ann's wind away as Rick fought the wheel.

"Flat," she gasped.

"Yeah." He pulled well off the track.

He stopped the Toyota and they jumped out. Ann reached the rear door first, tossed Rick the tire iron. He started loosening the lug nuts as she pulled one of the spares and the jack out of the back. By the time he had the lug nuts loose, she had the car jacked and was ready with the spare. The operation took less than five minutes. Then they were back on the road.

"Straight out two clicks, no problems, then a sharp left, then a gate," Ann said as he sped through the gears.

"Let's hit it." He accelerated until they were sailing along at a hundred and sixty kilometers per hour.

"Slow down, dust ahead, too slow to be another racer."

"Camels," he said.

"A herd," she said.

Slowing to match the speed of the desert beasts, he punched the horn, scattering the camels.

Passing through the terrified animals, he started to pick up speed, anticipating the sharp left. Then he was downshifting and lightly riding the brakes into the turn. Once through it, he brought the car to a complete stop. Ann jumped out and opened the cattle gate. He drove through and waited for her to close it.

They were racing across vast cattle stations, one of them rumored to be larger than the state of Texas. The owners received no compensation for the use of their lands. All they asked was that the racers close their cattle gates when passing through. No racer liked losing time, but they all did it. They wanted to use the lands again next year.

* * *

They were five days into and halfway through the "Australian Safari" desert raid, sixty-five hundred kilometers of desert off-road racing from Sydney to Darwin, and the hard days and desert nights were taking their toll. Ann knew her husband was dog tired, but she also knew he wouldn't quit. When he started something, he finished it. That's the way he was.

The day was only half over and they were already getting edgy. They had been driving hard since six-thirty in the morning and they had done well. His driving was improving and so was their position. She was looking forward to getting in before dark for a change and thinking of the early start they would get tomorrow, starting with the pros, when she saw the dust cloud. Another cloud of bull dust and they were gaining on it. The closer they got to the lead, the harder it was to pass. The speeds were faster, the drivers were more determined.

This was the part she hated, passing in the dust. The red bull dust in central Australia is one of the finest powders in the world and when a car going a hundred and forty kilometers per hour flies through it, it creates a dust cloud that turns a clear bright day into a red haze, visibility zero.

Passing in the dust is an art. The driver has to try to see the road ahead of the cloud, remember where it goes, then plow into the dust as fast as he's able, pass and hope the road is where it's supposed to be when he gets there. While in the dust, he's driving blind.

"Ann, can you get his numbers?"

"I have 'em." She picked up the mike, shouted into it, "Two-fifteen, two-fifteen, pull over, car behind wanting to pass." The dust cloud slowed and they drove into the red haze, passing the competitor. Ann got a quick glimpse of her as they passed. "It's the girl singer from Japan."

"Up ahead," Rick said.

She looked, saw another cloud of dust and tightened her stomach as Rick tightened his grip on the wheel in anticipation of the possible danger ahead. She knew he hated the passing part just as much as she did.

The track made a thirty degree turn to the right and Ann caught the numbers on the right side of the auto ahead. She grabbed the mike. "One-two-four, one-two-four, pull over, we want to pass." This time the dust cloud didn't slow and give way.

"What's wrong with the son-of-a-bitch? Call him again."

"One-two-four, do you copy? We are on your tail,

wanting to pass. If you don't pull over, we will push."

"His radio's out! Lord, I hate this. Hold on, here we go!" He eased down the accelerator and headed into the dust. "Can you see anything?"

"No! Yes, take it easy. Now!"

Gently, but not gently enough, he nudged the car in front, causing it to squirrel.

"Rick, he knows we're here. Look out! He's losing it! Come on fella, get it back. He's got it Rick. He's pulling over now."

"That was close!" Rick shouted as they passed.

"One more click, then a hard left," she called out. "I'll let you know." Less than a minute later she let him know. "Okay, make your left now." And as they made the turn, she saw tracks heading straight out and she wondered if she'd gotten it right.

They followed the track for two kilometers, then they slammed into a gully that wasn't on the rally instructions. The Land Cruiser bottomed out, hard, smashing the oil filter into the front differential, cracking it and spraying precious engine oil over the undercarriage and the ground. Rick, unaware of the damage, kept driving. The engine blew before he completed another kilometer, leaving him no choice but to pull off the dirt track.

Within seconds they knew they were off course. The gully wasn't on the rally instructions.

"No tracks," Rick said.

"Off course, I messed up. Sorry."

"I should have stopped when we hit. If I'd been checking the gauges, I would've seen the pressure drop."

"What now?" she asked.

"Radio for help."

She heard him using the radio as she checked under the car. After confirming that the oil filter was out of commission, she went to the back and opened the tailgate, but it was no use, they had no spare filter. If only she'd paid better attention to the rally instructions, she thought, as she heard Rick trying to raise someone on the CB.

"Radio's broke," he said.

"Are we in trouble?"

"Not really. We have plenty of oil. We'll drive slow and keep pouring it in as we lose it. We should be back to the course well before the last car goes by. The sweep car will pick us up."

"It's my fault," she said. "If I'd called that last turn right, we wouldn't be here."

"Plenty of blame to go around," he said. "If I'd paid better attention to the gauges, we wouldn't be here either."

"It's more my fault than yours," she said.

"Someone's coming," Rick said.

"Who could it be?" She followed his pointed finger with her eyes, saw a slow moving cloud of dust coming toward them.

"Beats me."

A few minutes later a vintage Jeep stopped alongside the stricken Land Cruiser. An old Aborigine was driving. Sitting next to him was an even older looking woman, obviously not well. The old man had a weathered, wrinkled face that spoke of great sadness. His silver hair, reflecting the sun's glow, gave him an angelic appearance.

"Can we help you?" Rick said.

"Yes you can." The aging Aborigine got out of the open top Jeep, taking every step deliberately, stiffly. "My wife is dying."

"What can we do?" Rick asked.

"Bury us."

"I'd rather go for help."

"I wish you could, but our time has come."

"You said your wife was dying?" Ann said.

"I won't live long after she goes."

"How do you know?" Ann said.

"I know."

"What can we do?" Rick asked again.

"Help make her comfortable."

Ann walked over to the passenger side of the Jeep. The door handle was hot to the touch, but it was more than just the heat that gave her a slight start as she grabbed it.

"Is there anything I can do to help you?" She asked.

The old woman opened her eyes and Ann looked into dark brown pools that spoke of a youth trapped in a decaying body.

"My time has come, child." She smiled, saying it with a thick Australian accent.

"How can you know that?"

"Take my hand." She had a firm grasp that turned Ann's knuckles white, then the old woman's grip went slack.

"She's gone," Ann said, tears welling up. "I don't understand."

"You can bury us off the road. There is no need to mark the graves." The old man grasped Rick's hand, then collapsed. True to his word, he was gone too.

"What's happening?" Ann said.

"I'm not sure, but I feel as if we should do what he asked."

"We don't even know their names," Ann said.

"We have to bury them." Rick kicked up sand as he walked to the rear of the Toyota.

"We can't just dig a hole and cover them with dirt."

"What else can we do?"

"Go and tell someone."

"That would be wrong."

"How do you know?"

"I just know." He started unloading the car, pulling out the spare tires, tool chest and the tent before he came to the shovel.

"We can never tell anybody about this, can we?" she said.

"No, I don't think so." He sighed. "We're through with the Toyota. Get what you think we'll need and put it in the Jeep."

He took twenty paces off the road, far enough that the bodies would be left undisturbed by the rare passing car, and started to dig into the dry, hard ground.

Ann finished unpacking the Toyota, taking out the emergency water, food rations, sleeping bags and their backpacks. She left the tent Rick had unloaded on the ground and put the rest into the back of the Jeep. Then she went over to Rick.

"Let me take a turn at the digging. I don't want you to have a heart attack and die, too." Ann, only a year younger than his forty-eight, was in much better shape. She ate better and did aerobics four or five times a week to keep up her figure.

"I'm going to get some water." He gave up the shovel. "Want some?"

"It's in the Jeep," she said, "and bring the tent when you come back."

"What for?"

"We're going to wrap them in it. We can't just throw dirt on them. It isn't right."

He walked the distance back to the car and Ann saw that he was done in. His heavy breathing told her that two months of swimming twenty laps in the pool every day to get in shape for the race hadn't made up for twenty years of meat, potatoes and prime time television.

She dug steadily for fifteen minutes, till he spelled her, then she dug again. It took two hours before they had a two foot grave. Another two, before they reached four feet, when they called it quits.

Ann lined the grave with their two man tent and smoothed it out so no dirt would touch the bodies. After she was satisfied everything was in order, she motioned for Rick to go and get the old man. He carried him like a child and with Ann's help, they lowered him into the ground.

"I'll go and get the woman," he said.

"No, let me." Ann got up and went to the Jeep, wondering if she'd be able to do it. She had expected the woman's skin to have the clammy feel of death that she'd read about in the Ken Douglas thrillers she liked to read, but it didn't. This old woman seemed to be resting, at peace, not dead.

She slid her arms under the body and carefully lifted her out of the Jeep. She was so light, so old and so comforting. All of Ann's doubts about whether or not they were doing the right thing vanished as she carried her to her final resting place and laid her beside her husband.

"They look so peaceful," she said.

"They do," Rick said.

"Let's do it." She knelt and wrapped the tent around them.

"Yeah." Rick started to cover them with dirt and sand and gradually their wrapped bodies disappeared from view.

"I hope we live up to you," Ann said when he finished and was patting down the top of the grave.

"Why did you say that?"

"I don't know."

"Let's go," he said.

"What about our car?" she asked. "If they find it, they'll find them." She pointed to the fresh mound of dirt.

"With a little oil it'll make it back to the race course. We'll leave it there."

* * *

Three hours later they were driving about twenty kilometers an hour over dry cracked ground, when Rick saw a pack of dingoes loping off in the distance. Although they were bundled well against the cold that comes with the night in the desert, the sight of the animals gave him a chilly, uneasy feeling.

During the race they had seen several of the wild dogs, but these were different, they seemed somehow menacing. Rick felt an electricity in the air and sensed that Ann felt it as well.

"Look!" she said. "They're running along with us."

He picked up the speed to thirty-five K. The wild dogs followed suit. Forty-five K and the dogs sped up as well, getting closer. He could imagine a point up ahead where they would meet. He turned right, away from the intersecting dogs on their left, and wondered how far off the road they were.

Looking back over his shoulder, he saw the dogs turn to follow, but they didn't appear to be gaining. He wished he could go faster, but he didn't want to take the chance of hitting one of the sharp rocks that peppered the dry ground. A flat he didn't need, but a flat he got.

Slowing, he was surprised to see that the dogs maintained their distance. And when he stopped the car, the dingoes stopped their pursuit, keeping a football field's distance behind, fading into the shadows of the sunset.

He didn't relish changing the tire and the biting desert evening would normally be enough for him to set up camp on the spot. He probably would have built a fire, made coffee, eaten and changed the tire in the morning. He was out of the race now. However, with the wild dogs so close in the shadows, it seemed best to get the spare on and get away before dark.

Keeping his eyes on the predators behind, he shut off the ignition, put on the emergency brake, jumped out of the Jeep, grabbed the jack and tire iron and unbolted the spare. His fingers burned with the cold as he loosened the lug nuts, while Ann jacked the car. They replaced the tire with race speed, then they hopped back in the Jeep. Rick cranked the ignition, popped the clutch, hit the lights and they sped off.

Once they started moving, the dogs started moving too. Fuck the rocks, he thought. He wanted to be back on a road before the sun faded altogether.

"They're gaining," Ann said.

"Don't worry, honey, they can't catch us." He hoped he was right.

He shifted into second, picking up speed, then into third and felt a surge of relief when the lights played over a road ahead. Keeping it in third, he turned a hard right onto the smooth dirt track, shifted into fourth and left the wild dogs in the distance.

Thirty minutes and thirty kilometers later, they were sitting by a campfire, watching flames leap into the night.

"I wasn't scared," Ann said.

"I know," he answered, but he thought maybe she was, a little. He certainly had been.

"Come over here, Flash." She patted her sleeping bag.

She only called him that when she wanted to make love.

"Now?" he smiled. "In the middle of the desert?"

"I can make all the noise I want," she said. "Nobody to hear."

He rose and put more wood on the fire. "All the better to see you with," he said as he watched his wife remove her clothes, down overcoat, sweat shirt, tee shirt, bra and Levi's.

"Come on over," she said, clad only in sheer cotton panties.

Eagerly he closed the distance that separated them and embraced her, marveling, as he had many times in the last twenty-five years, at the large breasts pressed against his chest and the firm body he encircled with his arms.

* * *

Ann raised a hand, brushed his hair aside and ran her tongue along the length of the scar behind his left ear. She knew that drove him crazy. It was odd that a scar left by a bullet that could have put him in a body bag, turned out to be one of the most sensual places on his body.

"Wait!" he said. "I think something's out there."

"I don't hear anything."

He held an index finger to his lips and they listened.

"Whatever it was, I think it's gone," he said after about a minute.

"I'm glad." She thought about picking up where they'd left off, but the mood had passed. Then she raised the wrinkles on her forehead, the way she always did when about to ask a serious question. "Do you think about what it's going to be like not having to work anymore?"

"I try not to, but sometimes I can't help it. I'm going to miss it."

"But it's what we've worked for all these years, so that

we could quit when we were still young. It's why we took all those chances."

"I know, but it was exciting. We traveled a lot."

"We'll still travel," she said, "and we won't be looking over our shoulders all the time or worrying if the phone is tapped. We're free now, nobody's after us anymore."

"I know you're right and I hate myself for wanting to get back into it," he said. She saw him tense up. "Ann, move over by me!"

"There is something out there, isn't there?"

"Yes."

"Is it the dingoes?"

"I don't know."

"Are you sure there's something there?"

"I'm sure."

"Oh, my gosh!" Ann saw the glowing eyes and dog shapes at the edge of the firelight. "The dingoes found us," she said.

Rick stood in time to block one of the animals as it raced toward the fire. He placed himself between the wild dog and Ann, taking the animal's flying charge. The dog closed its powerful jaws on Rick's arm, dragging him down. He hit the ground hard and was knocked unconscious, blood spilling from his forehead. The animal shook him for a few seconds, before releasing him and returning to its companions in the dark.

Ann sat, still as death, by the fire, staring unblinking at five pairs of dingo eyes, limpid pools of red, reflecting the fire's glow. She wanted to go to Rick, see if he was okay. She wanted to crawl into her sleeping bag and hide. She could do neither, she was frozen, dead still.

A scream roared out of the dark, tearing into her soul, but still she couldn't move, other than to wet her pants. Another scream, closer, so close it shook her body as well as the night. Another roar rocked her as something leapt over the dingo dogs, landing in the fire. It spun around, a miniature tornado, shaking flames and embers as a wet dog does water, eventually coming to a stop, standing still in the middle of the flames, front paws resting on a blazing log.

She could feel its breath, smell its hate, see its gaping mouth with canine teeth that were unnaturally long. The animal was huge, big, black, powerful and somehow beautiful. Beautiful and horrible at the same time. It wasn't at all like the dingoes she was used to. Much bigger and its claws resembled those of a big cat. It looked at home in the fire.

She thought it was going to attack, to kill her, but instead the most horrible looking man she had ever seen walked in out of the night. He had skin like burnt toast and breath like rotten fish. His clothes were shabby and torn, falling off his wasted body. He was short, old and evil. He captured her eyes with his and she was afraid.

"Smell—your—fear," the ragged man hissed.

She felt a blast of hot air and all of a sudden the fire was consumed by a star-white light, engulfing the screaming creature, causing it to leap from the flames. Then the light was gone and where only a moment ago the beautiful, horrible animal had been, there was only the charred smell of death.

"Smell yours!" a deep voice attached to a man behind her said to the ragged man.

Without a word the ragged man fled, followed by the dingo dogs.

"Are you all right?" He was the oldest man Ann had ever seen in person. An aborigine, but he didn't dress like one. He wore Levi's with a red checkered flannel shirt and cowboy boots. He was tall. His skin was rough and cracking. His hands were large. His arms were long. He had light brown skin, dark brown eyes and silver-white hair. He was thin and needed a walking stick to help him stand and Ann knew that he was a friend.

"I guess so," she said, "but my husband is hurt."

The old aborigine bent over Rick, touched his head and said, "He'll be all right in the morning."

Ann looked disbelieving and said, "There isn't any blood. Where did it go?"

"Just a nasty bump, he'll be fine."

"Will you stay until he comes to?" Ann asked as she searched her backpack for a fresh pair of panties.

"I'll stay, but you have to do something for me." He reached into his pocket and brought out a small wooden box and handed it to Ann. She opened it and looked inside.

CHAPTER TWO

THE ALARM ON MARK DONOVAN'S WATCH went off for the last time at 6:45, the way it did every morning. He stretched, rolled out of bed, stumbled into the kitchen.

He opened the refrigerator, recoiled when the light hit him full in the face, blinked and reached into the cold for the coffee and set it by the coffeemaker. He yawned again and opened the pantry without closing the fridge. He took out the coffee filters, dropping one on the floor. He bent to pick it up without bending his knees.

The fridge light cast ghostly shadows through the kitchen as he put the fallen filter into the machine. He made the coffee strong, the way Vicky liked it.

He tapped his fingers while he waited, poured his first cup before the machine had finished working its magic. He gulped the hot liquid, racing the machine. He won. He poured another cup as the machine was steaming. He took a sip from his second cup, before pouring a third, for his wife. He added cream to hers and took the two cups into the bedroom.

Vicky enjoyed waking to coffee in bed, but probably not as much as he enjoyed waking her. He loved the way she looked with the morning light sneaking in through the curtains, basking the room in soft shadows. Vicky slept on top of the covers, in the nude, and the filtered light and morning shadows gave her sleeping form an artful, erotic appearance.

"Coffee's here," he said, smiling.

"So soon, can't I sleep a little longer? It's Saturday."

"No."

"But the bed is so soft."

"I know and the bathroom is so cold."

"Can't we skip the riding today?"

"If I had my way, we'd skip it everyday and sell the bikes. You're the health nut. I was perfectly happy with donuts for breakfast and cheesecake for lunch."

"Don't forget the steaks for dinner."

"Yeah, and steak for dinner."

"I don't want a husband dead before he's forty."

"I'm not going to die."

"You were eating yourself to death and you were getting fat. Look at yourself now."

It was true, he had to admit it, since she'd put her foot down and made him ride with her every morning, he'd lost weight and had even started to regain the body he'd had in college. People were starting to notice and to comment on how good he was looking.

"Honey, I'm worried about J.P.," he said, changing the subject.

"Why?"

"I think he spends too much time with Rick."

"And what's wrong with that?"

"I don't think Rick sets the right kind of example for the boy."

"What are you talking about?"

"He's a criminal," Mark said.

"Was a criminal, which is more than I can say for your precious brother."

"But Judy divorced him and now J.P. is hanging around someone just like him," Mark said.

"Rick is not just like your brother. Judy didn't divorce Tom because he sold a few concert records, she left him because he couldn't keep his thing in his pants. He was cheating on her every chance he got. She found out and dumped him and I say good for her."

"They could have worked it out if she really wanted to," Mark said.

"The only thing that kept her sane through it all was Rick and Ann. She moved here because she was able to rent the house next door to them. They were there for her when she needed them most and they still are."

"She should have stayed in Toronto."

"Come on, Mark, your brother loves Led Zeppelin more than he ever loved her."

"He does not," he said. She was angry now and Mark was beginning to feel that he'd crossed the line.

"You should be glad Tom brought Rick and Ann up last year for the Reggae Festival, because if he hadn't, Ann never would have fallen in love with this place and they never would have bought that house. They would have stayed in L.A. and Judy would probably be living next door to them down there. You wouldn't be able to see J.P. at all."

"I don't see him that much now."

"Listen, Mark," she said, calming down, "you're not the jerk your brother is and Judy knows it, but you look an awful lot like him. Every time she sees you it has to remind her of the man she's trying to forget. Give her a little more time and before you know it, you'll be complaining about J.P. spending too much time here and not enough time with his mother."

"I hope you're right."

"And one more thing," she said, "Rick doesn't do that stuff anymore, but your brother still does."

"But Rick got him into it."

"Oh come on, Tom was selling Zep bootlegs when you guys lived in Canada, before he ever met Rick. Rick just made it possible for him to make a living at it."

"Okay, I give up." He raised his hands in mock surrender.

She laughed.

"Come on," he said, "let's hit the shower."

"Right behind you."

They took their coffee to the bathroom and showered together. Vicky was feeling a little frisky, so when Mark began soaping her breasts, she reached between his legs and the shower lasted longer than usual.

"That's a great way to burn calories, maybe we should do this every morning and leave the bikes in the garage," Mark said after they finished making love.

"In addition to, but not instead of." Vicky laughed.

Mark stepped out of the shower and reached for a towel.

"Throw me one too," Vicky said and he complied. She toweled off before leaving the tub. She hated getting the floor wet, but didn't mind when Mark did.

"Do you want to wake Janis or should I?"

"You do it, she loves the airplane noise you make in the morning."

Mark put on his robe, then held out his arms, with hands and fingers extended, and started making a buzzing sound as he flapped down the hall to his daughter's bedroom. She was sitting awake, laughing as he came through the door and jumped into his arms.

"Okay, Janis on with your sweats." He dropped her on the bed. "We're out the door in ten minutes."

"Do I have ta?" She giggled.

"Yes, you have ta." He tickled her tummy. "Get a move on. We don't want to keep Mommy waiting."

"I bet I beat you."

"I'll bet you don't." He buzzed out of her room. Back in the master bedroom he caught a glimpse of his wife's breasts as she slipped on her sweatshirt.

"Better put those brown eyes back in your head and hurry or she's going to beat you again."

"Not today." He threw open his robe, jumped into his sweatpants and shirt.

"I win, I win, I win," Janis squealed, bursting into the room as Mark was lacing his running shoes.

"You win again, but I'll get you tomorrow."

"Let's go." She ran toward the front door. She loved riding on the back of her father's bike.

"Right behind you." Vicky and Janis were out the door ahead of him. He wasted a few seconds getting his keys. He wore them around his neck when they rode in the mornings, because his sweats had no pockets.

"Seven-thirty," he told his wife as he unlocked the garage door.

"Seven-thirty?" she questioned.

"Seven-thirty, don't you get it? Up only forty-five minutes and look what we've already accomplished."

"Wash your mouth out." Vicky laughed.

They brought the bikes out and Mark locked the garage. Janis was laughing as he lifted her up to her seat and strapped her in. Then they were off, pedaling down Seaview Avenue toward the bike path. They turned right at the end of the street, onto the bike trail, and started picking up speed on the way to the Wetlands. Mark's heart was beating fast as they turned into the nature preserve. Vicky hadn't broken a sweat.

They usually made four laps of the Wetlands, the first and last at a slow, leisurely pace, because they thought Janis liked to look at the ducks. The second and third laps were the fast laps, and the ones that Janis really liked.

Peddling into the early morning mist was the best part of Mark's day.

A half mile into the Wetlands, they started their turn to the right, past the duck ponds, back toward the entrance. Janis squealed with delight, leaning into the turn, urging her father to go faster and Mark picked up the pace, passing Vicky as they neared the entrance turn and the completion of their first lap.

"Yeah, Daddy, we're winning, go, go, go!"

Mark pedaled furiously, keeping his lead for the next half mile and started to pull away from his wife. Both Mark and Janis leaned expertly into the turn around the ponds for the second time, and leaned again around the entrance turn when Vicky started to gain on the straightaway, heading toward the ponds.

"She's catching! Pedal, Daddy! Pedal, pedal, pedal!"

Vicky passed them just before the ponds and kept the lead all the way back to the entrance turn, where she braked hard, hopped off her bike, laughing, and waited for her panting husband to puff his way to the finish, before starting their cooling down lap.

"She always wins, Daddy."

"That's because I have you on the back."

Mark laughed, chugging his way to the finish.

"I think I can, I think I can, I think I can," Janis sang as they slowed down.

"Wanna rest a second?" Vicky said. Mark nodded, sucking in great breaths of the crisp morning air.

"Daddy sounds like a broken engine," Janis said.

"He sure does." Vicky laughed. "We'll just have to wait till the engine's all rested up and ready to go before we do our last lap.

"All right you two," Mark said, trying to laugh and control his breathing at the same time, "let's go."

"Can we feed the ducks?" Janis asked as they were approaching the duck ponds on their cooling down lap.

"How? We don't have any food," Mark said.

"I sneaked some bread."

They parked their bikes by the turn and walked down to the duck pond, Janis in the lead, breaking up the bread. "Here ducks, here ducks," she sang.

"Stay out of the water," Vicky said, cutting Janis' stride short. The girl waited till Vicky caught up and they went down to the pond together, where Vicky watched as the ducks took the bread from her daughter's hand.

Mark stayed back with the bikes.

* * *

Janis was chasing after the one duck that always refused to take the bread from her hand. It was the same every morning, the duck ran and she chased, but this morning as Janis ran behind the waddling bird, it stopped. Something caught its attention and Janis followed its eyes to the bike path and saw the beggar man.

He looked like one of those homeless people that hang out in the park during the summer, except she had never seen a homeless man that dirty. Dirt and grime were mixed up in his scraggly hair and it looked like he had wet his pants so many times that the wet place the pee makes was covered in black, like old engine oil.

The man turned her and she almost screamed when she saw the blotchy skin and bloodshot eyes, but suddenly the duck turned and was running toward her. She forgot about the beggar man and grabbed on to the duck she'd been chasing after for as long as she could remember.

"I got you," she squealed. She didn't wonder why the duck didn't fly or why it didn't struggle and she didn't see the Bowie knife in the beggar's hand, gleaming silver as it reflected the sun's rays.

* * *

Vicky turned to wave at her husband as the scrawny man stepped behind Mark, grabbed him by the hair, jerking his head back. He ran a knife across his neck, slitting his throat from ear to ear. The ragged man smiled, even as blood washed down the front of Mark's sweatshirt.

She wanted to scream out, but she was struck dumb, paralyzed in place, as planted as any of the trees in the forest. She could only watch as the ragged man brought the giant knife up to Mark's left ear and made another ear to ear incision, this time along the jaw line.

Then he ripped the skin off of her husband's face.

Then he slashed the knife around Mark's hair line, separating the skin and scalp from the head, pulling them off in a filthy clawed hand.

Then he jumped back as Mark Donovan, with only a bloody stump for a head, danced a quick, herky jerky, death jig, before collapsing on the dew damp ground.

That galvanized Vicky into action. Without thinking she grabbed the duck out of her daughter's arms, threw the screeching bird aside, wrapped an arm around her daughter's waist, tucked the child into her side like a football and started to run. Her system was working again, she was in excellent shape and the pumping adrenaline gave her added strength and endurance. She was an animal mother fleeing with her young.

She scattered ducks in her path as she ran flat out, hard and determined. She ran with the pond to her left and the bike trail to her right, seeking to put distance between herself and the evil thing that was carving up her husband's body. She harbored no doubt as to what it would do when it finished with Mark. It would come after her and her child.

She broke right and crossed the bike trail into the forest. Brush and branch whipped against her, tearing into her sweatshirt, but she kept on. She tasted her own blood when a low branch ripped a gash in her face, but she ignored the coppery taste and slicing pain in her attempt to get away.

Then she was through the brush and on a deer trail that she'd walked many times with her husband and daughter. She turned left, picking up her pace, thinking now that maybe she had a chance. She knew these woods.

Then she heard the scream, up ahead to the left, probably on the bike trail. The wail, coming from the belly of whatever was up there, wasn't indigenous to these woods. It was a bad thing. It was the evil that killed Mark and it was ahead, waiting for her.

It screamed again, a lightning blast to her heart. She stopped, fought her panic, turned to double back, when she heard something coming through the brush. "Another one," she moaned under her breath. "There's two."

Then she saw it, a tall pine with ladder like branches. If she could reach those branches, maybe she'd have a chance. She could hold them off till help came. She ran to the tree and saw the futility of her plan. She could never squeeze through the closely packed branches, but Janis could, if she could hold her high enough to get a hold.

"Janis, I'm going to lift you up to that branch. I want you to grab it and climb as high as you can. Do you understand?"

"Yes, Mommy," the terrified girl said.

"Don't come down for anyone or anything. Stay up there and hide, till I come back."

"When will you come?"

"Soon, now come on." She picked the child up and held her above her shoulders. She heard the thrashing in the brush getting closer.

"I can't reach," Janis cried with her arms extended. "I can't reach."

Vicky was standing on her toes, holding Janis as high as she could. "How close?"

"Real close, Mommy. I'm real close."

"Listen, baby, I'm going to jump and I want you to try and grab that branch, okay?"

"Okay."

Another scream ripped through the morning mist, closer, coming from the other direction. They're closing in for the kill, she thought. Then she muttered to herself, "But they're not going to get my baby, not Janis."

She lowered herself, bending her athletic legs and jumped, straightening, pushing off the ground, holding Janis aloft. She felt the weight lessen and felt a moment's satisfaction, knowing that Janis had grabbed onto the branch. But the satisfaction was short lived.

"Mommy, I can't get up." Janis was trying to pull herself up onto the branch, but her child's muscles weren't developed enough to lift her body.

"Let go, I'll catch you." Vicky could feel the evil closing in.

"I'm afraid."

"You have to do it, honey."

Janis let go and fell into Vicky's arms

"This is the last chance we'll have, baby," Vicky said. "I'm going to try and throw you. You have to grab on and climb or we'll die."

"I'll try."

Vicky bent her knees and back and lowered Janis as low as she dared, an inner instinct told her not to let her daughter touch the ground, just in case the creature was following her scent. She straightened her legs with an adrenaline rush, throwing her hands above her head, and Janis flew up. Vicky's aim was true. Janis sailed by the branch and came to a stop and started her descent. When it was at waist height, she reached out, grabbed hold and pulled it to her. She threw her leg over the branch and scrambled up on it.

"Climb," her mother said from below. She added, "I love you, baby." Then she left the trail and went into the thick woods and was gone.

* * *

Janis started to climb and almost fell out of the tree when she heard the noise coming from the direction they'd been headed. She strained her eyes and looked down the deer path. The noise was getting louder, heavy breathing, like the sound made by the air machine on her fish tank, only louder and it was getting closer. She heard the scream again and knew that it was coming from the thing that made the fish tank noise. Then she saw it, a black blur coming fast, toward the tree, toward her. It ran past. She saw its slick black hair as it glided over the path beneath her. She held her breath and watched it go away. Then it stopped and turned. It was coming back.

It wasn't running this time. It came slowly and stopped below the tree with its nose to the path. It was smelling the ground, smelling the ground and looking for her. It sniffed the area where her mother left the trail. It wasn't looking for her, it was looking for her mom. She wanted to yell, to tell it to go away, but she was afraid, so she stayed still.

There was a breeze coming from the direction of the monster animal. It smelled like fish, not the fish from her tank, but the ones the fishermen brought in on the *Seawolf*. She could smell it, she hoped it couldn't smell her. She stayed quiet, afraid to move, afraid to breathe.

She heard something else coming down the deer path. She hoped it was her father coming after them, he would take care of the monster below. Her father could handle anything. She started to yell, to tell her dad where she was, but she caught the words in her throat as the beggar man came into view.

He was skinny and reminded her of the stickmen that her kindergarten teacher drew on the blackboard, but he wasn't wearing the stickman smile or carrying the flowers that those stickmen always carried. Instead he had a giant silver knife, a knife big enough to be a sword. The sun reflecting from the bloody blade, and the man's crusty skin, combined to scream one word to the girl above, and the word was, *bad*.

She only saw the sores on his dried up face and his bloodshot eyes for a flash of a second, before he followed the scary animal that made the fish tank noise into the forest. She was afraid she would never see her mom again. Then she worried about her father and she started to climb higher.

It seemed like she had been up in the tree forever, but the sun said that noon was hours away. She wished her father would come and chase away the bad things.

Then she heard the fish tank noise again.

"Oh, no," she cried, "they're coming." She wiggled between the branches, climbing as high as she dared, tearing her sweat suit and scraping her skin, but she was afraid she wasn't high enough. She strained, trying to squeeze between another branch, ripping a cut on her right arm. She wanted to scream, but didn't dare.

She wondered again why her father didn't come for her. She was sure he didn't run away, but if he didn't, where was he? And she was afraid for her mom. The things that had chased her into the woods were bad and now they were coming after her. She burrowed farther up the tree.

She saw something move past below and she squeezed her eyes shut till it passed, but it didn't go far before it turned around and came back. She opened her eyes. She felt it getting closer. Then she saw her arm and the blood. Strange, she didn't feel anything. It didn't hurt. It should hurt. Always before whenever she cut herself it hurt.

She looked down.

"Oh, no," she cried, "it's one of the monsters." She tried to climb higher, but couldn't.

The dog-like animal raised its head and Janis saw into its deep red eyes and right into its mouth, all the way to its belly. It had teeth longer than her arm. She hoped that it couldn't climb trees.

It could.

CHAPTER THREE

J.P. SAT ON THE COOL BEACH SAND and wondered if he'd see his birds again. Good racers homed for life and these had been born a long way from the Northern Californian town of Tampico. The five birds were sixteen months old and had never flown free. He hoped that because they were only six months old when he and his mom moved, that they would home to the new loft. There was no loft left in Toronto, fifteen hundred miles east, for them to trap into.

At one time he thought about keeping them caged forever. They were his best birds and he didn't want to lose them, but Rick told him they were bred to fly and he had to agree, keeping them caged would be cruel. He couldn't put it off any longer, if they wouldn't home by now, then they never would.

He got up, dusted off, reached into the gunny sack. He liked the smell of the bag. He associated the dusty bird smell with the far away poster places on the dusty walls of Tampico Travel. He liked to imagine that he could fly to those places with the birds. His small fingers found Dark Dancer with natural ease. He wrapped them around the bird and pulled it out of the bag.

Dancer was his favorite, a big, black check racer whose sire was a hammer tough bird that had heart. J.P. would find out soon enough if the bird was made out of the same stuff as his father. He hoped so.

He smoothed back Dancer's feathers and thought for the thousandth time that the white corn on his beak and around his black eyes contrasted with his dark face to make him look like a dark hooded terrorist. Then, with clenched lips, he whispered, "Go, Dancer," and he lowered his right arm, hand holding the racer, bringing the arm behind his back, parallel with the ground, stretching his muscles, feeling the strain. Then he whipped it forward in a fast arc, releasing his fingers as the arm flew past his eyes, letting the bird slide out of his hand. He felt the burst of wind caused by the strong beat of Dancer's wings.

Four more times he repeated the ritual. Four more birds, Ballerina, Cyclone, Thunder and Lightning, followed Dancer into the air, forming a great circle above J.P., stealing his heart as he tried to keep them in sight. He watched as they circled for bearing and smiled when they headed south, into the wind, toward home, Dancer in the lead.

J.P. turned and saw a large black man standing on the

boardwalk. He was watching J.P.'s birds with a smile on his face, so that made him okay as far as J.P. was concerned. The man waved. J.P. waved back, wondering if the man had had pigeons when he was a boy. Rick had told him that a lot of people did in the old days.

He turned from the black man and picked up his binoculars. He tried to follow the birds, but it was too hard to keep them in sight, so he faced the binoculars toward his mother. He yelled and waved, but she was too far away to hear.

* * *

Down the beach, Judy Donovan wandered listlessly, occasionally picking up a shell or two and dropping them into a fringed straw sombrero. She had been in a daze for over a year. She had loved her husband and the thought that he didn't love her back tore at her heart. Fortunately, when she flew with J.P. from the never stopping pace and traffic of Toronto, they landed next door to Rick and Ann.

J.P. took to Rick like a bird to the sky and, to her great relief, Rick returned the boy's affection. In addition, Ann's friendship had become an important building block in the foundation necessary to put herself back together and make her life whole again.

She shivered. Somebody was looking at her. She looked right and gave a start. Red eyes, blazing with fermenting hatred, glared at her. They were a window to a soulless heart. She looked into the red ringed pools of anger and wanted to run, but she was frozen.

She felt an ache in her chest and swallowed back rising bile. She tried to rein in her fear. If anything happened to her, who would care for J.P.? She concentrated on the nauseating taste as she held back the vomit and sought strength, and failed. She closed her eyes and felt the man approach.

* * *

Satisfied that the birds were headed home, J.P. again trained the binoculars down the beach. He saw the man approach his mother and he saw the Jim Bowie knife clutched in a gnarled hand held behind the man's back. A Jim Bowie knife, bright as a mirror, reflecting the morning sun.

He screamed a warning, but his mother couldn't hear. He screamed again, louder. He was afraid the man was going to cut her. He was going to slice through her Levi jacket and kill her.

He dropped the binoculars, screaming in desperation. Then he saw Rick's red Jeep, the old Jeep that he had brought back from Australia, coming down the hill and turning onto Across The Way Road.

"Rick!" he screamed, running toward the Jeep. He didn't want to run from his mom, but Rick couldn't hear. "Help!" He waved his arms, but Rick didn't see him. He ran as fast as his new Nikes could carry him, but the sand slowed him down. He stumbled, fell, skinned his hands, got up and ran. He screamed again, but still Rick didn't hear. He ran harder, breathing too fast to shout anymore, but he kept waving his arms, hoping to attract Rick's attention.

Then he saw Ann pointing.

"Help," he choked, the word burning raw in his throat. He was fighting to hold back tears. "Please let him come," he cried. "Please let him come." And he yelled "Yes!" when the Jeep jumped off the road and came toward him.

Rick drove the Jeep alongside J.P., sliding to the right

as he stood on the brakes, throwing sand as an ice skater does ice.

"What's wrong?"

"Homeless man down the beach, going to kill my mom." J.P. gasped, fighting for air.

"Stay here."

"No." J.P. jumped into the back as Rick popped the clutch. "Get him!" He was slammed against the back seat as the tires spun and dug into the sand.

* * *

Judy tried to scream, but her throat was numb and the morning breeze chilled her sweat drenched body as she stared at the man coming toward her. She was used to the winos who begged quarters at the mall, but the thing she saw getting closer, ever closer, made them seem appealing. His dirt stained, tattered clothes hung from his corpse-like body, like rags on a line, but it was the piercing laser-look shooting out from his red-rimmed eyes that set him off from a wino begging a drink. No wino's eyes had ever burned with the steaming evil she felt from his glare.

Then a wave, louder than the others, crashed on the beach and the sound reverberated through her, snapping her out of her shock. She ripped her frozen feet from the sand and she ran.

* * *

"He has a knife." Ann was holding on to the roll bar as the Jeep bounced and jerked over the sand.

Rick shifted into third.

"Get him," J.P. said again.

"Hit the horn," Ann shouted as she clenched her stomach against a stab of pain.

Rick punched the horn, stabbed his foot to the floor and Ann flinched as they bore down on the man with a knife. Although Rick was many years away from combat, Ann knew he was still able to make a life or death decision in less than an instant. The man with the knife was going to die, the accelerator was the trigger, the Jeep the bullet. Rick punched the horn a second time, but something told Ann that death was the only thing that would stop that evil looking man.

The man kept on.

The Jeep kept on.

"Hurry!" J.P. urged.

The man leapt aside, scant inches before collision, and they shot by. Rick made a sharp right to avoid hitting Judy, downshifted into second and spun the Jeep around. Ann hoped he had discouraged the man, but in her heart, she knew he hadn't. The man had resumed the chase, oblivious to the red Jeep.

Ann caught a quick glimpse of bloodshot eyes, liver-blotched skin and stringy hair as Rick pushed the accelerator to the floor, aiming the Jeep, and for a third time he punched the horn. This time the man stopped and turned when he heard the blast. His screaming eyes were as red as the car that bore down on him. He flung his hands in the air, losing the knife and Rick stomped on the brakes, but they were too close and too late. The Jeep hit the man head on, waist high, breaking his back as it flung him aside, a lump of clay tossed on the sand.

Rick stopped the Jeep, jumped out and hurried to the man he had run down. J.P. hopped out of the back and ran toward his mother. Ann remained seated and silent, too shaken to move, doubled over, arms wrapped around her chest, the pain intense.

* * *

"Mom," J.P. yelled as her seven-year-old son leapt into her arms and Judy wrapped him in a great hug.

"It's okay," Judy said. "It's okay."

"He was going to kill you. Why?"

"I don't know."

"I was scared. I yelled but you didn't hear me. Then I saw Rick's Jeep and I yelled and yelled and he came."

"Are you okay?" Rick said.

"Is he dead?" Judy asked.

"He's dead."

"What do we do now?"

"Get the sheriff. Come on, get in."

"Shouldn't somebody stay here with that?" Judy pointed to the dead man.

"I'm not going to and I know Ann won't, so that leaves you and J.P. It's up to you."

"Let's go," she said.

Straining, Judy lifted her son over the tailgate. Then she climbed over herself, grabbing onto the roll bar to pull herself in.

Rick started the car, pushed in the clutch, shoved it into first and drove off the beach, going through the gears, driving fast.

The car bottomed out as it flew over the curb and hit the street. "Needs shocks," Rick said, spinning the wheel to the left and going into a slide. He corrected by turning into it and adding power. Then they sped down Across The Way Road, turned right on Kennedy, and left the beach behind.

* * *

It was water clear to Gundry that the man was dead. Maybe he had a wallet. Maybe he had money or a watch.

Maybe his shoes would fit. Maybe. Only one way to find out. Scratching his head, chasing the lice, Gundry rose, unzipped his fly and urinated. Then he started toward the corpse.

He had been a dentist before he'd started to burn his brain cells. An easy and safe career. A tooth doctor didn't have to tell a mother her child had died on the table. An easy job for an easy man. A man who loved children and life. However, unfortunately, somewhere along the line he started to drink and, as it happens so often, he found that later on down the line he couldn't stop.

Now he was little more than human refuse. A bum always on the lookout for a drink. An ape-like man, who walked with his face to the ground in a kind of simian shuffle. And like an ape, he was constantly scratching at the lice and fleas that fed off him.

Pushing his long, stringy hair out of his eyes, he looked down at the man. "Dead," he muttered. "Dead for sure." With large, swollen hands, he flipped the corpse face down into the sand. Then he went through the pockets.

He found a wallet, opened it, saw money, then stuffed the wallet into his rear pocket. The shoes were too small, but he saw a watch. He started to pull it off when the dead man's hand grabbed Gundry's arm in a dead man's grip.

Malcolm Gundry screamed, tried to jerk away, but the grip held. He pulled harder, but still the dead man held on. He kicked the corpse, but still it held on. Again he kicked, but to no avail. His weak heart started pumping more blood than it was used to. His head hurt and his arm, held in that devil grip, felt like it was being crushed. He was going to pass out. He was going to die. Then, all of a sudden, he was blinded by light as he felt a white hot stab of pain in the back of his neck. He jerked back, free. He screamed, grabbing the back of his neck, feeling the wetness of his own blood, but this time it was a scream of triumph. He ripped off the dead man's watch, picked up the dead man's knife, then shuffled off the beach in search of a drink as the wind picked up, blowing sand.

* * *

"Let me get this straight," Sheriff Sturgees said, "he attacked Judy and you ran him down?"

"Yes," Rick Gordon said.

"Where's the knife?"

"It was here."

"Where did it go?"

"Someone took it." Rick raised his collar against the wind. He was a head taller than the portly sheriff, but he didn't let that distract him. Many people, to their everlasting regret, misjudged the sheriff, finding it hard to accept such a keen mind in his short, overweight body.

"Who?"

"How should I know?" Rick met his stare head on.

"Don't get upset, I'm not accusing you of anything."

"It was probably taken by the same man that turned the body."

"Say again."

"The body was on its back."

"That's right," Judy said.

"He was laying on his back," J.P. chimed in, "and he had a knife. A Jim Bowie knife."

"How do you know it was a Bowie Knife?"

"Captain Wolfe has one. I know what they look like."

"Wolfe Stewart," the sheriff asked, "the captain of the all day fishing boat that runs between here and Palma?

"Yeah, the captain of the *Seawolf*," Judy said.

"And Captain Wolfe has a Jim Bowie knife like the one I saw," J.P. said. "He wears it in a knife holster tied to his leg."

"It's called a scabbard," Judy said.

"All right," the sheriff turned to Rick, "the man had a knife."

"And he meant Judy harm," Rick said.

"How do you know?"

"He would have cut me, Sheriff. I know it. He would have cut me and killed me. I was helpless. I couldn't move."

"He was gonna kill my mom."

"J.P., get away from there!"

"I'm not gonna touch him, Mom."

"Now J.P.!"

J.P. moved away from the dead man.

The sheriff bent over the corpse. "No wallet and he had a watch."

"How can you tell?" Judy asked.

"Look for yourself." He pointed to a white ring set off by a deep outdoor tan around the dead man's left wrist.

"Wow, that's police work, isn't it?" J.P. said.

"Sheriff, can we go now?" Judy asked. "I'd rather J.P. didn't have to see this."

"He was a witness, but I guess we can do without him here. I'll talk to you after I'm done. Why don't you take your boy and wait up by the cars."

"Thanks," Judy said, overcoming J.P.'s objections.

"Okay," the sheriff said, after they were out of earshot, "now let's talk about the Jim Bowie knife that isn't here."

* * *

Two blocks away Mr. Jaspinder Singh was ringing up a pack of Marlboros when the customer asked him a question.

"Do you know Rick Gordon?" The man asked like a policeman.

"I am truly not knowing him."

"About six feet, green eyes, maybe hazel. Brown, wavy hair, probably cut a little too long. Got a scar behind his left ear, here." Storm touched the spot with a finger. "Wife named Ann, a looker, just a little shorter than him, shoulder length hair, Barbie Doll looks, the original blue-eyed blond, you'd seen her, you'd remember. That's what everyone says. You know anybody like that?"

"Not that I can recall."

"I heard they come in here."

"Many people are certainly coming in here. I cannot be knowing each and every one. Why are you asking?"

"My name's Storm, Sam Storm. I'm a private investigator."

"That is a very private eye kind of name you are having, Mr. Storm."

"Yeah, well I've heard that before."

"What has this person been doing to cause your looking?"

"He makes bootleg CDs."

"And for this you are coming here? My eleven-year-old son makes them on my computer, is he in trouble too?"

"I work for the RIAA, the Recording Industry Association of America. They represent the music business and they're mighty unhappy with Mr. Gordon. They'd like him to find a new line of work. As for your boy, if he's just making them for himself, we don't care."

"Why would anybody be buying something anybody can be making?"

"The bootleggers are making collectable CDs now,

with original packaging that's hard to duplicate. The FBI busted someone in New Orleans last year, five agents, ten local cops and me. Quite a collar, but he wasn't one of the big guys that started up the biz."

"Five FBI agents, how impressive. I guess the FBI hasn't heard about what happened on September 11, 2001 or the war on terror. And ten local cops, that's impressive too. I guess they don't have murder, robbery or rape in New Orleans." Jaspinder Singh snorted. "And now you're thinking we have a dastardly criminal here in Tampico, pumping out these CDs." Singh shook his head, what a sad excuse for a man this Sam Storm was.

"No, I was following up a lead, that's all. My brother-in-law thought he saw him up here last month. I thought I'd check it out." That putz Herbie, Storm thought. This was the third time in as many years that he thought he'd sighted Gordon. Maybe he never should have shown him the pictures.

"I am certainly sorry that I cannot be helping you. I do not know the man you are looking for," he lied. Jaspinder Singh had heard enough—as far as he was concerned Rick Gordon had done nothing wrong. He would continue on the prudent course that he had set out for himself very early in life and mind his own business.

Sam Storm paid for his cigarettes with a twenty, pocketed his change and walked out the door, pausing for a second to check the magazine rack to see if there were any nudies. There weren't.

* * *

After the sheriff had dismissed them with the warning that he would be coming up the hill later to get full written statements, they stood next to the Jeep, talking around the events that had left a man dead on the beach.

"Can we stay and see what happens next?" J.P. asked.

"I think we should go home and let the police do their job," Judy said.

"Aw, Mom!"

"I think your mother is right, the police have enough to do without us getting in the way," Ann said.

"Can we get some Ding Dongs then?"

"J.P. loves frozen Ding Dongs," Judy explained.

"So I've learned," Rick said.

"Rick likes 'em, too," Ann said.

"Does Rick like everything you like?" Judy asked.

"Pretty much," Rick answered for the boy.

"Rick doesn't get on with too many people, but he's really taken to J.P.," Ann said.

"Not fair, I like people." Rick brushed hair from his eyes.

"In great moderation. It's good this isn't a big city or we'd have been long gone."

"So I like small towns."

"Is that why you bought the house on the hill?" Judy asked.

"It's always been our dream to settle down in an isolated house in the woods. Quiet and private, with nobody around."

"But you like to be around me, don'tcha?"

"J.P., we couldn't have a better person to share the hill with. We're glad you moved next door and we like being around you. You can come over anytime you want," Ann said.

"I'm glad, because I like doing stuff with Rick. He doesn't treat me like a kid." J.P. was squinting, trying to see what the policemen were doing on the beach. He turned away and looked down the street. "Can we get the Ding Dongs now?" He pointed to Singh's Bait and

Convenience Store.

"I don't think so, J.P.," his mother said.

"But we're out," the boy pleaded.

"We need milk anyway," Ann said.

Rick thought Ann was making an excuse, so they could stay longer and see what happened next, without feeling like freeway rubberneckers. He decided to help her out by starting off in the direction of the convenience store, leaving the three others to drift along in his wake.

* * *

They entered the store to the ringing of three golden bells. Jaspinder Singh looked up and smiled at one of life's coincidences and wondered if he should tell Rick Gordon about the man that had just left.

Then the warning bells went off again and one of life's many burdens came through the door for the second time that morning. "Can I be helping you, Mr. Gundry?" Jaspinder Singh asked.

Gundry ignored him, eyes wandering over the store.

"You are not wanting more wine?"

"No."

"Then for what are you wanting?"

"Something to eat." He shuffled toward the breakfast cereal, picked up a box of Wheaties with his left hand and held it in front of his face, like he was reading the back of the box.

"Can you guys come over for coffee?" Judy Donovan said as the group was approaching the counter.

"Sure," Ann Gordon replied, "no way would we leave you two alone after what happened out there."

"What happened out where?" Jaspinder Singh asked.

"A man tried to kill my mom and Rick ran him down."

"Big city crime in our little town?" Singh shook his head. "What is this world coming to?"

"Right on the beach. Killed 'em," J.P. said.

"Can we get some wine?" Ann asked from the back of the store.

Gundry tried to replace the Wheaties with a shaking hand and caused an avalanche of cereal boxes. Startled, he jumped back and dropped something on the floor. The clank of metal on cement riveted Singh's attention. A man at the magazine rack took his face out of Field and Stream. A man with a bag of bait froze. Judy gasped, Ann stared wide-eyed.

"It's the knife!" J.P. shouted.

And Jaspinder Singh saw Sam Storm enter the store and take in the situation as Rick Gordon started for Gundry, then he grabbed for the gun he kept on the shelf under the cash register.

Gundry looked confused as he snatched the knife from the floor and charged Rick with his right arm extended, hand holding the blade like a jousting knight. Rick stopped, stood his ground, stepped out of the way of the stumbling Gundry and brought a bottle of red wine down on his head. Gundry folded, all tension leaving his body as he went down.

Singh had his gun trained on the action, felt his arms shaking as he held the automatic in a two handed grip, saw Rick Gordon dive for the floor.

"It's okay, Mr. Gordon, I won't be shooting you."

"You're sure?" Rick Gordon said.

"Absolutely." Despite the circumstances, he was tempted to laugh as he lowered the weapon. He wasn't a coward, but he wasn't an idiot either, he'd been afraid. However, he didn't back down. He'd acted like a real American.

"Big gun," Rick said as he got up.

"He was coming at you with a big knife." Singh put the weapon back on the shelf under the register.

"Yes, he was." Rick dusted off as the store came to life.

Everyone crowded around Gundry. Sam Storm bent to take his pulse. "Dead," he said.

"Somebody better go for the police," the man that had been reading Field and Stream said.

"Sheriff Sturgees is across the street," Ann said. Then added, "I'll go." But light flashed through the store before she had a chance to move. Then the lights went out.

* * *

In the excitement no one saw Sam Storm pick up the Bowie knife. They didn't see the dead Gundry's hand close on Storm's arm, They didn't see him jump away and they didn't suspect a thing when he eased himself out of the store.

He tossed the knife on the passenger's side of his old, brown Ford Granada, started the car and drove. Something was happening. He felt light headed. He reached and scratched the itching sensation on the back of his neck. Something wasn't right.

He made the first left without thinking, then the next left, then the next, and he found himself driving past the convenience store. Something was drawing him back. He continued on and found himself driving around the block for a second time. This time he parked across the street and down the block from the store.

He lit a cigarette and thought about Gordon.

He would sit tight and see what developed. He'd been after Rick Gordon for years, not that he could do much unless he caught him with a smoking gun, but he was convinced that he hadn't retired. Once they taste the easy money they never quit.

It had taken him over twenty years to put it all together, but he'd done it. From that first scratchy record in the plain white cover, to the current rash of bootleg CDs, he had been on the case, and behind most of it was Rick Gordon. He was sure of it.

* * *

"So the electricity goes out in a great white flash and the knife disappears," the sheriff said through a frown of disbelief.

"Yes, sir. That's about it," Jaspinder Singh said.

"I'll ask it again. Where's the knife?" the sheriff said.

"Not here." Ann was the first to speak.

"There was a knife," J.P. said. "I saw it."

"Me, too," his mother said.

"That enough for you, Sheriff?" Rick said. For a short moment he thought he was in trouble, the kind of trouble he didn't need.

"No, it's not. What I'd like to see is the knife." He bent to see if it might have slipped under one of the food counters. "Not here."

"There was a knife," Judy said.

"It's not here now."

"Somebody took it, that's for sure," Jaspinder Singh said. "It was right there, bigger than life."

"Well, if there was a knife, then one of you took it."

"No, sheriff, there were two others here. A man reading the magazines, who is now gone and a private detective. They are not here now."

"That's right," Ann said.

"Private detective?" The sheriff turned to Singh. "What did he want?"

"He was asking if I saw a certain person in town," Jaspinder Singh said.

"What person? Who?"

"I am not remembering."

"How could you forget?" the sheriff asked with the edge of anger creeping into his voice.

"I would remember if it was somebody I was knowing, but a name I have never heard is a thing easy to forget, especially after what has happened this morning."

The sheriff turned toward Rick.

"You know I'm going to have to hold you for this."

"No, I don't know that. I've done nothing wrong."

"Two men are dead because of you."

"That's absolutely not true. That bum on the beach was going to kill Judy, and that bum there," he pointed to Gundry's body, "came at me with a knife. There's a world of witnesses to both events."

"You used deadly force."

"Come on, Sheriff. I hit a man who was trying to kill me with a bottle of wine. It's not like I used a gun."

"Sheriff, it is without a doubt that the dead Mr. Gundry was going mad. He was going to kill Mr. Gordon," Jaspinder Singh said.

"Without doubt," Rick added.

"Even if I agree, I'm going to need you to come in and make a statement."

"And I'll be glad to do it," Rick said.

"J.P., get away from there," Judy scolded. Her son was bent over the corpse, the second dead body he'd seen that morning.

"There's blood," the boy said.

"He was hit hard, J.P." Rick pulled the boy away from the body. "Why don't you wait outside."

"Blood on the back of the neck," J.P. whispered under

his breath, "like the man on the beach." But nobody was listening.

CHAPTER
FOUR

ANN CLENCHED HER FISTS, then fumbled in her purse for her keys. The day hadn't even started yet and already she was fighting the pain. She found the keys, then took J.P. by the hand, looked both ways, threw a quick glance behind and caught Rick looking, as she knew she would.

"He always watches when you walk, doesn't he?" J.P. tugged on her hand.

"Yeah, he does," she said. The group had decided she would take J.P. home, while Rick and his mother answered more of the sheriff's questions.

"Why?" J.P. pulled her into the street, toward the Jeep parked on the other side.

"He likes the way I walk." She opened her door, but J.P. climbed over.

She heard the distant blast of a fog horn.

"Can we go?" he asked. "You've never been, Mom and Rick take me all the time and they like it. I bet you would too."

The single blast of the foghorn told the town that it was 9:00 and that the *Seawolf* was docking at the pier, like she did every morning, rain or snow. Holiday anglers didn't like going out too early and they didn't like coming in too late.

J.P. loved the *Seawolf* and Captain Wolfe Stewart. He'd been out so many times that the bearded captain thought of J.P. as his lucky charm. Lately the boy had been having breakfast three or four times a week in the ship's galley. If his mother didn't want to go, Rick did.

The ship's cook, under captain's orders, had bacon sizzling every morning when they docked, just in case J.P. showed up for breakfast. He had become the ship's unofficial mascot, and both crew and boy enjoyed the arrangement.

Ann waved to Rick, bit back the pain, let out the clutch and sped away. Soon she wouldn't be able to conceal it anymore, but every minute of happiness she could give him, before the awful truth surfaced, was a minute worth fighting for, and she was a fighter.

"Of course, the *Seawolf*," she said. "I should have known." She knew he loved the bacon and egg burgers and told herself she probably would, too. A few weeks ago she would have shuddered at the thought of so much grease and fat. She always ate healthy. Low fat, high fiber for her, exercise for her, aerobics for her, vitamins for her, she wasn't going to get the big C, no sirree. Well she did, so this morning she was going to have a bacon and egg burger, maybe two, grease, fat, cholesterol and all.

She sat back in the seat and ran her hands over the leather steering wheel cover. Thank God she was still fairly fit, but soon she would start to lose her strength and she wouldn't be able to hide it from Rick any longer.

"Are you thinking?" J.P. broke her train of thought.

"Yes, I was thinking, remembering actually."

"About what?"

"I was remembering the time I gave Rick this old steering wheel cover."

"Why?"

"Because sometimes it's the little things that are the most important."

"And it's important that you gave that to Rick?"

"No, it's important that he kept it."

"I don't understand?"

"It's a symbol, it means he loves me. He says he only keeps it for luck, but I know better. Every time we get a new car—or in the case of this Jeep, an older one—he takes this old leather cover off the old one and puts it on the new one. This cover is important to him."

"Why?"

"Because I gave it to him and he loves me."

"Oh." Then a few seconds later he asked, "Did he keep everything you gave him?"

"Every lickin' stickin' thing."

"He must love you a lot."

"He loves me very much. So much that it's sad."

"How could that be sad?"

"It's sad because if something happens to me, Rick will be all alone, and I think he loves me too much to be alone."

"That's a lot of love," J.P. said.

"Yeah, Rick and I couldn't have any children, so we

only have each other."

"That's Susan Spencer's car. She goes out on the boat. You can park behind it," J.P. said, changing the subject.

Ann parked behind a yellow Ford Courier and smiled when she read the bumper sticker on its tailgate. *Fishermen do it deeper.* She knew Susan, she owned the Tampico Diner, but Ann hadn't known she was into deep sea fishing. She shut off the ignition, leaving the car in gear, and put on the parking brake. "Short drive," she said.

"We could've walked."

"We could have, but I felt like driving."

"Just a few blocks?"

"I don't get to drive the Jeep very much. Rick likes to have all the fun."

"Really?"

"He thinks he's a rally driver. He turns into a little kid when he gets behind the wheel of anything that has four wheel drive." Judy opened her door and J.P. jumped out of the back. They were both too preoccupied with their own thoughts to notice the aging brown Ford Granada that pulled up and parked behind them. "Come on," J.P. said, "we don't have much time."

"I'm coming." Ann followed J.P. across the parking lot. By the time she reached the pier, he was halfway toward the end and the waiting fishing boat. He looked so small compared to the big men fishing along the wooden pier, who all seemed to know him. This was a part of his life she knew little about.

J.P. turned when he reached the ramp and waved. "Hurry, Ann," he hollered. Ann quickened her pace. She was almost to the ramp when she slipped on the wet wood and started to fall. Strong hands saved her from an embarrassing spill.

"Thank you," Ann said, looking up to see her savior.

"Don't mention it." The man had a rugged outdoor tan and he had a Bowie knife in a scabbard strapped to his right leg.

"You're Captain Wolfe."

"At your service."

"Has anyone ever told you that you're a brown-eyed handsome man?"

"Not for a lot of years, but I'm glad to hear a pretty lady talk about these old bones in that light."

"You're not so old and I'm not so pretty." She smiled, becoming lost in his eyes.

"I'm sixty-seven. Where I come from that's old and you're very pretty. On that I won't be argued with."

"Okay, you're old and I'm pretty. I'm also Ann, a friend of J.P.'s."

"You're Rick's wife?"

"That's me."

"Annie, tell him about the murders," J.P. chimed in, interrupting.

"Murders?" the captain questioned.

"I'll tell you all about it over one of those famous bacon and egg burgers I've heard so much about."

"I'll show you to the galley," the captain said.

Ann had never been on a sport fishing boat before and the notion that one would have a galley that resembled the inside of a roadside diner had never dawned on her. She wondered if the captain and Susan Spencer had something going. The decor in his galley wasn't that much different than the decor in her diner.

Captain Wolfe yelled for the cook, then he apologized to Ann. "The galley is usually empty till we get out to sea, unless of course our good luck mascot comes on board."

He ruffled J.P.'s hair and the boy grinned wide. He would never need braces, Ann thought.

They watched the cook throw the extra bacon on the griddle and J.P. wiggled with anticipation when he heard the expectant sizzle the cold meat made against the hot surface.

"God knows why, but he really loves our *Seawolf* breakfast burgers." The captain smiled before shifting the subject, "Now, you were talking about murder?" As suddenly as it was there, the smile was gone.

"Two of 'em," J.P. said.

"Let the lady tell it," the captain softly said.

And Ann told him. She told him how Rick ran down the bum that had tried to kill J.P.'s mother, then she told him about the other one that had attacked Rick in the bait shop.

"In your honest opinion, could your husband have done anything else than act the way he did?" the captain asked, when she finished with the story.

"Not and have left Judy alive."

"How about after, in the store?"

"I don't think so. He wasn't trying to kill the man. He was defending himself."

"Do you think he could have defended himself without hitting the man on the head?"

"I don't know, maybe, but he didn't do it on purpose. Rick would never hurt anybody on purpose."

"He was in Vietnam," J.P. said. "That bum picked on the wrong guy to mess with."

"Your husband was in Nam? He can't be old enough."

"He's fifty-seven."

"He doesn't look much older than you," the captain said, "and you can't be a day over thirty."

"Off by fifteen years, but I love you for saying it."

"So not only is your husband a combat veteran, he's also apparently in pretty good shape. That explains his quick reflexes and why he killed the man that attacked him. I would have acted the same."

"Really?" Ann said.

"Yeah," J.P. said, "Captain Wolfe was in Vietnam too. You don't mess with guys like him and Rick."

"It that so?" Ann said to J.P., but it was Wolfe Stewart who answered.

"When you've been in combat, you learn that when somebody is trying to kill you, you try and kill him first. If you live, it's something you never forget."

"Can I go on deck and talk to the guys?" J.P. asked.

"Sure, go ahead, we won't be leaving right away. Take all the time you want."

The boy scurried up the stairs to greet the fishermen on the deck above.

"You're not hanging around longer than usual on my account?" Ann asked the captain after J.P. was out of the galley.

"You bet I am. It's not everyday when a lady pretty as you, with a tale of murder on her lips and a pain in her eyes like I've never seen, takes the time to talk to old Wolfe Stewart."

"I'm glad my husband isn't as perceptive as you."

"You want to tell me about it?"

"I have cancer."

"How long?"

"A few weeks, two months if I'm lucky."

The captain rose from the table and shouted at the cook. "When J.P. comes back, feed him and tell him to wait, I'm taking the lady up on the bridge for a bit."

For reasons Ann was unable to fathom, she felt a bond

with the captain. He was loud, blusterous and lovable, all at the same time. She also couldn't help notice that he was a man used to getting his way and, although he was a big man, he didn't throw his weight around. People did what this man asked because they wanted to.

She followed him up to the bridge.

"Careful going up," he told her. "It can be slippery." She felt him behind her as she went up the steep steps. When she reached the top, he showed her through a door that opened onto the bridge.

"From up here you can see over the dunes." She pointed. "That's where Rick ran down the man that was after Judy." She was able to see the spot down the beach where a small crowd surrounded the body, including two of the sheriff's three deputies. "And that's the store where that second wino attacked us." She pointed to Singh's Bait and Convenience Store.

They looked over the dunes for a few seconds, then she asked, "Why did you bring me up here?"

"I wanted to show you this." He showed her a framed photograph that was fixed to the bulkhead.

"She's very pretty."

"Was very pretty."

"I'm sorry."

"She's been gone ten years now. She had cancer, like you, and like you she kept it from me. She wanted to spare me what she was going through and she managed to do it almost right up to the end."

"Why are you telling me this? You don't even know me."

"I want to spare your husband the pain I suffered. I want to help you not to make the same mistake my wife made."

"I don't understand," she said, but she was beginning

to.

"It broke my heart when my wife died. It hurt more that she didn't share it with me. We were a team, but she didn't let me be there for her. It took me years to forgive her. Can you imagine that? She was dead and I couldn't forgive her. If you love your husband and he loves you, tell him. Don't let him waste time by going to a movie alone, or to a friend's for a card game, or even out to buy a paper, when you should be spending what precious little time you have left together. That was the hardest to forgive, the time we missed, because she kept her illness from me."

"Captain Wolfe Stewart, you're a perceptive man. You saw the pain in my eyes and knew I was hurting. How is it you didn't see it in your wife?"

"I don't know. I suspect she worked very hard to conceal it from me, like you probably do to conceal it from your husband."

"That's true. I don't let down my guard for a second, for fear he'll see through me."

"Tell him and you won't have that problem."

"Thank you, Captain, I'll think about it," but she already knew she was going to tell Rick as soon as possible.

"I like Rick. Why don't you bring him fishing sometime, on me."

"Why thank you again, that would be nice, we'll do it."

After they left Wolfe Stewart and his boat, they came straight up the hill, even though Ann desperately wanted to go by the bait shop and find out what was going on, but she didn't want to be responsible for dragging J.P. into any more unpleasantness than was necessary. He had already, in a space of a few hours, seen more than most see in a lifetime. If there was more evil afoot, she wanted to keep him out of it if she could.

Home, she shut off the Jeep, went over to Judy's front porch and sat on the front steps. It seemed too nice a day to waste it away inside. J.P. sat beside her and was unusually quiet for about a minute.

"Wanna watch television?" he said

"Not really."

"Wanna take a walk?"

"Yeah," she said, "it's a good day for it."

She had to do something, she couldn't just sit on the porch with a seven-year-old boy on a nice day and expect him to be still, though it amazed her how little he'd been affected by what had happened earlier.

"Let's walk down to the park and back," J.P. said.

"My brother and I had pigeons when I was a kid," Ann said, making conversation as they walked side by side down the shady road.

"What kind?"

"Tumblers, rollers, fantails, helmets."

"Wuss birds!"

"Wuss birds?"

"Show birds are wuss birds, you know pussy birds, real men have racers, my dad said."

"Well, I didn't know."

The half mile walk to the park took about fifteen minutes with J.P. blasting rapid fire questions the whole way, as usual, and Ann doing her best, as usual, to field them.

He seemed to run out of questions as they reached the park and turned left to cross Seaview Avenue and just as Ann thought she was going to get a breather, a stab of white hot pain ricocheted through the back of her head. A pain that had nothing to do with the cancer that was ravaging her body.

"There's something bad over there." She pointed toward the dunes.

"How do you know?" J.P. said.

"I don't know, but I know."

"The park," J.P. said.

"Okay."

They turned, sprinted to the park and dropped in front of the backstop, sharing their hiding place with two empty bottles of Red Dog wine. Ann felt a little better once J.P. was shielded from what or whoever was over there.

"Wait here, I'm going over to take a look."

"Don't leave me here by myself," J.P. said.

"Don't worry, I won't leave your sight and I'll be right back." She got up and jogged across the street to the beach. At the sand, she crawled on her belly up the dune and peered over the top and saw him. It was the man from the bait shop, only now he reminded her of the Ragged Man from the outback and he was headed in her direction. She slid down the dune and ran back to the backstop.

"Just in time," J.P. said with his eye to a knot hole.

"Let me see," Ann said, replacing his eye with hers. "It's the man from the store."

The man sat on the dune and studied the beach.

"It doesn't look like he's gonna move for awhile," Ann said. Then she added, "He reminds me of the Ragged Man."

"What's the Ragged Man?"

"I met him once in Australia."

"Are you afraid of him?"

"Yes. He's very bad, very evil."

"The town," J.P. said.

"Let's go."

Keeping the backstop between them and the man across the street, Ann and J.P. walked across the baseball diamond, where the Tampico Pirates played, then the football field, where the Tampico Bullets played. Then they went into the Elm's section of the park, where the high schoolers went to make out. Exiting the Elms, they found themselves at the corner of Kennedy and Second Avenue.

"Let's go by Ken and Dub's Records and see if they got the new Dylan CD in yet," J.P. said.

"I don't think it's open."

"We could look in the window," he said.

"Since when did you start liking Dylan?"

"I don't, really," J.P. said, "but I was gonna buy it for Rick. I've been saving up."

Ann smiled and they started out for the used record store that catered to a diminishing group of people who still preferred vinyl, but they didn't get far, because J.P. turned for a look behind.

"Look, he's coming," he said. "Over there, by the corner. I don't think he's seen us."

Ann grabbed him by the hand and pulled him into Susan Spencer's Diner. The only other soul in the restaurant was Jesse Hernandez, the morning cook. He was dressed in kitchen whites, long hair in a bun under a cook's hat and headphones, his back was facing the door and he was singing at the top of his lungs about being dazed and confused.

Like spies in the night, they walked through the diner, past booths with blood red Naugahyde and into the corridor that led to the back exit, past the women's, past the men's, past the pay phone, and out through the open door in back as Lola, the morning waitress, exited the woman's restroom, never knowing that Ann and J.P. had passed by.

Ann looked left, then right. They were in the alley between First and Second Avenues. The east side was dotted with dumpsters and trash cans situated near the rear doors of Second Avenue's merchants. The west side fronted on the garages and fenced backyards of the modest homes on First.

"Is he still coming?" J.P. asked.

"I think so," Ann said.

Then they heard the front door of the diner crash open.

"Is there anybody here?" Someone yelled in a raspy voice.

"Nobody's been here for the last half hour," Lola answered.

"Are you sure?" The raspy voice boomed loud.

"We're going over," Ann whispered. She hoisted J.P. up to the top of a five foot brick fence. He grabbed on, rolled over the top and dropped into the yard on the other side with Ann right behind him.

Ann took J.P. by the hand and led him across the backyard to the back door of a two story house. Checking the door, she found it unlocked and they quietly went inside. Ann locked the door behind them. They heard the sound of a shower and a woman's voice humming a tune Ann wasn't familiar with. Putting her index finger to her lips, indicating to J.P. to be quiet, Ann looked through flower print curtains and saw the man coming over the fence.

"He's still coming," she whispered, taking J.P.'s hand again and leading him through a modern kitchen, then a dining room, then a sitting room, then an entrance way and finally out the front door as they heard the man banging on the back.

Once they were out the front they turned left and sprinted down First. Without slowing, they crossed Kennedy, back into the Elms, back across the football field and the baseball diamond, back onto Seaview Avenue, and back up the hill toward home.

Once they were back at Judy's Ann felt safe, at least for a few minutes, she told herself. She was exhausted, the cancer stealing her strength. She had to lay down, just for a few seconds. She literally fell on the sofa.

"Are you all right?" J.P. asked.

"I'm fine, I just need a little rest."

"Okay.

* * *

J.P. settled back in his mother's favorite chair, remote in hand, and channel surfed, changing channels at least three times a minute, but he couldn't get that Ragged Man out of his mind. How could Ann rest at a time like this? She must really be tired. He didn't want to think about it, so he decided to get something to eat, but before he got to the refrigerator, he heard an animal sound from outside. He pulled a kitchen chair over to the sink, climbed up and looked out the window and saw the black shape of a big dog slide into the bushes that grew between the garage and the house.

J.P. loved to play in there.

Like a flash he was off the chair and through the kitchen to tell Ann. Halfway to the sofa he heard the scratching at the front door and screamed, "Annie, something's outside!"

* * *

"What?" she said, nerves taught.

"Listen," he whispered.

Ann heard the scratching at the door.

"It's the Ghost Dog," she said. "It belongs to the Ragged Man."

"What are we gonna do?"

"Sit tight for a second," she said.

For the longest minute in her life, Ann sat, J.P. by her side, listening to the scratching and scraping at the door. Then whatever was out there growled a low rattling, rasping whisper, barely heard by the duo inside. "Smell—your—fear." A hideous phlegm-filled gurgle.

"That's the Ragged Man," Ann whispered.

J.P. shuddered.

Ann's adrenaline was flowing before her feet hit the carpet, her racing mind taking her back to the night with the dingoes in Australia. She was afraid then and she was now, afraid that fear meant death and she wasn't ready.

"Are you okay, Annie?"

She couldn't answer, because she wasn't okay, her hands were trembling, her skin was clammy with sweat and a searing pain was ripping through her chest.

She knew the end was near. She wished she could see Rick and his beautiful smile one last time, but instead all she saw was the glint of the summer sun reflected into her eyes from the silver, shiny blade of the Jim Bowie knife the Ragged Man was holding up for her to see, just outside the window.

J.P. picked up the phone. "Annie, the phone doesn't work," he whispered and she heard the fear in his voice. "Someone cut the line." He looked Ann in the eyes and she saw the boy fight the fear away. "I'm going for help." He dashed to the door, slid the bolt and screamed when he saw the Bowie knife sitting on the front porch. Then he jumped over it and ran.

* * *

Jaspinder Singh watched as Sheriff Sturgees cradled the phone, then turned to Rick Gordon and Judy Donovan. The phone call had done something to him. The straight shoulders now sagged. The hard set of his jaw was gone. His glaring eyes were now dim. In thirty seconds the call had transformed him from a steaming battleship to a lumbering barge. He started to say something, then stopped. He turned away from Judy as he fished out some bills from a shirt pocket and faced Jaspinder Singh behind the counter.

"Can I have a pack of Camels?" he asked, handing over the money.

"It's that bad?" Singh knew the sheriff only smoked when he was severely upset.

"It can't get any worse, Mr. Singh," the sheriff said. It was plain for them all to see that the Sheriff was suffering some kind of mental anguish. He was fighting hard to control the tremor running through his hands and it took him a few seconds to get the pack open, and a few more to get a cigarette from the pack to his mouth, and still a few more to get it lit.

"They're here," he said, exhaling a cloud of blue-gray smoke as an ambulance was parking out front.

"Isn't it a little late for that?" Rick said.

"We don't have an undertaker, don't even have a morgue. They'll transport both bodies to old Doc Willets in Palma. Doc will do the autopsies and sign the death certificates."

They watched as the two attendants rolled Gundry's body onto a stretcher with no more concern for his earthly remains than they'd have for a dog in the gutter.

After they were gone and it was just the four of them again, the Sheriff again looked like he'd swallowed something bad, then Jaspinder Singh thought he'd cry and he fought the tears as he listened to the Sheriff tell Judy Donovan that her brother-in-law, his wife and daughter had been found dead in the Wetlands.

As soon as he'd finished the horrible telling, the phone rang again. This time it was the boy, J.P. Donovan. He was out of breath, wanted to talk to the Sheriff and Jaspinder Singh knew, as he handed the phone over, that it was more bad news, so he wasn't surprised when the Sheriff said, "It's J.P. He's calling from your house, Mr. Gordon. He had to break a window to get in. Seems like there's trouble up there."

* * *

Rick jumped from the police car and ran into the house. Ann was stretched out on the sofa, looking ashen. "I'm here, Annie," he said, brushing the damp hair from her face.

"Judy," Ann whispered. She was fading fast and she knew it.

"I'm here," Judy said.

Ann struggled, held out her hand.

Judy took it and gave her a gentle squeeze.

"Thank you." Ann sighed as she took her hand back. Everything was going to be all right now.

"Annie, what's wrong?" Rick said.

"Come closer, Flash." She reached out, rubbed her husband's cheek. "Give me your scar," she whispered, barely loud enough for him to hear. He bent his head low, offering the scar under his ear and she ran her tongue along it. "Smile for me one last time."

He did and she died.

CHAPTER FIVE

SIX HOURS TILL SHERRY. Evan was lost in the thought of her. The creamy brown eyes and full lipped smile hung in the haze of his memory as he rolled the hundred dollar bill.

Smiling with anticipation, he bent over the table, put the rolled bill to his nose, and inhaled. Then he sat back and felt the calm course through his body. The first line was always the best. He listened to the sounds of the Stones playing low in the background. For a few seconds he was one with the music. He was completely aware.

He opened his eyes and bent to inhale the second line, when he heard the bell. He inhaled quickly, annoyed that the anticipated rush was being interrupted.

"Who is it?" he called downstairs.

"Rick."

"Come on up." He heard the door open and footsteps on the stairs. He covered the residue on the table with a magazine and stuffed the rolled hundred into his shirt pocket.

"I thought you would be jogging," he said, as his friend came into the living room.

"Not today," Rick Gordon said, "I'm going back to California."

"You know you can stay as long as you like."

"Hey, New York's great, but I belong somewhere on the Coast. Besides, I've been abusing your hospitality for almost six months. It's about time I got on with my life."

"You've been paying rent on the apartment. If it wasn't for you, I'd probably be renting the downstairs to starving students. You know the kind, always late on the rent. Parties, girls, noise."

"I gotta go, Evan."

"When are you leaving?"

"Tonight, I'm going to stop in L.A. for a few days and see Christina, then it's back to Tampico. I was hoping you'd give me a ride to the airport."

"I can't, I got a date with Sherry. I'll get my father to do it."

"You sure?"

"I think he likes you better than me. He'll be glad to do it."

Evan Hatch walked across the room to the phone and tapped the buttons.

* * *

Rick dropped on the divan, closed his eyes and listened to

Mick Jagger's voice coming out of his friend's speakers.

"*You can't always get what you want,*" repeated the chorus, "*You can't always get what you want, but if you try sometimes, you just might find, you get what you need.*"

Very true, he thought, before Ann's death, he'd managed to get anything he'd ever wanted out of life. And he hadn't been born with a silver spoon in his mouth, he'd earned what he'd wanted. He was no stranger to hard work. He'd taken risks and they'd paid off. But since Ann's death, the only thing he wanted was her back, and the only thing he needed was food and water and a place to sleep.

"What time you wanna be picked up?" Evan's voice snapped him out of his reverie.

"Two, my plane leaves at 5:00, that should be plenty of time."

"Can you be here by 2:00?" Rick heard him say, then he watched him hang the phone up.

"Thanks," Rick said.

"You sure you're ready?"

"I've got to go back. I have to put the house on the market, deal with her things and sell the Jeep."

"You sure that's the best?"

"I can't live in that house without Ann. Everything there reminds me of her, the house, the furniture, the Jeep. I have to shed it all."

"Maybe that's not such a bad thing, being reminded of her. She occupied a large chunk of your life."

"What time you seeing Sherry?" Rick asked, changing the subject.

"Lunch at one."

"When are you going to let it go?"

"Never."

"Jeez, you gotta get her out of your mind."

"I can't. It must be love."

* * *

Evan had been in love with Sherry Quilvang since a cold New York winter day in 1986 when he'd stumbled into her at the Record Rack. He had been making a cold call and she had been the girl behind the counter. Although he had fallen in love with her at first sight, she had been in love with her employer, who also happened to be her husband. Over the years he'd become her friend and confidant, and, during her rocky marriage, had spent many an hour over a bottle of wine acting the big brother.

"I gotta pack." Rick offered his hand and Evan grasped it. "Thanks for the use of the place, you're a good friend."

"You'd do the same for me," Evan said.

"Will I see you before I go?"

"No, I have to go to the Village and drop off some CDs before I meet Sherry."

"Good luck." Rick turned and went down the stairs.

"I'll see you in California next month," Evan yelled after him.

"Looking forward to it," Rick shouted back, then he was out the door.

Alone again, Evan removed the magazine, laid out two more lines, then inhaled them. Feeling as good as he thought he was going to get, he donned a black leather jacket and bounced down the stairs and out the front door. He walked around to the back, flicking the button on the garage door opener and climbed into his BMW. He was halfway down the street before the door thudded shut.

When he rounded the first corner, a red Toyota started and followed. It stayed with him all the way to the train station.

* * *

Sitting across from Sherry in the restaurant, he felt the tension, something was different. She kept changing the subject and fidgeting with the menu, and the way she kept crossing and uncrossing her legs was putting him on edge. He wondered what was bothering her.

"Would you like to start with a drink?" the approaching waitress asked.

"I'll have a double vodka martini, straight up, no olive," Sherry said.

Evan was taken aback. She usually only drank wine. Something was definitely up.

"And you, sir?" the waitress asked.

"Make it the same." If she was going to drink doubles, then he was, too.

The waitress left and Sherry buried her face in the menu.

"What's up?" he asked her.

"Nothing." Her perfect teeth barely squeaked through a loose smile. He noticed a drop of sweat making its way from her hairline down her forehead. She was wound up tighter than Mick Jagger's pants.

"You sure?" he asked her.

"You know, we've never been on a real date."

"I don't think your husband would appreciate it."

"You're probably right, but I don't think I care anymore."

Evan was stunned, he felt like he'd been hit with a hammer. In all the years that he'd been having lunch with her, she hadn't once suggested that she was interested in anything more. Greg and Sherry were the perfect couple. He was a great guy, confident and sure of himself, allowing Sherry to have her own friends. The man hadn't once hinted that he objected to his twice a month lunches with his wife or their frequent phone calls. If Sherry was his wife, he'd watch over her like the environmental wackos watched over the California gray spotted owl.

"We took in a mint copy of *London Roundhouse* last week, the original *Trade Mark of Quality* version," she said.

"Really?" she had his full attention. He had one of the best collections of Rolling Stones records in the world, but he was missing that one.

"That's the second TMQ Stones record, isn't it?" she twinkled.

"No, the third, *European Tour* was the second."

"And Rick really didn't save any copies of his stuff?"

"No."

"Doesn't he know that some of the original TMQ records are worth hundreds of dollars?"

"He doesn't care."

"He should, he could have made a fortune by just hanging onto three or four copies of every record he made."

"He has enough money."

"It must be nice."

"He has problems, like everybody else," Evan said, pushing his chair away from the table. "Excuse me, I have to go to the restroom." She smiled at him as he rose. God, he loved her, he thought, as he made his way through the restaurant toward the men's room at the back.

He pushed open the swinging door, glad the restroom was empty. He took the first stall, flipped down the toilet seat and sat without taking down his pants. Anticipating the rush, he took a small paper bindle out of his shirt pocket, carefully opened it and set it on his knee. Then he eased a crisp hundred out of his hip pocket and rolled it into a tight pencil thin tube. Already loose, he lifted the bindle of white powder and, with the rolled hundred to his nose, he inhaled twice, once in each nostril. Feeling better than he had in years, he closed the bindle and put it, with the hundred, into his shirt pocket.

If he was going to be drinking doubles, he'd need the coke. The white powder kept him sober, but it was a delicate balancing act, walking a thin line between the stimulant and the depressant.

On his way out of the bathroom, he stopped by the wash basins to check his hair. He quickly ran a comb through it, making sure there were no tangles. Then he bent forward, into the mirror, to inspect a pimple forming at the bridge of his nose.

"Those are the worst kind," a voice from behind said. "You don't know if you should pop them or leave them alone." Evan checked out the voice's owner in the mirror.

"I pop them," the man said.

"I tend to leave them," Evan said.

"You're Evan Hatch, aren't you?"

"Do I know you?"

"We met at Beatlefest, last year." Beatlefest was the yearly gathering of New York's Beatle fans. They swarm into the Hilton Convention Center to buy, swap, and sell Beatle collectibles. Like the Star Trek conventions, which Evan also attended, they got bigger every year.

"I met a lot of people there, it's hard to remember them all."

"Storm, Sam Storm." The big man held out his hand and Evan shook it.

"I gotta go, I got a girl waiting."

"Maybe I'll see you around," Storm said.

"Maybe." Evan turned and left the restroom.

"What took so long?" Sherry asked when he returned

to the table.

"I met a guy in the john that I knew." He didn't want to tell her that he'd been sitting in a toilet stall, finishing off the gram of coke that he'd started earlier in the day.

"You know I was thinking," she said, "if I went through your Stones collection, I would know exactly what you had and the next time we got something in, I'd know for sure whether you had it or not."

"What do you want to do that for? You know exactly what I need."

"I know, I'm just looking for an excuse to go to your place."

"Why?"

"Evan, you silly, can't you tell when a girl wants to go to the submarine races?"

"I don't understand."

"That's what we called making out in high school, the submarine races."

His tongue was planted firm against his bottom teeth, temporarily frozen. This was a moment he thought would never happen.

"Come on, say something."

"I just never thought—"

"Well, don't think now. Drop some money on the table and let's get the train to Great Neck. It's about time I saw your place."

* * *

She slept with her head on his shoulder during the train ride and was sexually silent as he shepherded her to his BMW, and the only thing she said on the ride to his place was, "I'm really looking forward to this." Her voice was electrifyingly erotic and he was euphoric.

"You take my breath away," he said.

"And you leave me breathless," she answered.

He was in heaven, spine-chilling, spine-tingling, spine-thrilling heaven.

As soon as they were in the door, they were in each other's arms. Evan scooped her up, carried her to the bedroom, dropped her on the bed.

"God, you look great," he said as he stood back to look at her.

"Come here, you," she said.

He jumped on the bed and they were instantly entangled, a mass of arms and legs. He ran his hands up and down her back, then with a daring he didn't know he had, he reached under her blouse and unhooked her bra. He hadn't done that since high school.

She moaned in his ear as her breasts sprang free.

He brought his hands around to them, cupping one in each hand.

She nibbled in his ear and moaned louder.

Trembling, he pulled the blouse over her head and gasped when he saw her breasts. "They're magnificent." He lowered his head to take a nipple into his mouth.

She arched her back and moaned still louder.

Without removing his mouth, he worked her skirt up and put a hand inside her panty hose. She wasn't wearing panties.

"Take them off, quick," she whispered with her tongue in his ear. He complied, rolling them off of her agreeing form, leaving her clad in nothing but her short checkered skirt.

"Do you like me like this, naked and waiting, wanting you?"

"I sure do." And he pulled her toward him. Their lips met, tongues jousting. She tugged at his belt and pulled down the zipper of his jeans.

Holding fast to her tongue, he pushed his underwear and jeans to his knees, then, kicking off his loafers, he shed the pants. She grabbed between his legs and it was his turn to moan, and to worry.

"What's the matter," she said, "don't I excite you?"

"It'll be okay," he said. He gently pushed her back, knowing that it wouldn't be. Why of all days did he coke himself up today. And why of all days, did she pick today to finally succumb. Life wasn't fair.

All of a sudden Mick Jagger and the Rolling Stones started to scream as his stereo jumped to life.

Evan sat bolt upright.

"Somebody's here," Sherry said.

* * *

Sam Storm cranked up the volume, and while the couple in the bedroom were still in a state of surprise, he burst into the room, grinning.

Evan jumped off the bed, determined to make a fight of it, but he was no match for Storm. He interrupted Evan's lunge with a blow to the face that knocked him out. Then he turned to face the girl.

"I'll do anything you want," she said.

"If you fuck good enough, I might leave you alive."

"I'll fuck great," she whimpered.

He reached into his coat and pulled out a length of rope and said, "Bring that chair over here."

She did it.

He picked up the unconscious man, set him in the chair and tied his hands behind it and his feet to its legs. Then he said, "Suck his cock."

She went down on her knees, took him in her mouth and began sucking on his limp member.

"If you don't make it hard, you die."

She ran her tongue over the tip and pumped her hand up and down the shaft. After about five minutes Evan came to and ruined Sam's fun.

"Sherry, what are you doing?" he moaned.

"If I don't make it hard he's going to kill us."

"Stop it, Sherry. He's going to kill us anyway."

She stopped, "But he said."

"He lied."

The woman turned to look at Sam. "You said."

"Your boyfriend is right, I'm going to kill you anyway," he said. Then he grabbed the kneeling woman by the hair and slit her throat with his razor sharp Bowie knife. She twitched, gagged, then slumped to the floor, drowning in her own blood.

"Why?" Evan asked.

"Because Rick Gordon ruined my life." Then he swung the knife in a great arc and removed Evan Hatch's head.

CHAPTER
SIX

RICK WAS THE LAST off the plane. He wasn't in a hurry. He said his good-byes to the flight crew with a smile he didn't feel, hoisted his shoulders and walked off like a man with nowhere to go.

"Uncle Rick, over here!"

He looked up, smiled a real smile at the two visions of teenage loveliness that came rushing toward him.

"Oh no, the Tees," he,d been calling the twins that since they were toddlers. T for Torry, the oldest by three minutes, and S for Swell. T & S, the Tees. Because the girls were identical, Christina gave them unique names.

He dropped his carry-bag, took a girl under each arm.

"Are you going to stay awhile this time?" Torry asked, "or are you going to pass through without taking us anywhere?" For the last twelve years, every time he came to Los Angeles, he took the twins somewhere big, Disneyland, Knott's Berry Farm, Magic Mountain, the zoo, or Mexico. The challenge was always to have a better time than the last time.

"I thought I might take your mother to dinner and leave you two home to wait up."

"We have to go someplace good," Torry pouted.

"No, we don't. You take Mom someplace good," Swell said, shooting her sister a look that said, "Shut up!"

"Where is your mother?"

"She's out front, parked in the red," Torry said, smiling.

"That figures." Rick remembered that Christina had told him once that the reason curbs were painted red was so she could always have a place to park. She paid about five hundred dollars a year in parking fines.

"How come she didn't come in with you guys?"

"A cop was hassling her about parking there, so she sent us in," Torry said.

"Did she move the car?"

"Don't bet on it. If I know Mom, she started an argument with the poor cop that won't end till she sees us walking out the door," Swell said.

"Your mother is one of a kind." Rick laughed. The last time he'd arrived in L.A. the twins were gangling girls who went careening through the concourse, causing travelers to take cover to avoid being run down by their rambunctious cascade. Now they were young women.

Squinting as they left the terminal, he curved his lips into a smile. Swell knew her mother, she was indeed arguing with a pair of police officers.

Seeing Rick and her daughters approaching, she smiled, said to the officers, "Okay you win, I'll move it."

The policemen, knowing they'd been had, shook their heads as Rick and the girls climbed into the red Toyota convertible.

"Pretty blondes always get their way," one of the officers said with a smile on his face.

"But they shouldn't." Rick laughed.

"But they do," the other officer said as Christina started the car.

Sitting in the shotgun position with the twins in back, Rick thought about Christina. When they first met she was pregnant and married to one of his best customers, and when her husband died two years later, he was pleased to let her continue buying his product. She paid on time and he had grown to love the twins as if they were his own.

"Time truly does heal all wounds," she said, as if reading his mind.

"That's what I hear."

"You know," she added, "I've been trying to get a hold of Evan all night and kept getting his machine."

"When I left he was on his way to have lunch with you know who. Maybe he finally got lucky."

"Maybe." She put a CD into the player. Christina was a devoted Beatle fan and collector, so, for the remainder of the ride to her house in Long Beach, he was treated to forty-five minutes of alternate versions of famous Beatle songs. Like most collectors, she preferred the bootleg versions to the originals.

Three hours later, after they had deposited his things and the twins at her house, they were sitting in a quiet restaurant.

"How long have you been a vegetarian?" he asked her

after the waiter had taken their order.

"I didn't say I was."

"You ordered the stir fry. I seem to remember you as a hamburger with lots of onions kind of person."

"When you get older you begin to confront your own mortality. If giving up meat can give me a few more healthy years, plus help me keep the pounds off, well, it's a small sacrifice."

He took in her figure. "You've lost quite a bit, haven't you?"

"Fifteen pounds."

"You look great and may I say you've lost it in all the right places," he said.

"Why, Rick, I believe you're flattering me."

"I guess I am."

"They say that flattery will get you anywhere."

"Will it?"

"Not with the twins at home."

"Yeah, the twins," he said and they both laughed.

For the next three hours they talked about everything from rock and roll to the state of the economy, staying well away from any more talk of a sexual or flirtatious nature, but as they were leaving the restaurant, he wrapped his arm around her waist and she answered back by wrapping her arm around his.

They made small talk on the short ride back to her place, each noticing a new kind of tension building a gap between them, and each wondering if it could ever be closed. Their years of friendship—instead of making their new-found awareness of each other's sexual identity an easy, natural thing—made them kind of awkward with each other.

Rick pulled her into his arms as they were mounting the porch steps, his lips on hers before she had time to react. She responded by opening her mouth and receiving his tongue. The kiss was passionate and long.

"Whoa," she said, stepping back, "I need air."

"I don't know what came over me," he said. "I'm sorry."

"Don't be, I'm not complaining. I'm just trying to get used to the idea."

"Well, what do you think?"

"I think I like it, but I need a little time."

"I understand." He also needed time and was thankful for her level head. "The girls left the lights off," he said.

"I think they wanted us to have a little time alone in the dark."

"Really?"

"Yeah and seeing that they're out, I think we should take advantage of it." She wrapped her arms around him, pulled him to her. This time she initiated the kiss.

When they broke away after the long kiss he said, "I think it's time to go in, the girls are probably waiting up."

"Sitting on the other side of the door laughing, if I know them," she said.

She turned, inserted her key and opened the door.

The living room was lit by a soft bulb, casting soft shadows from an amber shaded Tiffany lamp.

"I read by that lamp, those imps changed the bulb."

"There's a note." Rick laughed, pointing to a sheet of lined paper taped to the glass lamp shade. He crossed the room and removed the message. "Listen to this," he chuckled. "Mom, we're spending the night at Donna's. You guys have fun."

"Those little brats." She tried to conceal her laughter.

"What do we do now?" he asked.

"How about we go out to the kitchen and have a drink, like two friends?"

"Okay." He followed her through the swinging door into the kitchen.

"What'll it be?" she asked, "more cabernet or Bailey's and coffee?"

"Bailey's and coffee."

"It'll have to be instant."

"That's fine."

She filled two cups with water and added a teaspoon of instant coffee to each and stirred. Then she put both cups in the microwave and set the timer for two minutes.

"I'll be right back," she said. "I'm going to let my hair down."

Rick watched as she left the room. He tried to imagine what she would be wearing when she returned. Would it be a sexy negligee or a simple tee shirt with nothing on underneath. His anticipation was high, but was soon dashed when she returned, wearing the same clothes she'd had on when she'd left. She had, however, let her hair down.

She took the coffee out of the microwave and added a generous portion of Bailey's Irish Cream, then handed a cup over to Rick.

"Have a seat," he said.

She drew a chair out from the table and sat down across from him.

"I've been thinking about you a lot lately," she said.

"And I you." He sipped the hot liquid.

"You wanna smoke a joint?" she asked.

"I didn't know you still did that."

"I don't. I haven't smoked grass in over fifteen years."

"Then why the question?"

"One of the girls left it on their dresser. I confiscated it."

"What did you say to them?"

"Nothing, I don't think they're smoking, I think they were just curious. Besides, even if they do smoke a little grass occasionally, I did when I was their age. It won't kill them."

"They didn't say anything about it being gone?"

"No, they know I found it and I know they know." She smiled and pulled the rolled marijuana cigarette out of her blouse pocket.

"So you didn't just let your hair down?" Surprisingly Rick found himself eager.

He watched in anticipation as she struck a match, then lit and inhaled the sweet tasting smoke. Holding her breath, she handed the joint across the table to him. He took a long drag and passed it back. After three hits he was as stoned as he'd ever been.

"This stuff is a lot stronger than what we used to get," he said.

"Yeah." She got up from the table. "I've been thinking about this for a long time." She pulled her blouse over her head. She wasn't wearing a bra. "Let's go to the bedroom." She held out her hand.

He followed her up the stairs and into her bedroom. He watched as she crossed over to the nightstand. She picked up a Zippo and lit it. The lighter fluid smell wafted over and zapped him, reminding him of the time when he used to smoke and of how intense your senses are when you're stoned.

She bent to light a candle and the combined effect of the lighter's and candle's light, both flickering, turned her breasts into twin nippled, bewitching yellow moons, casting a spell that shot straight through to his loins. Still leaning forward with her breasts dangling, she lit an incense stick and then she straightened, clicking the Zippo shut.

The pungent smell of the incense overpowered the sharp smell of lighter fluid and reminded him of his hippie days in the Sixties. Civil rights workers marched and fought in the South. John, Bobby and Martin were shot. The North Vietnamese were fighting America to a standstill in Southeast Asia. He grew his hair long, smoked dope and demonstrated in front of draft boards. Then his older brother was killed in Vietnam and he joined the Army and it all changed.

"Brings you back," he said.

"To a happier time?" she questioned.

"To a different time."

She came over to him and started to unbutton his shirt. He was speechless. He felt so good and Christina looked so right, topless in the flickering candlelight. When she reached the final button, she crossed around behind him and pulled his shirt off.

Then she pressed her body into his, rubbing her breasts into his back as she lowered her hands to undo his button fly Levi's. The sound of the buttons popping open echoed throughout the room.

"Are you sure you want to do this?"

"Hush." She went down on her knees dragging her breasts down his back and buttocks as she pulled his Levi's and boxer shorts down.

"I'm hung up on the shoes." She laughed as she untied them. "Raise your foot."

He raised his right leg and she pulled off the shoe and the right pant's leg.

"Raise the other one."

He complied and she repeated the procedure, leaving him standing naked with her behind him on her knees. She put a hand on each leg and spun him around. Then she surprised him by taking his stiff penis into her mouth and before he had time to think, he was spurting and she was swallowing.

"I'm sorry," he said. "I couldn't hold it."

"That's okay." She smiled. "We have all night."

"No one's ever done that to me."

"Really? Ann never did that?" she asked, getting to her feet.

"No, never."

"Why not?"

"I don't know. We just never did that kind of stuff."

"How often did you guys have sex?"

"Almost every night."

"Was it good sex?"

"It was always great." He felt a pain in his heart. He would never be over her death. She was the first thought in his mind when he woke and the last before he fell asleep. Their sex, by some people's standards, may have been routine, but it was full of love, and love, he thought, was never routine. If more people enjoyed the kind of sex life he'd shared with Ann, then the world would be a better place.

She took his hand and gently led him to the bed. They cuddled in each other's arms and kissed. She broke away and stripped off her skirt and panties, allowing Rick to revel in her body.

"I haven't been with anyone since Ann died and it's been only Ann for the last twenty-five years."

"Then I'm going to do my very best to make this special," she whispered, lowering her lips to his, while at the same time reaching between his legs, making sure he was hard again. She let go of him and rolled onto her back, guiding him into her and they began a long, slow, easy kind of love-making that continued for the better part of an hour, ending with them climaxing together.

And at that final moment, for reasons he didn't understand, a picture of Judy Donovan flashed through his mind.

CHAPTER
SEVEN

THE ENGINE CHANGED from a smooth rumble to the rough chugging of idle. They were there. It was still dark. On Fridays the *Seawolf* left the Palma Pier at midnight on its weekly overnighter for the serious anglers. Judy, like most of the fishermen, slept till they reached the fishing grounds.

Steeling herself, she rolled off her bunk onto the deck, put on her shoes and headed for the galley. Coming from the warmth of below to the cold of a morning at sea snapped her awake. Sometimes she asked herself if it was worth it, but J.P. loved to go out on the all day boat.

Drinking a cup of coffee, she picked up her rod with

its five hooks and headed toward the bait tank, trying not to slip on the slimy deck. She set the coffee by the tank and, with a quick count to three, thrust her hand in, grabbing for an anchovy. The bait net was gone. She latched onto one of the fast moving little fish and jerked her hand out of the cold water, spilling her coffee.

She baited one of her hooks, repeated the process four more times, then sighed when a smiling man returned the net without a clue that he had committed a gross rudeness by taking it away from the tank. She felt like telling him, but instead took her rod over to her position.

Looking overboard, she saw a school of silvery mackerel swim by and uttered one word, "Shit," under her breath. They'd try to steal her bait before it hit bottom, where the unsuspecting cod lay waiting to become dinner. She hoped she had enough weight on the line to get her hooks down before she lost her anchovies. Crossing her fingers, she dropped the line into the water and watched it sink.

She smiled when the bait slid by the mackerel without a strike and she spun out her line. Five hundred feet to the sea floor. Then she wound up five turns and waited. She thought about a cigarette as she watched the gulls soar overhead, backlit by the rising sun, but it had been almost a year and she didn't want to start back up. Settling in to get comfortable, she felt the first quick tug, then another, then a third. She started winding.

"Fish tonight!" she yelped.

Then she saw it, six feet of graceful glory, circling twenty feet away. Blue shark. Shifting her gaze skyward she saw three pregnant looking birds gliding into position. Pelicans. It wasn't going to be easy. When she judged she had only about fifty feet of line left, she stopped winding and watched the shark. It seemed an eternity, the animal had done this thousands of times, she was an amateur compared to it. She watched as the shark turned and headed toward her line. There was nothing she could do if it decided to take it. Then without warning it turned and struck.

"Damn!" an unlucky fisherman cursed as Judy wound with all the fury she could muster.

Forty feet, then thirty, then twenty, ten.

"Oh boy!" she squealed.

Another shark, coming fast. Five feet, closing rapidly.

With a jerk she pulled the line, winding furiously and grinning as dinner, eyes bulging, burst from the ocean. But the grin was short lived, because a pelican, diving like a kamikaze, swooped out of the sky and grabbed her fish. It swallowed, fish, hook and all. Then it went limp and waited. Waited to be cut loose. Like the shark, it too had played this game before, it was like the birds knew they were protected. Gone was her dinner. There was nothing left to do, but cut the bird free, curse and try again.

Such are the perils of rock cod fishing, she thought as she heard J.P. shout out, "Mom, that was almost beautiful." Hearing him say that made it all worthwhile.

"Did you catch anything yet?" she asked her son.

"Naw, I slept in." It didn't even occur to her to look for him when she got up. She thought he would be up front at his favorite spot fishing with the regulars. The fact that he wasn't, meant that something was wrong.

"I'm sorry, I didn't notice. I just assumed you were up and at 'em. You always are."

"I was sleeping too good to get up early."

She was worried about that. She wanted to know why and though she didn't want to pry, she thought that maybe now was the time to bring it up.

"You haven't been sleeping well lately, have you?"

"What?" J.P. snapped his eyes away from the blue Pacific and looked at his mother.

"Come on J.P., I hear you get up during the night and go to the kitchen. And I see the way you drag your butt around the house. What's wrong?"

"Nothing."

"Come on, you can tell me."

"You'll think I'm stupid."

"I would never think that."

"Dick Rainmaker told me that he saw the Ghost Dog."

"What?"

"You know, the Ragged Man's dog."

"J.P., that was just a silly superstitious story that Ann believed in."

"It killed her, and I really did see a knife that day. I did."

"It did not kill her. She had cancer. She was sick and she had a stroke. We've been over this knife business. It was a bad day, you saw those poor souls with a knife and you imagined they had something to do with Ann's dying."

"No, I didn't, and I saw something big and black go into the bushes. It was the Ghost Dog." He was convinced.

She'd thought J.P. was over that horrible day. He was resilient and she'd thought, no hoped, that he'd bounced back, but apparently that story about the Ragged Man gave his memory something to hang on to. She wished he would let it go.

"Maybe you saw a dog or something out back, but that doesn't mean it was the Ghost Dog and who started calling it that anyway?"

"All us kids call it that."

"If you and the other kids are seeing anything, it's probably just someone's big dog running loose."

"Okay, Mom, let's not talk about it anymore."

"Okay." She felt like he was shutting her out and she hated it.

"J.P.," came the booming voice of Wolfe Stewart, "we missed you this morning." Judy turned and saw the bearded captain approaching.

"I didn't feel like getting up, Captain."

"Really, you?"

"J.P. hasn't been feeling well lately," Judy said.

"Well I got some news that will perk you up."

"What?" J.P. asked.

"Rick called a couple of days ago. He said he'll be back soon."

"Oh boy! Mom did you hear that, Rick's coming back. He'll know what to do about the Ghost Dog."

"What?"

"It's nothing Wolfe, just a fantasy."

"Is not."

"J.P.!"

"It's nothing, Captain," the boy said, understanding the tone of his mother's voice.

"Coming up front, J.P.?" the captain asked as he turned to leave.

"Mom, I'm going up front to fish with the guys. Okay?"

"That's fine J.P., I think I'll get some breakfast. You want to use my rod?"

"Okay."

Judy handed him the rod and watched as they started for the bow.

"Wolfe," Judy called after the captain.

"Yes." He turned back to face her.

"Where is Rick now?" She didn't know why she wanted to know.

"He's visiting a friend in L.A."

"Christina Page?"

"I wouldn't know. All I do know," he said, with an unmistakable twinkle in his eyes, "is that he called and asked how you and J.P. were doing." He paused for a second, as if in thought. "Oh yeah, and he told me he'd be back soon."

"Thank you."

"It's nothing," the captain said, dodging a fisherman on his way to the bait tank.

"Oh, Captain," she called again.

"Yes."

"Why didn't he call me if he wanted to know how we were?"

"That's a good question." He smiled his answer, then with a wave, he left and went back to the front of the boat, leaving Judy to ponder what he'd said.

She suspected that Rick was staying with Christina Page. Christina was one of his old bootleg cronies and bootleg cronies stuck together.

Having been married to one of them, Judy knew about Rick's four big customers: Evan, the Rolling Stones collector in New York; her ex-husband, Tom, the Led Zeppelin collector in Toronto; Danny, the Bob Dylan collector in New Orleans; and Christina Page, the Beatle collector in Long Beach.

She stopped her reminiscing and made her way to the galley to replace the spilled coffee. She took the steps down to the galley, bouncing through the door, smiling at the old men playing poker in one of the four booths.

"How's it going, guys?"

"Great," a bucktoothed man named Henry said,

"except for the fact that I'm losing my shirt."

"You guys paid to fish," she said.

"And we're gonna, right after this hand."

Judy took the booth across from the poker players and watched as Henry won the hand with a queens over tens full house. She wished them luck as they made their way topside to wrestle with the Pacific for their dinner.

"I'll be back in a flash." The cook dropped a plastic menu on her table. "Nature calls and I need a break."

"Take your time, I'm not in a hurry."

"Coffee pot is behind the counter, I'll be back in fifteen or twenty." He took the steps two at a time, leaving Judy alone in the galley, studying the menu.

"Mind if I join you?"

She looked up to see a big man with close cropped hair.

"No, of course not, I'd appreciate the company." She was drawn to his steel gray eyes.

"I don't like fishing," he said.

"Then why come out on an all day fishing boat?"

"I'm in town awhile, kind of on vacation, and I was bored. But now instead of being bored in a nice warm motel room at six in the morning, I'm bored on a freezing cold fishing boat in the middle of the ocean."

"I'm a little bored myself." Judy laughed, catching his smile.

"Then let's be bored together," he said.

"What a marvelous idea. Would you like some coffee?" She rose and walked behind the counter, without waiting for his answer, and poured two cups.

"Black."

"Two black coffees coming up." She carried the cups back to the table and set them down.

"Thanks," he said.

"My name is Judy Donovan." She held out her hand.

"Sam Storm," the handsome gray-eyed man said, taking her hand.

* * *

Judy hung up the phone with a smile. It had been a long time since she'd been out with a man. She was looking forward to dinner. The dinner didn't really seem like a date, more like extending the long conversation that was interrupted when the *Seawolf* docked. She checked the wall clock, 4:30. An hour and a half and she had much to do.

She waltzed out of the kitchen and danced up the stairs. She was acting like a girl on her first date and it felt good. Sam Storm might be closing on sixty, but he was still a head turner, and he was a charmer. The way he looked at her made her feel wanted. Of course, she told herself, she was probably imagining it. Men didn't go out of their way to meet a small town woman with a child.

At the top of the stairs, she entered the bathroom, whirling in front of the full length mirror, keeping her eyes on her reflection as she spun around. Her new figure looked good. She had been without sex for so long, she wondered what it would be like.

She unbuttoned her shirt and slid it off with a fluid motion. Her jeans and panties followed. She kicked them out of the bathroom and shivered into the shower. It wasn't cold, but goosebumps ran up, down and around her body. The hot shower failed to calm her. She was excited.

She shampooed her hair and rinsed. Conditioned her hair and rinsed. Added more conditioner, shaved her legs, rinsed again. Changed blades, shaved again. Shut off the water, toweled off. Dried her hair, smiled at the mirror.

She was ready.

Ready but naked, she laughed to herself.

She padded out of the bathroom to her bedroom. She thought for an instant about what to wear, then selected a lavender silk blouse and tight CK jeans. She decided against bra, panties or panty hose.

She slid her bare feet into a beige pair of low heels and dashed down the stairs. Only thirty minutes had passed since she'd hung up the phone. An hour to go. Forever.

"Wait a minute," she told herself out loud. "What am I doing? I'm not that kind of woman!" Never had she planned on sex before a date. And this wasn't a real date. It was dinner, nothing more.

She marched back upstairs, unbuttoning the silk blouse as she took the steps. She shucked it off as she entered the bedroom. Then she dropped the CKs. Moving toward her dresser, she thought that maybe she was going a little crazy. A year and a half without a man was a long time. From her top drawer she found a frilly bra and matching cotton panties. The next drawer down yielded a cotton Hawaiian print dress. She put it on, then plucked an elastic out of a box on top of the dresser and pulled her hair back into a ponytail.

A horn honked. He was early. Grabbing her purse on her way to the door, she hoped she wasn't doing something stupid. All thoughts of a smooth prince vanished when she saw the dusty Ford. She put on a brave smile and jumped in the car. He honked the horn, she thought, he didn't even come to the door.

"Hi," he said, "I'm a little early."

"That's okay, I was ready."

"I didn't see any sense pacing the motel room waiting, so I grabbed the bull by the horns and here I am."

"I'm glad you did. I was a little anxious myself."

"Anxious? I wasn't anxious, I was sweating. I haven't been on a date since my wife died fifteen years ago."

"Really, Sam? It's been eighteen months for me. Eighteen months since my divorce, but you can't expect me to believe that you haven't been with a woman in fifteen years."

"I didn't say I hadn't been with a woman. I said I hadn't been on a date."

"You have been with a woman then?"

"Well sure, a woman here and there that I might have met in a bar, but when you wake up next to someone you don't know, who couldn't care less if you were alive or dead, it hardly qualifies as a date."

"And when was the last time you met a woman in a bar, here or there?" Judy laughed. She was beginning to like Sam Storm. His honesty was refreshing.

"So long ago I can't remember." He laughed back.

He drove straight to the Tampico Diner, taking the alley shortcut off Kennedy, like he'd lived all his life in Tampico.

"How did you know about the short cut?"

"Whenever I come to a new town I make a habit of getting the lay of the land. I like to know my way around."

He parallel parked in front of the diner and jumped out of the car. He had her door open before she started to reach for the handle. A very interesting contradiction, she thought. He honks me out of the house, but he springs out to open the door. Mr. Storm was consistently inconsistent.

They spent the next three hours eating, drinking and talking about everything under the sun. He told her about his hopes and dreams, his successes and failures, his beliefs and fears, but he also listened. It was a two way conversation.

"This has been one of the nicest evenings I've had in a long time," she told him as they were getting ready to go.

"I'm glad you're enjoying yourself."

"I don't eat out often, in fact, I don't eat out at all. This was a real treat for me."

"I still think we should have brought your son," he said.

"I tried, but he didn't want to come." Judy was impressed with this man. Not many men would want a seven-year-old boy along on a dinner date.

"Why not?"

"He's staying at a friend's in town. It had been planned for a long time." She wondered why she'd told him that. Was she unconsciously trying to tell him that nobody was home at her house.

"Would you like another drink before we leave?"

"I don't think so. I'm ready if you are."

"I'm ready." He signaled the waiter and paid the bill with a credit card. Then he got up from the table, came around to her chair and eased it back as she rose.

"Very gallant," she said.

"Your arm, my lady," he said, offering his. She took it and they made their way out of the diner to the parking lot and his brown Ford Granada.

"You know, from our conversation on the boat, I would have pictured you in a flashy sports car," she said as he unlocked the passenger door for her.

"Why is that?" He seemed amused.

"You seem so independent, in control, a sports car kind of guy."

"Well, I guess I like all this pig iron around me. No question if I get in an accident with one of those little Jap cars who the winner is going to be."

For a second she felt a twinge. Was that a racist statement? She hoped not, he was such a caring man, she couldn't imagine that it was.

As if answering her thoughts he said, "I hope I didn't sound like I have a problem with the Japanese, I don't. I just don't like tiny, tinny cars. I spent a good deal of my Army time in Germany in a tank and I guess it rubbed off. I feel safer in a big heavy clunker."

"I can understand that," she said, getting into the car. She leaned back into the worn Naugahyde and closed her eyes. She couldn't remember when she'd felt so good.

"We're here," he said.

"What?" she opened her eyes.

"You fell asleep."

"I'm sorry."

"Don't be. You don't snore."

"Would you like to come in for a drink?"

"I was hoping you'd ask." He seemed tense to her.

"What are you thinking about?" she asked.

"Happier times," Sam Storm said.

"And times aren't happy now?"

"They're getting there." He smiled, getting out of the car. He walked around to her side and opened the passenger door.

"I don't think I've ever known a man that's done that for me," she said.

"A lady pretty as you should never have to open her own doors."

"Why thank you," Judy said, leading him up the walk to the front door. She fumbled with her keys at the porch as he stood by and watched. "Got it." She opened the door.

Once inside he reached for her shoulder, spun her around and covered her lips with his. She tried to protest, but he hugged her to him and it was all she could do to breathe. She reached her hand up to his shoulders and was starting to push away, when she felt his hand cup her buttocks and pull her in to him. She gasped when she felt his hardness.

He broke away from the kiss and lowered his mouth to her ear, "Will you obey me?"

Judy knew that she was at a crossroads. Something from down deep told her to say yes, or else, and besides she told that inner voice, a part of her wanted to submit to this man.

"What do you want?" she asked.

"Music, something slow." He opened his arms to let her go to the stereo.

She toyed with the idea of running, the situation was getting out of control, but realistically, she asked herself, how far could she get. Maybe it wouldn't be so bad, and still there was that part of her that wanted to submit, to abandon her problems and worries and wallow in a night of sexual pleasure.

She went through her CDs and decided on *Saxuality* by Candy Dulfer, a soft, soothing saxophone piece.

"I like that," he said.

"So do I."

"Dance."

"With you?"

"No, with the music." He crossed over to an easy chair and sat down. "I want to watch you."

She looked into his eyes and saw a touch of evil and started to dance. Whatever this man wanted, she decided, she would do.

She closed her eyes and started to sway with the music, moving her hips with the rhythm. Humming along with the saxophone, she tried to imagine that she was dancing for Rick Gordon, surprised that his image planted itself in her mind. She smiled coyly, kicked off her shoes and began moving with the music.

She was getting into it when he said, "Take off your dress."

Without opening her eyes or breaking her rhythm, she reached and grabbed her dress below the waist and lifted it over her head. She continued to dance, clad only in her bra and panties. She knew he could see her nipples and pubic hair through the thin fabric and she was both thrilled and terrified.

She reached behind her head, swaying with the music, and took out her ponytail. She swung her head back and forth, fanning her hair and waiting for his next command. She felt goosebumps on her skin and a tingling sensation running up and down her spine. She was dancing on the edge, sliding on a razor with no end in sight, more alive than she could remember.

Now she knew what freefall felt like, the stark terror of wondering if the chute would open or if she would Roman candle into the earth. She had no idea where this night would lead or how it would end, but she knew she would remember it always.

"Take off the bra."

She felt her smile broaden, in spite of her reservations, as she reached behind her back and undid the clasp. She gasped as her breasts sprang free and began to wonder what this big man would be like in bed.

She started to think about Rick in a sexual way about two months after Ann died, but she was tired of waiting for him to come home. This man was here now, and he obviously wanted her. Her fear was gone, she was enjoying herself and she was going to enjoy herself even more.

"Play with your tits."

She opened her eyes, meeting his dark glare, and she widened her smile, showing her perfect teeth. Then she did a slick bounce, bouncing her breasts like buoys on the water. She cupped one in each hand, pointing the nipples at him and she gently squeezed, moaning along with the saxophone.

Then she started to involuntarily undulate her hips. She felt her panties start to dampen as the orgasm approached. It hit her hard, almost knocking her over. She opened her mouth and let out a pleasure scream. She was unashamed and unable to stop. She stayed with the music till the orgasm ran its course, then started to slow as the rhythm slowed.

"Take off your panties and keep dancing."

She pushed them down, stepped out of them and faced him totally nude. She raised her hands toward the ceiling, spread her legs and swayed her hips, letting the jazzy sound rule her. Never in her wildest fantasies did she think that a man's cold stare could make her come.

"Play with your cunt."

She lowered both hands to her pubic region, inserting two fingers of her left hand, massaging herself with the beat.

"I'm going to do it again," she moaned. "It's coming, it's coming, it's coming." Then she screamed and collapsed to her knees, keeping her fingers in place, eyes locked all the while on the big man's steel grays.

Satisfied, but wanting more, she watched as Sam Storm stood and stripped off his shirt. He was a muscular man who obviously worked out. His biceps bulged without trying. His stomach was as flat as a high school athlete's and he had a thin mat of dark hair on his chest which accented his masculinity. She was a little afraid, a lot excited and she wanted to run her fingers through those hairs.

He kicked off his loafers and bent to take off his socks, while she watched, salivating like a dog in heat, all fear gone, ruled only by excitement and anticipation, watching, wanton and wicked as his hands went to his belt buckle and unclasped it.

Still on her knees, she started massaging herself afresh as he slid his zipper down. She picked up the pace, leaving the beat of the music far behind as his pants fell, leaving him clad only in bulging Jockey shorts.

"I want to see it," she mouthed, eyes glued to the bulge. He must be huge, she thought.

Pumping her fingers furiously, she gaped, mouth open, making animal sounds as the Jockey's went down and his manhood came into view.

"Oh, my," she moaned as the third orgasm tore into her, and despite the racking pleasure running through her body, she wondered if any woman could take in something so big.

Then it happened. Something stole into her mind, pushing her into the background. All pleasure left her body as she fought to stay in control. A tortured pain ripped into her brain, causing a scream that had nothing to do with ecstasy or euphoria to shoot out of her mouth.

And then she was gone.

"Smell—your—fear," Sam Storm said.

"Smell yours!" Judy Donovan said.

"I don't understand," Storm said.

"We've met before, you and I." She glared into his eyes.

"No," he croaked.

"We have, and we'll meet again." She sensed his fear. "I'm going to the bathroom to clean up. When I get back, be gone."

He was out the door before she started the shower.

She felt the water, prickly cold, cascading down her back. She reflexively grabbed the hot water spigot to warm up the beating spray. She was in the shower, safely enclosed by the stone brown tiles and the sliding glass door. Familiar surroundings, but how did she get there?

She remembered the dinner and remembered that maybe she'd had too much to drink. She remembered leaving the restaurant. After that everything was a blank. Except for that horrible black out.

She was revolted. She must have had a lot more to drink than she thought. Blacking out was a new experience for her, and one she didn't want to ever repeat again. She felt used, abused and incredibly thirsty. She raised her mouth to the spray and drank, hoping that the nauseated feeling would vanish with her thirst. It didn't.

She thought of Sam Storm, charming and delightful. She remembered the tempting thoughts she had of enticing him to her bed and she realized that she was sore. So she did have sex with the man, and from the way her body felt it must have been wild and wonderful.

"Damn," she muttered. Wild and wonderful sex and she couldn't remember it. Over a year without it and she couldn't remember it. Did she politely resist, then let him persuade her or did she submit willingly and jump straight into bed? She wished she could remember.

She opened the shower door slightly and reached out for the shampoo. She poured a generous amount on her wet hair and soaped it thoroughly. Then with a soapy hand, she rubbed herself between her legs and winced. She really was sore. She vowed never to drink again and she wondered if she would ever see Mr. Sam Storm again.

She rinsed herself off and stepped out onto the cold

tile. She was kind of glad the mirror was covered with steam, because she wasn't in the mood to look at herself and she was afraid that tonight she might not be the fairest of them all.

She toweled herself off, wrapped the towel around her hair, turban style, then padded into the bedroom and was startled to see the bed still made up. She'd expected it to be rumpled with the covers and pillows tossed on the floor. Where had she done the deed if not in the bedroom?

Trying to puzzle it out, she left the bedroom, crossed the hall and went into the living room, where she found her clothes strewn all over the floor.

Did she grab him, pull him down on top of her and do it right here on the floor? She didn't think so, more than likely she walked in alone, drunk, tore her clothes off and made straight for the shower. Therefore, she concluded, they must have gone to Sam's motel after dinner for fun and games and after they were finished, he probably dropped her at the door without coming in.

He probably didn't want to be here in the morning when J.P. came home. What a gentleman, she thought.

Maybe it would all come back to her after a good night's sleep.

She made her way back to the bedroom, satisfied that she had the evening figured out and eager to hit the pillows. She turned down the bed, turned off the lights, unwrapped the turbaned towel, shucked the robe, climbed between the sheets, and wondered why she was thinking about Rick Gordon as she dozed off to a deep, dreamless sleep.

CHAPTER

EIGHT

HE SAT FOUR TABLES AWAY from the stage and brooded. Damn the woman. How dare she? How could she? How did she?

Everything had been going along just fine. She had been doing exactly what he'd wanted, but when the time had come to kill her, she'd made him do what she'd wanted. It wasn't the way things were supposed to be. Ever since that day in the convenience store, he had been in control of his destiny, right up till three days ago.

Now he was tormented with confusion. New York had been easy. Tonight would be easy, but something had happened and that woman was responsible.

The next time he would tie her, blindfold her and make her suffer.

He felt the knife under his jacket and a hot glow coursed through him.

He could be whatever he wanted. Do whatever he wanted. After he rid himself of Rick Gordon. But before Gordon died, he would know that everyone he loved had been destroyed. Gordon would suffer before Storm captured him and skinned him alive.

That was his task, make Gordon and all his bootlegger friends pay for the humiliation he'd suffered all these years. Nobody made a fool out of Sam Storm and stayed alive.

And he owed it all to the knife. The knife gave him the strength. No longer was he hampered by liberal laws. He was Sam Storm and he would stamp out the bootleggers. And then, when free of those that had shamed him so often, he could finally rest.

He pulled his thoughts back to the task at hand and watched the man on stage, who he planned on killing before the evening was over. He was tall, gangly, bearded and in the middle of an Irish folk ballad, his fingers running up and down the neck of the guitar like a tape on fast forward.

Like with the one in New York, he had no set plan for killing Danny Morrow. He would wing it, but he was beginning to soften toward Danny, the Dylan collector. He liked Irish music and Danny Morrow played it well.

He had been drinking draft beer in the Bourbon Street Irish Pub for the last three sets, clapping and stomping with the music, enjoying himself as he hadn't done since college. He luxuriated in Danny's New Orleans brand of Irish folk humor and was laughing and clapping at the end of a bawdy joke, when he noticed

Danny signaling the audience to silence with raised hands.

"Ladies and gents, I have to leave early tonight." He was interrupted by shouts of "No," "Stay," and, "More," but he kept his hand raised till the audience quieted. "Sorry, but I've got a date with a river tomorrow in West Texas. We do, however, have what I think is a pretty fair replacement for you tonight. Ladies and Gentlemen, may I present Susan O'Malley."

Storm gasped as a stunning blond ascended the stage with an electric violin in her right hand. She was wearing an A shaped, white muslin skirt that fell halfway between her knees and the floor, allowing a hint of shapely legs, but what really tore at Storm's eyes were the twin globes of her rising breasts, reflecting the stage light as the moon does sunlight. She was both girl-like and woman-like in her peasant Spanish blouse. Her bare shoulders and creamy skin stole the looks of every man in the audience.

He was so taken with her that he didn't notice the man he'd come to kill leave the stage, nor did he feel Danny Morrow brush past him as he made his way through the crowd on his way to the exit.

Storm, captivated by the girl's Southern beauty, sat through four sets, applauding each song like a teenage lover. He wanted the night to never end, but at the end of the fourth set another band took the stage and his heart growled in protest. He jacked his head round the pub, but she was nowhere to be seen.

He paid his bill and left.

Once on the crowded walking street, he headed in the direction of the Sonesta Hotel. Bourbon Street was thronged with tourists, buskers and prostitutes, and flashing signs promising burlesque, boylesque, voodoo, female mudwrestling, tee shirt boutiques, bars and more bars.

He stopped at the crowded bar across from the Sonesta and looked in at all the people who seemed to be having a good time and he felt a pang. He didn't want the good time he was having to end. It had been so long since he'd been able to enjoy himself. He fought through the haze of his memory and tried to recall an earlier time when Rick Gordon and bootleg records occupied only a fraction of his life. A part of him was tugging him toward his hotel, where his car waited in the underground parking garage, but another part dragged him into the bar.

He pushed his way to the bar and ordered a Hurricane, the tall red drink that every tourist seemed required to try at least once. The heavily alcohol-laced drink caused him to stretch his facial muscles and reminded him of the last time he had been in this city of fun and excitement. He had been young and handsome and his wife had been alive.

Hurricane lips, he thought, Louise had Hurricane lips, her lipstick matched the red of the drink he was holding. He smiled at the memory of her. She loved New Orleans and New Orleans was the last happy time for her. She went into labor two weeks after their return to California and died in childbirth. The baby, born dead, had been a girl.

He raised the drink and drained the glass. The drink itself was too sweet for his taste, but the soothing effect of the alcohol was welcome. He chewed on the ice while he waited for the bartender to notice his glass was empty.

Two drinks later he left the bar and crossed the walking street to the hotel. He pushed through the door into the lobby with a slight nod to the girls at the reception desk. He continued to the back of the lobby and the stairs down to the garage below, where his rental car was parked.

Ten minutes later he drove by the big corner house where Danny Morrow lived. He turned the corner and parked. The house looked unoccupied, but Morrow left the pub more than three hours ago, maybe he was asleep. Storm shut off the engine and got out of the car. The street was middle-of-the-night silent and Storm took care not to make any noise as he crossed it and lifted the latch to the back gate. He eased himself into the backyard and studied the turn of the century house and, for a fleeting second, thought about returning to the car and leaving town.

He banished any thoughts about turning back. He'd come to kill a man. The mission demanded it, so he wondered how he was going to get into the house. He tried the back door. It was locked. He checked the two windows that were accessible from the back porch and discovered that they were also locked. It was a big house, with a lot of windows. He started working around to the side and discovered a window with a broken pane on his fifth try. He reached his hand through the opening, unlocked it, raised it, and climbed into the house.

While his eyes were getting used to the dark, his nose told him that the house was a dusty, dusky kind of place. He knew Morrow lived alone and that he was reconditioning the house, bringing it into the twentieth century, but he had no idea the place would be covered with a decade's worth of dust. When his eyes allowed limited sight, he saw paint peeling from the ceiling and walls and that the room was devoid of furniture.

He reached into his pocket, took out a disposable lighter and flicked it. The flame showed him the door across the room and he followed its lead to a hallway that lead into a kitchen. Through the dancing shadows he saw a fully appointed modern kitchen, complete with built in dishwasher, oven and oversized refrigerator. There was a note stuck on the refrigerator door with a Daffy Duck kitchen. He crossed the room and read it.

Susan

You'll find plenty to eat in the fridge. I can be reached at 713-555-3487. See you in 5 days.

Love ya - Dan

He turned on the light. He was furious. He scanned the kitchen and found the phone. He grabbed it and dialed the number.

"King's Pride Inn," a female voice with a German accent answered.

"I'm trying to reach my son, he left this number."

"What's your son's name?"

"Sam Storm," he lied, giving the only name he could think of on the spur of the moment.

After a few moments the woman with the accent said, "Sorry he's not registered, but maybe he's staying with someone else, most of our rooms have two or more kids staying in them during the summer."

"Why?"

"We're one of the cheapest motels in town and we treat the river rats right."

"River rats?"

"The kids who go tubing down the Comal River."

"Tubing, what is tubing?"

"They sit in inner tubes, you know, those things they used to put inside of tires before they invented tubeless." The woman had a smart mouth. She coughed, then continued. "They float down the river and drink beer all day long."

"Where are you located?" Storm had heard enough.

"New Braunfels, near San Antonio."

"Thanks." He hung up.

He stood for a moment in thought. Then he left the kitchen to explore the house. With the exception of the living room, all of the downstairs rooms, he counted ten, were empty. Upstairs only one of the six bedrooms was furnished, all the others had wallpaper or paint peeling off the walls, and the hardwood floors were in serious need of repair. Many of the upstairs window screens were torn or missing and the upstairs bathrooms, with the exception of the one off of the master bedroom, were not functioning. Danny Morrow had a long way to go to get his money back from this white elephant, he thought.

Irritated, because now he had to drive the rest of the night, he made his way down the stairs. Outside he heard a car door slam. Instinctively he knew it was the girl the note had been addressed to. He turned out the light and hastened out of the kitchen to the dark hallway, where he hid in the space under the stairs.

He was cramped, but from his darkened position he could see into the kitchen and he had a clear view of the back door. He waited silently, like in ambush. He heard footsteps on the back stairs, heard a key inserted into the lock, heard the door latch click and he saw the door open.

It was the girl from the Irish Pub, Susan. Of course, he should have made the connection earlier when he read the note. She was wearing the same white skirt, but she'd changed out of the peasant blouse that had revealed so much into one that had sleeves and buttoned up to the neck.

The girl went to the refrigerator, read the note, then opened the door. She took out a quart of chocolate milk and drank from the carton. After she finished it, she tossed the carton in a waste basket. Storm readied himself for the attack, but before he moved, she turned round again, closed the refrigerator and started in his direction. He looked at her pouting lips as she approached his hiding point, and he clenched his fists, biting into his tongue. Her lips were the color of a New Orleans Hurricane. She had Hurricane lips.

She came into the dark hallway and stopped, inches from his crouching form, searching for the light switch. Her skirt brushed against his face. He could kill her so easily, but he didn't. He held his breath, hoping she wouldn't look down and see him, a coward below the stairs.

She found the switch and the hallway burst into light, allowing Storm to take in every weave of the cotton fabric. He started to reach for her, but something held him back. She had Hurricane lips. Louise had Hurricane lips. In the bar, behind the stage light, her lips were lighter, but now he knew they were Hurricane red, that special red that till now he had only seen on his wife. He was powerless.

She moved away and mounted the stairs. He remained until she reached the top, then he allowed himself a breath. He waited till she went into the one furnished room up there and imagined that she was using the working bathroom, probably to take a shower.

When he thought she was safely out of earshot, he eased his cramped body out from under the stairs and silently made his way to the kitchen. He opened the door with a burglar's soft touch and made his way out of the house.

He crossed the street, a man torn in half, and slid behind the wheel. The fire inside him raged, he wanted to go back to his room and sleep, but forces beyond his control were driving him on. He reached under the seat for the road atlas and turned on the map light.

New Braunfels was about thirty miles north of San Antonio. He lay back, closed his eyes and asked himself if driving all night to kill a man he didn't know was what he wanted to do.

Danny Morrow had done nothing to him. In fact, he told himself, if Gordon and his gang hadn't set up their underground network, he wouldn't have had a job for the last fifteen years. It wasn't their fault that they were too smart to get caught in the act. It wasn't their fault that the crime they were committing wasn't felonious enough to keep the police interested. It wasn't their fault that collectors all over the country clamored for the bootlegs. And it wasn't their fault that everybody in the record industry laughed at him behind his back.

But he hated being laughed at. He started the car and drove the night away and half the next day. He was tired and sleepy when he turned off the interstate, but he still managed to find the King's Pride Inn in less than five minutes.

He stretched, yawned and stepped out of the cool air conditioned car into a hundred and three degree West Texas summer day, where breathing was the only thing one had to do to work up a sweat.

He undid the top buttons of his sport shirt and wiped the sweat from his brow. He felt lousy. He hadn't slept in over twenty hours. He hated the heat and he was beginning to question his actions. He was no longer sure he was fighting the good fight, but gritting his teeth, he made his way to the lobby.

He pushed open the glass door and again entered air conditioned comfort. And with the cold, the rightness of what he had done and what he was going to do flooded through him. The death of Gordon's gang of four, followed by the death of Gordon himself would send a shock wave throughout the international bootleg community. Fear of finding themselves in the same shoes would send the other bootleggers scurrying for cover. Then, when the world was free of these record and CD pirates, he would finally be able to rest.

"Can I help you?" He recognized the accent from the phone last night.

"I'm dead dog tired and I need a room," Storm said, putting on a smile.

"Usually we're booked for the summer, but we had a cancellation yesterday, so you're in luck. One hundred and twenty a night." The woman was older than God and her face was covered in rouge.

Storm dropped six twenties on the counter and jumped back when a large cockroach scurried over the bills.

"Will I be sharing the room with his relatives?"

"This isn't the Hilton." The rouge-faced woman scooped up his money, without asking for ID and handed him a key. "Room twelve, down the hall." She didn't ask why he had no bags, but said instead, "You'll need a bathing suit if you want to go down the river."

"Where can I get one?"

"Sporting goods store across the street."

Storm thanked her and made his way to his room. The air conditioner didn't work and he suspected that was the reason for the cancellation. He opened the sliding door and stepped out onto a fenced patio. The room next door had a makeshift clothes line with wet towels and bathing suits hanging on it. He reached over and took a black suit that looked like it might fit.

He was about to slide the door shut and take a shower

when he heard a young girl's voice call out, "Hurry up, Danny."

He went out on the patio and looked over the fence. A young redhead in a bikini that matched her green eyes was loading the biggest inner tube he'd ever seen on the back of a fully restored '65 Impala convertible. Another girl was rolling a similar tube toward the car. She was blond, thin, and looked like she'd just stepped off the cover of Vogue. And then he saw Danny Morrow, with both arms wrapped around a tube.

"Where's Ronny?" the redhead asked.

"Bathroom," Morrow answered. "We'll have to wait."

Storm tore his clothes off, jumped into the stolen bathing suit, grabbed a tiny hotel towel and started for his car. But he tripped over a cooler in the hall, landing on the seedy carpet with several cold beers.

"Hey," a young man complained. He was carrying a dive tank to the room across the hall. The corridor was littered with his things, scuba gear, a giant inner tube, a suitcase and the spilled cooler.

"Sorry." Storm pushed himself from the floor.

"Why don't you watch where you're going? You spilled my beer and ruined the ice." The boy had an athletic body and an attitude.

"I said I was sorry," Storm repeated.

"Yeah, well sorry doesn't quite cut it, does it?"

"Here, let me help you with this stuff." Storm picked up the beer and put it back in the cooler. Then he carried the cooler into the boy's room.

"I can do it!" the boy said.

"No, I spilled the ice, the least I can do is help you load this stuff into your room and buy you another bag." He went back to the hallway, picked up the wetsuit and weight belt, carried them into the boy's room and dropped them on one of the sagging beds. The boy followed with the suitcase. Storm closed the door after him, picked up the scuba tank and brought it down on the boy's head

There wasn't any blood.

And now Storm had an inner tube, too.

He had just finished stuffing the tube into the back seat and was getting into the car when Morrow's friend joined the group. Either I'm a fast killer, he thought, or that boy's a slow shitter.

Morrow started the convertible and put a tape in the cassette player. Storm heard Bob Dylan, backed by Tom Petty and the Heartbreakers, belting out *Positively Fourth Street* and his blood ran hot. The son of a bitch was playing a bootleg cassette. The son of a bitch was going to die.

He followed them through the small town to a wooded campsite. He stayed behind as they entered the campground, entering only after they were parked and were unloading their car. He parked far enough away that he could watch without being noticed.

The park was full of college kids, waiting in line to jump into the water with their tubes. The slow current carried them down the river. Many of the kids had a smaller tube with a cooler full of beer tied on to the larger one they rode in. It was one giant party.

He saw two men with scuba gear slip into the river and he smiled, remembering the dead boy in the room across the hall. The snot nosed bastard had it coming. It wasn't Storm's fault. His attitude killed him.

"Scuba diving?" Storm heard Danny Morrow say.

"They go along the bottom and gather up beer cans," his friend Ron said.

"They get paid for that?"

"No. Every summer guys into scuba go down the river and every now and then they pop up and scare the girls. They usually make one or two trips gathering up the cans."

Storm hadn't been under in years, but he still remembered how. It was like riding a bike.

He watched the group as they headed for the wooden landing and the river. Morrow's friend dropped his tube into the water, then climbed down the ladder after it. The two women, younger, were more daring. They threw their tubes in and jumped after them, squealing as they hit the cold water. Morrow was the last in. He went down the ladder with his tube in hand. Storm watched as he slipped into the tube at the foot of the ladder—buttocks in the center, legs draped over one side of the giant donut and resting his back over the other without falling into the water.

"Didn't even get wet," he said.

Storm watched them drift away with the current, then he followed Morrow's example, climbing down the ladder one handed, with the tube in the other. At the last second he put the tube in the moving water and let go of the ladder aiming his buttocks for the tire's center. He was a big man and he got wet as he splashed into his target and he enjoyed it.

He paddled against the current, so that the four young people slowly drifted away. Within a few minutes they floated around a bend up ahead and were out of sight. He had no desire to stay with them any longer. He only wanted to learn the way of the river.

Every other minute he was passed by a group of college kids, the smallest consisting of two people, a pair of young lovers, and the largest, a group of about fifteen boys and girls laughing and drinking beer. So early in the morning and so many people, he could imagine the zoo the river would become in an hour or so, when the sun burned off the early morning cloud cover.

He lay back in the tube and watched the clouds go by. Convinced there would be no opportunity to get at Danny Morrow on this trip, he decided to relax and enjoy and the ride.

He studied the backyards of the large shaded Southern homes that jutted up against the riverbank. Places where kids grew up sheltered from the violence of modern America. He watched children swinging from a tree rope into the river. Their laughter and squeals of delight stabbed at his heart and he cursed. There had been no happy home when he had been a child.

He spotted a small pool of still water where two men were fishing from a rubber raft. He paddled over to them.

"Fishing any good?"

"In the morning, but once the river fills up it's slow going," one of the fishermen said.

"The water here always this still?"

"Unless it rains. When the river is up, the current reaches the banks."

Storm looked across the river and noticed that the man was right. The areas by the riverbank were relatively still.

"Hey, mister, you going down the chute?" a young boy, about ten, floating by asked.

"I guess so."

"You ever been down it before?"

"No." Storm waved to the fishermen and paddled back out into the current with the boy.

"You're gonna love it. You go real fast and your tube spins around and it shoots you into the river below the dam and you get all wet and everything."

He wanted to reach out, grab the boy and shove him under the water till he turned blue, but he held himself in check.

"Get ready," the boy said.

Storm felt the current as it picked up speed. He looked ahead and saw that the river was dammed and that part of the running current was funneled down a man-made chute that appeared to be sucking in the shouting, yelling, happy tubers. They were having fun and so was he. He clutched onto his tube and followed the summer revelers into the chute.

The chute was a collaboration of man and nature, an unpredictable waterslide that whipped around the dam, depositing the tubers in a small lake below. The smooth flowing river, when compressed into the funnel, churned and foamed, spinning the tubes and spraying the riders. Children loved it. The college kids loved it. And Storm loved it.

He started paddling to shore the instant he shot out of the funnel. It had been years since he'd had this much fun. He reached the bank and trudged out of the water, carrying his tube behind. He spotted a lifeguard and asked. "How do I get back?"

"The bus leaves from over there every fifteen minutes. It's a free ride if you parked at the landing."

Storm's eyes followed the man's pointing finger to a group of people in wet bathing suits stuffing their oversized tubes into the back of a blue painted school bus.

"That thing still runs?"

"Since 1963."

He slung his tube onto his shoulder and walked over to the bus. He handed the tube to a tanned youth who stuffed it into the back, then he got into line behind a group of young people. By the time he got on board there was standing room only, but he was still able to search out and find Morrow and his friends seated toward the back of the bus, near the tubes that were piled to the ceiling. They were involved in a conversation that had them all laughing.

Their laughter stiffened his resolve.

Back at the landing, he watched as Morrow's group headed back for another ride down the river. When they were out of sight, he carried his tube to the car. The hot West Texas sun had him dry by the time he got the tube in the back.

He drove to the motel, stopped at the desk and asked the rouge-faced woman if she knew where he could get a strong bag. She sent him to the kitchen and the cook gave him a gunny sack. Then he went to the dead kid's room, stuffed the scuba gear into the sack and hauled it out to his car. He sang along with the radio on his way back to the landing.

He made his way to the river landing with the gunny sack over his left shoulder and his right arm through the tube. Once in the water, he set the sack in his lap and floated down river. When he reached the pool where the fishermen were on his first run, he was pleased to see that they were gone. He paddled into the pool and continued on under the overhanging trees to the riverbank. He waded out of the river, squeezing between the copious bushes, where he concealed his tube and donned the scuba gear.

He lowered himself back into about two feet of water, hidden by tree and bush, and waited. Forty-five minutes later his patience was rewarded. He spied Morrow and his friends floating toward him. The two girls with their red and blond hair acting as beacons made them easy to single out. Like a shark, he lowered himself into the water.

Three separate groups of river runners passed him, unaware of the danger he represented. He swam out to the center of the river as the two girls grew closer. The blond passed three feet overhead and he thought of her cover-girl looks as he eyed her legs through the murky water. He let her float on by, waiting, a still predator set on his kill.

The redhead floated over next, kicking her feet and splashing water with her hands. Storm imagined her chewing on her hair and clowning around. Morrow's friend Ronny floated over with his belly down, paddling furiously with his arms. Storm watched, worried that the boy might see him, since he was floating face down, but the boy was more interested in catching up with the girls than checking out what lay below.

Then came Danny Morrow, sitting in his tube, buttocks hanging down through the middle, arms and legs dangling over the sides. Here was a man without a care in the world, Storm thought, just floating down the river, watching the sky go by.

Storm swam under Morrow's tube, coming to the surface behind him. He reached out of the water, clamping a strong right hand over Morrow's mouth and with his left, he brought the Bowie knife up through the center of the tube, up between the young man's legs, driving it point first into his belly. Then he dragged the head below the water and held it there, to make sure.

He held on to the body as it went through the dancing spasm of death and when it was still, he pulled the tube over to the calm water. He felt a slight twinge of guilt, but he shrugged it aside, and brought the knife around the dead man's neck, pulling it through, severing the head.

Then he swam back to his hiding place, removing the

weight belt, regulator and tank on the way, letting them drop to the bottom of the river. He left the mask and fins at the river's edge, grabbed his tube and went back into the water, heading for the chute. He gave the tube with the headless body a slight shove as he passed.

He entered the current behind a gaggle of giggling girls from Texas A & M. He listened to their banter and smiled when the giggles turned to screams of delight and anticipation as they neared the chute.

He followed them into the churning water, holding fast to his tube as it spun in the spray. He came out of the chute paddling with the current, directing himself to the opposite bank. He dragged the tube out of the water and made his way to the blue bus. He shoved his tube into the back and climbed on board. He took his seat as the bus started and didn't look back when the screaming began.

CHAPTER NINE

RICK WOKE ON THE LIVING ROOM SOFA to the smell of coffee. He thought about Christina upstairs and he wondered if last night had been a dream.

"Morning, Uncle Rick," Torry said.

"Yeah, morning," Swell echoed.

"Morning." He yawned.

"We gonna do something today?"

"Does your mother have anything planned?"

"Yeah, she's gone flying." Torry smirked. "She said you'd entertain us today."

"She's gone flying?"

"Yeah, on Sunday some people go to church, Mom

goes flying."

"Every Sunday?"

"Never misses, thanks to you."

"Thanks to me?"

"Well, you sold her the plane."

"How long does she stay in the air?"

"All day. She says it clears her head."

"Yeah. She needs the time to herself, at least that's what she says," Torry added.

"I had no idea."

"There's a lot about Mom you probably don't know," Swell said.

"Like what?"

"Like she's in love with you."

"Come on."

"No, really, she is," Torry spoke up.

The girl's words tore at his heart. He thought of Christina as a special person and he loved the twins. They were the children Ann and he couldn't have.

"We're just very good friends."

"Come on Uncle Rick, how can you say that?" Torry said.

"Yeah, especially after last night," Swell said with a knowing smile.

"Look, Mom's back," Torry said, looking out through the living room window. "Guess she changed her mind about flying."

"Went to the airport and came right back," her twin said.

"We should go to the mall."

"We should go now."

"Right."

The girls grabbed their purses and headed for the front door in time to greet their mother.

"Hi, Mom," they said as one.

"Where are you off to?"

"The mall." Torry held out her hand.

Christina dropped her car keys into it.

"No drive safely speech?" Torry asked.

"Go."

"We're gone," both girls said and they were out the door.

Rick watched as Christina closed the door after the girls. She was wearing Levi's and a faded red tee shirt. Her shoulder length hair was tied back with a matching red bandanna. In the fifteen years that he'd known her, she had never looked better.

"God, Chris, you look great."

"I love you. I've been in love with you for years. I just thought you should know."

It was one thing to hear it from the girls, another to hear if from Christina herself.

"You don't have to say anything. I've always known you were in love with Ann and that all we could ever be was friends. After she died I was so used to the relationship, you know, the friends thing, that I never imagined anything else. But after last night I can imagine more. I don't know what exactly, but I can imagine something else."

"I love you too," he said.

"No you don't." She smiled. "Well, maybe you do love me, but you're not in love with me. There's a difference."

"So what do we do?"

"Take it one day at a time and see if you fall in love with me."

"That shouldn't be too hard."

"Will you keep living in Tampico?"

"No. There's nothing holding me there now." He felt a twinge as soon as the words left his lips.

"Nothing? How about the girl next door?"

"There's nothing between us. And say," he laughed, "what do you know about the girl next door?"

"Come on, Judy's a good friend. They spent last Christmas with us. I know how you love J.P. You must feel something for his mother."

"That's not fair."

"Last night was great, probably the best night of my life, but let's face it, there were times when you weren't all there. Admit it."

"I was there, all there, enjoying every second."

He saw the lines of tension leave her face and the determined set of her lips relax into a smile and he realized he had a problem. He cared for Christina and was maybe even in love with her, but until she put it into words, he wasn't aware of how strongly he felt about Judy Donovan.

"So where do we go from here?" she asked.

"I don't know. Ann hasn't been gone that long. She's still the first thing I think about when I get up in the morning, the last thing on my mind before I go to sleep."

"It's been six months," she said, "but I understand you still need more time."

"And I plan on taking a little more, not too much, but a little. I'm going to buy a new Jeep and take awhile. driving back up to Tampico. I'm going to stay at cheap motels off the freeway and check out all the small towns along they way. Maybe I'll find a new place to live," he said.

"Look, I don't want what happened last night to come between us. I've seen too many situations where sex ruined a perfectly good friendship. I don't want to lose you," she said.

"You could never lose me."

"Oh yes I could. I could pressure you into something you're not ready for and drive you away and I'll be damned if I'll do that. So here's what I'm proposing. We go on like we did before. Friends. When you come to L.A. or Long Beach, and I hope you'll come often, you stay here, only you sleep with me instead of on the sofa. That is, if you want to."

"I want to," he said.

"And if you should choose to be with someone else, the girl next door for example, I'll deal with it."

"I don't think you have anything to fear. I'll go to Tampico and make arrangements to sell the house. It shouldn't take more that a couple of weeks. Then I'll be back."

"Where will you live?"

"Why don't we talk about that when I get back." He smiled. "I'm sure we can work something out. Who knows, maybe I'll have found that small town on the edge of nowhere. How would you like living somewhere with the desert for a backyard, or maybe a small town on the sea coast in Oregon or Washington? Someplace large enough for a bookstore, but too small for a movie theater."

"Really?" she jumped into his arms and hugged him tightly.

"Really." He squeezed her in a strong embrace.

* * *

Rick guided the new Jeep along the two lane road, getting into Tampico before the sun, with his mind full of Christina, the future and the twins.

He started to run through what he would have to do. He had to box the personal possessions he wanted to carry over into his new life with Christina and the girls. He had to contact a broker and put the house on the market. And he had to start living the rest of his life.

He made the left off of Solitude River Road onto Seaview and started up the hill, when something darted in front of him. He cranked the wheel hard to the left, stomped on the brakes as he shoved in the clutch, but the moves were unnecessary, because it was too fast to be hit by a car doing less that thirty miles an hour. However, the brakes locked the rear wheels and he found himself screeching to a stop on the wrong side of the road. Shaken, he downshifted into first and eased the car back on the right side of the road and parked to catch his breath and his wits.

It must have been a mighty frightened bear, he thought, because he had never seen one move so fast. If it made its dash across the road a fraction of a second later, he would have hit it head on. He counted to ten, released the clutch and drove on.

By the time he pulled into his driveway his adrenaline rush was as dead as he felt. He shut off the ignition and hauled himself out of the Jeep. He grabbed his overnight grip from the back seat, closing the door without locking it. He looked next door and noticed the light was on in J.P.'s upstairs bedroom.

He opened the door and entered the living room, turned on a lamp and stared in stunned disbelief. Someone had been living there. Empty beer cans littered the living room and foil dinner trays, left over from frozen dinners, filled a waste basket. The remnants from daily newspapers lay throughout both the living and dining rooms. The television was on and there was a note taped to the flickering screen.

He walked over to the set and read a childish scrawl.

Your wife saw the knife
before she died.

In the kitchen, he found dirty dishes and uneaten food on the breakfast table and counter tops. He emptied filthy water from the sink and rinsed the dishes, worrying and thinking about the note as he worked. Then he turned on the disposal, grinding the rotting scraps into the city sewer system. He filled the sink with clean soapy water and started to wash the dishes, when he was interrupted by the doorbell.

He dried his hands, wondering who wanted him so early in the morning. He decided not to take any chances. He hadn't told anybody when he was coming back and his house had been broken into, two good reasons to exercise caution.

He went out the back door, into the cover of the forest that encircled the two houses on the hill. He worked his way around the back, to the west side of the house, trying to move as quietly as possible, using tree and bush as cover. He paralleled the house, till he was opposite the front porch and saw her. His caution hadn't been necessary after all.

"Judy?" He stepped from behind a tall pine.

"I saw the light," she said.

"I had a break in. The burglar left a note."

"They must have been awfully quiet, we didn't hear anyone."

"You want to come in?" He mounted the porch, inviting her inside.

"Sure." She followed him in.

She saw the beer cans and refuse, but her eyes quickly fastened on the note taped to the television screen.

"That's the note?" she asked.

"Read it."

She crossed over to the television. "Oh, no."

"Yeah."

"You think maybe she was killed?" she said.

"I don't see how."

"Maybe J.P. really did see a knife," she said.

"I did."

The pair turned to see J.P. framed in the open doorway.

"You scared me," Judy said.

"Sorry, I didn't do it on purpose. I saw Rick drive up, so I got dressed and came over."

"Have you seen anybody around here?" Rick asked.

"No," J.P. said.

"That's hardly surprising, you've been gone a long time. He could have been here six months or six days ago," Judy said.

"More like six months," Rick said. "The food scraps have started to come alive with mold."

"I saw an animal though, the Ghost Dog," J.P. said. "It comes sometimes at night and sniffs around. Mom says it's a dog, but I know better. It's the Ghost Dog."

"There have been some reports of a large wild dog," Judy said.

"The Ghost Dog," J.P. repeated.

"J.P., there's no such thing as ghosts or ghost dogs," Rick said. "Your mother's probably right, it's a dog. I've seen it too."

"Really?"

"Yeah, it ran in front of my car this morning. I almost hit it."

"Did you think it was a bear?"

"At first, but it was too fast. It looked more like a big

dog, maybe a black lab."

"Maybe the Ghost Dog?"

"It wasn't a ghost dog. It was just a big dog. Right now it's probably asleep in a nice warm house."

"Really, you think so?"

"I know so."

"I'm glad, I was kinda scared, but I'm not now."

"Good boy."

"I'm glad you're back," he said.

"I'm glad to be back."

"You wanna go fishing?" the boy asked.

"I'll get my gear," Rick said, "but first I've got to call the sheriff."

Within minutes Sheriff Sturgees was in Rick's living room, reading the note.

"Probably kids," he said.

"How can you say that?" Judy said.

"Nothing missing, no real damage done and the note looks like a kid wrote it."

"I can't believe anybody around here would be cruel enough to write a note like that," Judy said.

"Me either," Rick said.

"You don't know kids," the sheriff said. "What we think is cruel, they think is good clean fun."

"I can't believe that," Rick said.

"Oh yeah, when is the last time you pulled the wings off a bee, or stuck a fire cracker up a frog's ass, or put a cherry bomb down a mailbox? Kids having fun can be cruel."

"Maybe?" Judy said.

"I have my doubts," Rick said.

"As long as I'm here I'd like to ask you something," Sheriff Sturgees said.

"Ask away."

"Tell me about the Ragged Man," he said.

Rick was stunned and the sheriff saw it in his eyes. J.P. bit into his lower lip and took his mother by the hand.

"That's a strange question," Rick said.

"In two months I'm throwing in with my brother, we're gonna buy the Chevy dealership in town. Ever since that day when Mark, Vicky and Janis were killed, the luster has gone out of this job, but I'd like to walk away knowing that I didn't leave any stone unturned. I've heard this nonsense about the Ragged Man and this Ghost Dog the kids have been talking about and I want to know more."

"Sheriff, you can't believe this stuff?"

"Didn't say I believed it, said I wanted to know more."

"And why ask me?"

The sheriff turned to J.P. "My boy says you told him a story about the day Mrs. Gordon was killed."

"Yes, sir," J.P. said.

"J.P.!" Judy said.

"That's okay Mrs. Donovan. Don't blame the boy. Kids talk, they don't mean nothing by it. I just want to hear the story from Mr. Gordon."

"Then we better all sit down," Rick said.

"Then there is a story?" The sheriff plopped down on the sofa.

"When you were a child, Sheriff, were you afraid of the Bogeyman?" Rick asked, his voice cracking.

"I don't have time for games."

"Ann was afraid of the Bogeyman. She had a name for him. She called him the Ragged Man. And her bogeyman has a familiar, a black dingo with saber-tooth canines and tiger-like paws."

"What's a dingo?" J.P. asked.

"A wild dog, like a wolf," Rick said. "They live in the Australian outback."

"Are you going somewhere with this?" Sturgees asked.

"You want to know about the Ragged Man?"

"Yes."

"Two years ago we were stranded in the Australian outback. Ann and I were racing in the Australian Safari. That's a desert road race, and we broke down. While we were wondering what we were going to do, an old couple, Aborigines, came along in an old Jeep."

"Like yours?" J.P. asked.

"It's the same Jeep, J.P."

Rick looked out the window, half expecting to see Ann, then continued with his story. "The woman was ill and we asked if they needed help. The man said we could bury them and then they died."

"Wait a minute."

"Let me finish, Sheriff, then ask me whatever questions you want."

"Sorry."

"We buried them off the road and took the Jeep. For reasons I can't explain, we decided not to tell anyone about the old couple. That may not have been the right thing to do, but that's what we decided.

"While we were driving back to civilization, a pack of dingoes started following us. We lost them and that night, when we were sitting by the campfire, they found us. I got up to protect Ann and one of the dingoes attacked me. It dragged me down and I was knocked unconscious. The rest of the story I learned from Ann.

"She told me that after I was knocked out, she was afraid that she was going to be killed. One of the dingoes lept into the fire and danced. The fire had no effect on the animal and, when it stopped its dance, it glared at her with glowing red eyes and saber-tooth teeth. She called it a ghost dog and she thought it was going to kill her."

"The Ghost Dog," J.P. said under his breath.

"Then the Ragged Man came out of the night. He was wearing foul, dirty clothes and she said she could smell his breath from twenty feet away.

"The Ragged Man told her to smell her fear."

"That's what the voice told us. I heard it from through the door," J.P. said.

"But before the evil man or his ghost dog could harm her, another man entered the glow of the fire and saved her. This other man healed my bleeding head and arm with his touch and stayed with her till morning.

"When I came to I was fine. No head wound where my head crashed on the ground. No gashes in my arm where the dingo dog ripped my flesh. Not even any bruises. Something happened that night. I don't know what, but something happened.

"Sheriff, I can't tell you who or what was responsible for everything that happened the day the Donovans were killed, but I can tell you what Ann would have said."

"Go on."

"It's a story of shamen and sorcerers, good and evil, magic, sorcery and ghosts that walk the land—and it's very probably not relevant. You still want me to go on?"

"Yes."

"Do you know what a shaman is?"

"A kind of witch doctor."

"You're not too far off. The Aborigines have a traditional healer, a shaman, a marangit in their language. It's his or her job to protect the clan from the evil of the galka and, if possible, to undo whatever evil the galka has done."

"Galka?" the sheriff asked.

"The Bogeyman. The Galka are sorcerers who use their power for evil. They're strangers who travel the land to seek out and kill. They like to ambush their victims in secluded places, where they kill them and mutilate their bodies.

"Galka is one of the first words a child learns and he is taught from infancy to fear it. 'Don't stray from camp or the galka will get you,' 'Don't go in the water or the galka will get you.' Sound like the bogeyman?"

"Yeah," J.P. said.

"But it's not only children, adults fear the galka, too. The galka is the reason a woman won't go to the river alone and why a hunter won't hunt out of eyesight of another. No one strays from camp at night for fear the galka will get them."

"Why does it want to get them?" J.P. asked, captivated.

"The Aborigines believe that people have two souls, a true soul and a false soul. When a person dies, the true soul goes to the clan's waterhole or their version of heaven, while the false soul goes into the bush where it turns into a bad spirit called a mokuy. Sometimes, if it's a strong spirit, and if a suitable human is present when it's released, it will turn that man into a galka and give him evil powers. The mokuy then becomes the galka's spirit familiar."

"Like a witch's black cat," Judy said.

The sheriff remained silent.

"Yes, only mokuy don't appear as anything so lovable. They usually take the form of deformed large animals that are sent out by the galka to kill and maim. The mokuy can't live without the galka, they make him what he is and then they do his bidding."

"Can anything stop a galka?" J.P. asked.

"Yes, two things, the first is a marangit. They get their power from the true soul. Sometimes, if a good person is present at the time of death, the true soul will touch him on its way to the waterhole, turning him into a marangit with the powers of good. Marangit use their powers to heal and protect.

"The marangit has a small dillybag or box that contains the ten healing stones which he uses to treat the members of his clan. Each stone has a different power. One, when placed in a glass of water turns the liquid into a healing potion for the stomach, liver or kidneys. Another heals internal sores, another, external sores and wounds, another is an X-ray stone letting the marangit see inside the patient. Oh, yeah, and one stone tells him the identity of the killer after a murder has happened."

"The sheriff could use a stone like that," J.P. said.

"I sure could." Sturgees turned to Rick and added, "Are you finished yet?"

"Not quite. There is a never-ending battle between good and evil, between marangit and galka. The galka causes illness and kills. The marangit heals and protects. A galka will never stop trying to kill the marangit and even though it's possible for a marangit to kill a galka, it almost never happens, evil usually wins.

"The power of both the marangit and galka is passed on after death, usually to one of their children, however if they die away from their family and anyone else is present, the power and personality is transferred to that person, and that brings me to the crux of the situation."

"I don't get it," Judy said.

"The man that chased away the galka had one of those dillybags. He opened it and let Ann look inside. She said that she saw the past, all of her lives, that is, all the lives of that old woman. She believed the old couple we buried were marangit and that they transferred their power to us and that the dingo with the canines was a mokuy familiar and the man with the bad breath, a galka. That galka won't rest till he kills both Ann and me in such a way that we are not able to transfer our powers."

"Who was the man that chased away the galka?" J.P. wanted to know.

"Remember I said there were two things that could stop a galka?"

"Yeah."

"The other is a wongar. The Wongar are the creators of the Dreamtime and all mankind. They live in the sacred sites and aren't dangerous unless they're offended."

"So the man that chased away the galka and fixed you was a wongar?" J.P. said.

"Bullshit," the sheriff said.

"I agree, Sheriff. In our lives together, it was the only thing that ever came between us. I don't know what happened that night, but whatever it was, it scared Ann so much that it scarred her mind and somehow she came up with that fantastic story to deal with it. We never talked about it after we got back to the States, but I always knew she never shed that belief."

"So why are you talking about it now?" the sheriff asked.

"You wanted to know about the Ragged Man."

"It was kids that left the note. Trust me." The sheriff got up and walked toward the door. When he reached it he turned and said, "I'm going to go back to the office and try and get a little work done."

The three of them saw the sheriff out and watched as he drove down the hill and out of sight.

"Are we going now?" J.P. asked.

"J.P., maybe Rick wants to straighten up first. He just

got back."

"No, that's all right. I'll be over in fifteen minutes."

"I'll be ready," J.P. said over his shoulder as his mother pulled him along back to their house. "Then you can tell me more about the Ghost Dog," he shouted, just before his mother dragged him inside.

He watched them till Judy closed her front door and, for a brief instant, he had the feeling that he was being watched, but he shrugged it off and went back into the house, unaware of the large dark animal watching from the forest at the edge of the clearing. An animal whose low rumbling breath sounded like the pump in a little girl's fish tank.

CHAPTER TEN

JUDY'S CLOCK RADIO CLICKED ON minutes before the sun. She rolled out of bed, glancing in the mirror as she passed it on her way to the bathroom. She was secretly pleased. She'd been dieting, doing aerobics and running for the last two months and she'd dropped ten of the twelve pounds she'd wanted to lose.

She passed into the bathroom and bounced on the scale. She looked at the digital read out and squealed with delight. One-fifteen. She'd lost the last two pounds. "And I'm gonna keep them off," she told the scale.

She rushed back into the bedroom, shut off the radio and donned her sweats and running shoes. She was in a hurry to beat the sun.

Happier than she'd been in months, she tiptoed to J.P.'s door and eased it open. Satisfied that he was still asleep, she closed it and went down the stairs. She unlocked the deadbolt and went out the front door to meet the crisp morning.

She smiled into the cool breeze and glanced up at the sun starting its morning peak through the pines. She loved sunup and the birth of a new day. For her, every dawn signaled the beginning of another twenty-four hours away from the bad times and another day closer to the good times that she knew were coming.

She worried about J.P. Lately he'd been spending most of his time in town. She knew there were one or two children his age that he played with, but what she gathered from her conversations with him, was that he was spending a lot of time with the older boys at the park. She didn't know if that was good or bad, but it wasn't like him to spend so much time away from her. They were a team. Now it seemed like the team was breaking up. She didn't like it, but she could understand why a boy would want to get out and play with other children.

If that's all it was, maybe she shouldn't worry, but he was neglecting the birds. He'd always enjoyed them and now it was like they didn't exist. She didn't mind taking care of them herself, she'd been taking care of pigeons all of her life, but it wasn't the same without J.P.

Something was different. She wanted to sit down with him and talk it out, but she was afraid. Afraid that she was the cause, afraid that she was different.

She did feel different. She was more determined. She'd lost the weight that had been bugging her since J.P. had been born. She was getting up every morning and running, something new for her. She was taking more care with her appearance, trying to look her best. She bought new clothes. Clothes with bright colors, the opposite of the dull tee shirts and Levi's she'd been wearing for the last ten years.

Now that she thought about it, she was different, but a good different. She couldn't see why any of the recent changes she'd made in her life would drive J.P. away from her.

This morning, she resolved, when he wakes up, I'll talk to him and we'll work this out.

She continued fifty yards through the pines to Clark Creek, a slim stream of water that ran year round behind the two homes. She hopped over the slow flowing water and continued into the forest, listening to the sounds of the early rising birds. She wished she could tell which ones made which sounds. She would have to buy a bird watcher's book.

She intended to wander through the forest until she came to a steep path that led down the hill to the beach below. She'd discovered it on one of her walks and she doubted that anyone else knew about it. She called it the sluice, because it was vee shaped, like a sluice. She had no idea what or who had carved the path through the trees. Maybe it was a former owner of one of the two houses, or maybe the creek overflowed in winter and this was a water path down to the sea, or maybe it was caused by animals seeking a way out of the woods, but she was grateful to what or whoever was responsible for it. She enjoyed the tricky, steep descent that provided her quick access to the beach, where she did her morning run.

But this morning, as she reached the beginning of the sluice, the forest turned quiet. She was instantly alert. She had become used to the various bird and insect sounds and their absence sent an eerie chill up her back. *Go home,* she told herself, and she slowly turned, trying to make as little noise as possible, and started for home. She was afraid.

She cringed at the crackling and crunching dried leaves under her feet. With every bird and creature silent, she was an elephant tramping through the woods and there was nothing she could do about it.

Winding her way through the trees, back toward the stream, she felt a presence behind her, something bad, maybe a bear. She picked up her pace, no longer concerned with the dead leaves cracking under her feet. Then she heard something and turned. She thought she saw movement behind, movement not caused by the soft, silent breeze brushing her sweating skin. She turned back toward the stream and home—and ran.

She saw the stream. She put on a burst of speed and flew over it. The forest noises picked up as soon as her feet hit ground on the other side. A bird or two at first, then the insect sounds followed by more birds. She slowed to a walk and chided herself. She had undoubtedly panicked over nothing. She felt foolish, like a little girl out after dark for the first time, but she wouldn't have felt so foolish if she hadn't been spending so much time alone up on the hill, with only her son and the pigeons for companions.

If she had been more in touch with the town, she would have heard the stories.

* * *

J.P. woke the instant the forest went quiet. Unlike his mother, he had spent time in town and was familiar with the stories, stories about the strange happenings. They started shortly after the day of the murders, the day his cousin Janis disappeared.

That same day, the murder day, the sheriff's two German Shepherds, Woodruff and Dandy, failed to show up for dinner and everyone assumed they had been stolen, or worse, poisoned. Sheriff Sturgees was in the habit of letting the dogs roam free around town. They were friendly, tame and everybody liked and fed them, but they would roam no more and now J.P. and a lot of the other kids were sure they knew why.

Two nights after the Shepherds vanished, some of the junior high school boys were playing baseball at the park, when Dick Rainmaker, out in left field, saw an animal across the street, running along the beach. He said it looked like a black cougar with a wolf's head.

The next night the Johnson's cat vanished and then the stray cats around town started disappearing. Then Johnny Miller's collie didn't come home.

The kids that played at the park credited the mysterious disappearances to the Ghost Dog, and they had taken to calling it Black Fang, because Johnny Miller was half way through Jack London's *White Fang* when his dog went away for good.

"Black Fang," J.P. thought, when the forest went quiet. He shuddered, despite himself, because he didn't want to believe in the Ghost Dog any more than he believed in Santa Claus or Green Lantern. But there was a lot of ground covered between the man with a bowl full of jelly and the Guardians of the Universe. Things like vampires, werewolves, Superman and aliens, and the more he thought about it, the more he was beginning to wonder if there wasn't something to the stories, because yesterday Dick Rainmaker's dad took one of their horses out for a ride and never came back.

The grownups said that old Andrew Jackson Rainmaker was plain tired of his nagging wife and kids. So tired that he saddled up and rode away. The sheriff wasn't even going to look for Mr. Rainmaker till he'd been gone at least two days, but the boys that played at the park, Dick Rainmaker included, knew that it would make no difference. The sheriff would never find him, and he'd never be back. Black Fang got him, sure as shit.

J.P. got out of bed, went down the hall to his mother's room and knocked on the door, expecting her to invite him in. When she didn't answer, he pushed it open, then he remembered that she had started running in the mornings.

He wished she believed him about the Ghost Dog. Dick Rainmaker believed. Dick was scared, and Dick was fifteen.

He'd wanted to talk to his mom about the Ghost Dog last night, but when he got home, she was in one of her moods. She hadn't eaten all day and was cranky. He didn't know why she wanted to get skinny all of a sudden. He thought she looked fine and he hated it when she was cross with him for being a few minutes late, even though she apologized to him minutes later. He wished she would just eat and be her old self.

So last night he forgot about the Ghost Dog and went to his room and watched television till after midnight. It was the latest he had ever stayed up by himself. Now, still sleepy and staring at his mother's empty bed, he had the sudden feeling that Black Fang was after his mom.

He ran back to his room and swiftly changed from his pajamas into jeans, tee shirt and high top tennis shoes. He didn't waste time with socks. He was in a hurry to get outside and find his mom. He wished he had told her about the Ghost Dog, because all of a sudden he was afraid his mom was going to disappear like Dick Rainmaker's dad.

Dressed, he ran from the bedroom. If he wasn't too late, he thought, he might be able to warn her and save her. He would tell her not to go running on the beach anymore. She should stay inside. It was safer inside.

* * *

The forest noises stopped again, as suddenly as they had started. She quickened her pace. Something was moving behind her, something that frightened the forest creatures into silence, something bad. She started to run, but before she hit her stride, she tripped over a fallen branch. She thrust her arms out to break her fall, skinning both hands on the hard ground. She felt a sharp stab of pain in her right arm as it buckled under her, but despite the pain, she lay still, afraid to move and afraid not to. She listened to the silence.

There is nothing there, she told herself. Then she rolled onto her side and saw the reddened swelling midway between her elbow and her wrist. Pushing off with her left hand, she stood. White hot pain shot through her arm. She tried to think through the haze of panic and pain.

The forest remained silent. Her skin was alive. She felt a cold chill as a vomit-like smell assaulted her. Nearby, bushes moved. She knew it wasn't the wind. The morning had calmed. She heard something behind the bushes. There was something there, scraping against the ground. The only audible sound in the forest, save for the sound of her heavy breathing. There was definitely something in there, and she felt like it was stalking her.

She darted her eyes in all directions. She was trapped. She wondered it if was a mountain lion. She had never heard of them in these woods, but she supposed it was possible. She heard a low growl and her mouth went dry.

Her eyes stayed glued to the bushes. They weren't moving now. Whatever was in there was being still. It growled again, more like a big dog, she thought.

Afraid to move and afraid not to, she inched away from the bushes on the other side of the creek toward home and safety. The thing in the bushes growled and started to move. She moved a little faster. The pain in her arm was like wild fire.

The thing roared and she saw a black blur leap the creek and vanish into the pines ahead of her. Oh my god, she thought, it's between me and the house. Thinking quickly, she reversed her direction—and ran. She was too afraid now to deal with pain.

She rejumped the creek and started pumping her runner's legs, dodging tree and bush the best she could, but still getting several scrapes. The thing roared again, giving her an adrenaline rush. Scratched and bleeding, she ran for the sluice with the thing behind her. She felt it closing as she neared the path down the hill. The adrenaline gave added strength. She lept off the hill, landing on her behind in the center of the vee in the sluice.

The landing knocked the wind out of her, but she had no time to catch her breath, she was sliding down the hill and it was all she could do to keep from tumbling head over heels. Instinctively, she lay back and tried clutching the dirt sides to slow her slide. Failing, she grabbed at thinly growing shrubs, but to no avail. She was going over loose dirt, small rocks were ripping at her clothes and there was nothing she could do about it till she hit bottom. She was frantic. She didn't think she was going to make it. She was about to give up, when the angle of slide leveled a bit. She used the opportunity to grab onto a shrub with her good hand and managed to stop her slide and catch her breath.

The few seconds it took her to grab a breath seemed like forever. Any second the thing was going to get her, she thought. She forced herself to turn and look up the hill. It wasn't easy. She had to push her tired, aching, and damaged body onto its side with her good arm. If the thing came for her, there was nothing she could do. She sat up, fighting the urge to cry out. Sitting, she turned, expecting the worst, but there was nothing there. Whatever it was, it apparently didn't want to leave the forest.

She felt exposed on the hill. She felt like she was being watched. Then the thing roared once more and by the sound of it, she was able to tell that it was going away, but for how long? Would it come back? She had to get off the hill. She had to get home to J.P.

She tried to move, but it was agony. Her arm was screaming. With great care, keeping her feet in front of herself to control her rate of descent, she went down the hill on her backside. It was agonizingly slow work, but she forced it upon herself. She couldn't afford the luxury of waiting for help. She wanted to get home to J.P. as quickly as possible.

After a few minutes, with not much progress, she slipped and started to slide. She was out of control, rolling and tumbling in the sluice, screaming against the fear and the stabbing pain. But the careening ride didn't last long, in short order she was thrown out of the sluice and deposited on the soft beach sand below.

She tried to stand and found that if she bit hard enough into her lip, it was possible. Then she saw the most beautiful sight, Rick's red Jeep coming down the beach. Once again he was going to be her savior.

* * *

J.P. shuddered when he heard the animal scream from the forest. He knew what it was and he was afraid, but his mom was out there. He ran toward his mother's bedroom, tripping on the oval rug in the hallway. He picked himself up and hurried on. He stopped for an instant in front of his mother's bureau, he was scared shitless, but again he heard that animal roar and he pulled open the bottom drawer.

He knew what was there, his mom had shown it to him and told him to never, never touch it, but he was going to touch it now. He knew the gun was loaded, because his mom had told him it was. "This is a thirty-eight Police Special," she had said. "I'm showing it to you, so you'll know what and where it is. It's not a toy," she continued. When he asked her why they needed a gun, she said, "We're alone now and you never know who might come calling in the middle of the night." She had gone on to say that she trusted him and his judgment, after all he was almost eight. That's why she wanted him to see the gun. She trusted him and here he was grabbing it out of her bottom dresser drawer, but he wasn't going to play with it.

With the gun in hand, he raced down the hallway, careful not to trip again. He left the hardwood floor and turned onto the wall to wall carpeting of the living room. He skirted around the davenport and coffee table, more afraid than sure of himself, with his little boy's hot, sweaty hand extended for the front door's big brass doorknob. He threw open the door, crossed the porch and went down the steps, skipping the last one.

He didn't have any farther to go. Standing in front of the house with the sun hanging in the early morning sky, he was confronted with silence. The woods were quiet.

He strained to hear the steady drone of forest noises, and hearing none, strained his eyes for movement. His eyes weren't disappointed. They fixed on the rustle of bushes behind Rick's house. There was something there. He saw a blur dart behind the pines that extended from behind Rick's house to the back of his house.

The birds are back there, he thought.

"You're not gonna get the birds!"

He bounded up the steps and again raced across the living room, but instead of going into the hallway, where his bedroom and safety were, he turned into the dining room, careful not to bust his shins on the one chair that was always pulled out from under the big round oak table. That table always reminded him of King Arthur and his knights. Now, he was Sir Lancelot on his way to protect his mother from the evil dragon.

He threw his shoulder against the swinging kitchen door, throwing it inward, without breaking his stride, running across the tile floor into the service porch. He grabbed the back doorknob and tried to turn it, but his hand slipped round the knob. Locked. He let go of the knob, and, with shaking fingers, tweaked the lever in the center of it and turned. Then he grabbed the doorknob and turned, turned and pulled. The knob turned but the door was still locked, deadbolt locked, double deadbolt locked.

Mr. Keeper at the hardware store told his mom that double deadbolts were better than singles. That way if a thief broke in through the window, he couldn't get the doors open to take their stuff out. He could hear Mr. Keeper's voice, plain as the gun in his hand. "There is a danger to double deadbolts though, you can't get out without a key, there have been children killed in fires, because they were trapped inside." He remembered old

Mr. Keeper telling his mom to be sure your boy knows where the key is kept.

He had his own key on his key ring, somewhere in his bedroom, but he couldn't remember where. Then he remembered that his mom had a spare, an emergency key. It was in the cupboard, next to the coffee filters, hanging on a coffee cup hook. He lay the gun on the dryer and ran into the kitchen. He opened the bottom cupboard and using the kitchen counter for a hand hold, stepped up on the lower cupboard shelf. He was too short to reach the top cupboard by himself. He opened the top cupboard door, grabbed the key and pulled on it, breaking the key chain. Then he hopped down and went back into the service porch at top speed, fighting the urge to be scared. Sir Lancelot was never scared.

Back in the service porch, he fumbled the key in the lock and turned the deadbolt. He started when it clicked, but only for an instant. He grabbed the gun and opened the door. Cautiously, not running, not in a hurry anymore, he stepped out onto the back landing. There was something out there. He felt it. He looked at the loft. The birds usually up and pecking the ground or billing and cooing were silent. Something in the air had frozen them statue still, silent sentinels warning him of the danger out back.

He descended the steps, no longer Sir Lancelot. He was a cautious Rambo, a nightfighter climbing down those wooded stairs, one hand on the railing, the other clutching the gun. The gun that his mother had forbidden him to ever touch. Leaving the steps, he crossed the silent yard to the loft. The sound of his footsteps rang through the quiet morning air. Now, he was only a boy, a scared boy.

Running his eyes through the inside of the loft, he saw

Maverick, a tough male blue bar and his mother's favorite, by the feeder, unmoving, head cocked, eyes alert. He sensed danger. Dancer, his favorite, was on Maverick's left in the same position. All the other birds were in their orange crate nests. Never had he seen them like this.

He walked around the cage, knowing something was out there. He wanted to turn and run back to the house and crawl into his bed, but something told him he was no safer there than he was out back with the birds. Besides, his mom was out there somewhere. He hoped she was okay.

He saw something move beyond the clearing, twenty feet from the loft. He turned to face it. Nothing there. But something was there, in the bushes. He knew it sure as Maverick and Dancer knew it.

He took a step forward, squinting into the morning sun. He remembered from the Louis L'Amour stories that his mom read him, that a gunfighter liked to have the sun at his back, and he was staring into it. What would a Louis L'Amour gunfighter do? He would move, try to get a better position. J.P. moved away from the loft, toward Rick's house, never for an instant taking his eyes of the area where he'd seen the bushes move.

He stepped sideways, one step, two, three and the bushes moved again. It was only the breeze, he told himself. Then he heard something, a low growl. Black Fang, he thought. Four steps, five, six, seven, the bushes moved again and this time it wasn't the wind. Eight steps, nine, ten, his angle was better, the sun no longer directly in his eyes. Eleven steps and then the largest animal that he had ever seen gracefully appeared from the bushes as if by magic. It seemed to be walking on air.

It was Black Fang, the Ghost Dog. Its blue-black, short fur glistened in the sunlight and its red eyes bore into him, like the electric drills that Mr. Keeper sold in his hardware store. He wanted to turn and run, but he stood his ground. Sure as a Louis L'Amour villain would shoot him in the back, this thing would come for him if he ran. He stood fast, meeting its glare full on, afraid to move and afraid not to. If the thing charged him, he was done for. He wasn't a gunfighter. No way could he shoot. He was a boy and he wanted his mother.

The blue-black beast raised its right paw as if it wanted J.P. to get a look at it, and he did. He saw the steel-like claws reflecting the sun's glow like diamonds. It was the animal's way of telling him it was going to rip him apart. Then it pawed the ground, digging, no not digging, demonstrating its power by ripping up great chunks of earth as easily as one of Mr. Keeper's buzz saws ripped through pine.

Paralyzed, J.P. watched as the beast glided toward the loft and the birds inside. J.P. felt a new fear, not fear for himself, but for the birds he loved. The Ghost Dog or whatever it was, was going to kill the birds before it came for him. It was going to rip through the chicken wire cage and turn his birds into blood pudding.

No way.

"No, you're not!" He was getting mad. The beast was halfway to the cage, taking his time, making J.P. suffer, trying to make him more afraid. But it wasn't working. J.P. was getting more mad than afraid. He raised the gun, holding it with both hands, like a TV cop. He pointed it at the beast and pulled the trigger.

The noise was louder than any firecracker and his arms were thrown up and back with the kick of the blast, but he held onto the gun and kept the animal in sight.

The animal faced J.P. The shot had gone wide and to the right, throwing up a divot of dirt halfway between it and the pigeon cage. The animal looked first from J.P. to the loft, then back to J.P., like it couldn't make up its mind to go for the birds first, then J.P., or the other way around. Then it turned back to the loft and continued its slow glide to the pigeon cage.

J.P. brought his arms back down, back into the TV policeman shooter's position, tried to aim and pulled the trigger again. This time the gun didn't jerk as much. He was ready for it and had tightened the muscles in his hands and arms. This time the shot didn't go wide. He hit the beast square in the chest, right where his dad told him to aim, when he'd taken him deer hunting. "Make the shot clean," his dad had said, "and you won't have to go crashing through all hell and gone trying to put a wounded animal out of its misery."

The beast stopped and regarded J.P. with its red eyes. J.P. saw that it was bleeding. He shot again and missed. The beast didn't move. He shot again and again hit it full in the chest. His dad would have been proud, but the beast didn't go down. It stood stock still, baring its fangs, longer teeth than J.P. had ever seen, and he shot again. Another miss. Another shot, another hit, again in the chest. He pulled the trigger again and heard the metallic click that told him the gun was empty.

He'd seen enough television to know that when the gun was empty you threw it at your attacker. They always did that in old cowboy movies. But that would be dumb, far smarter to run, but that would be useless. He could only stand and watch as the hot breath closed in on him. The animal advanced slowly, no longer interested in the birds. This was no television monster. This was real.

He saw the Ghost Dog prepare to spring and knew that he was finished. Then he heard the car coming fast. The blue black Ghost Dog heard it too. The car was getting close. It was out front. The Ghost Dog, with a bullish snort, turned and vanished into the woods.

CHAPTER

ELEVEN

TOM DONOVAN LEFT THE FREEWAY at Colorado and turned north toward Pasadena City College. The rented Chevy came with a broken air conditioner and it was hot. He made a mental note to complain to the company about it as he wiped the sweat from his forehead. Even with both front windows cranked down, it was a gesture he had to repeat every few minutes.

He had been coming to Southern California off and on for the last five years. He didn't like it. It was too hot and too smoggy, but this time he was excited, as excited as he was the first time he had seen Led Zeppelin that great day in 1975 at Earl's Court in London.

He patted his shirt pocket, feeling the folded letter. The letter that was a gateway to a lot of money, maybe a quarter million or more, but the money was secondary, as it always would be when it came to Led Zep. It was the board tapes that he was after. The fact that he would make a small fortune was bloody great, but to hear stereo soundboard recordings of the greatest band on earth before anyone else, that was to die for, and the letter promised him that.

In his heart he had never forgiven Rick Gordon for scoring Zep board tapes and putting them out. The man cared nothing for the band, didn't even like them. He was only in it for the money. If anyone should make money off the band, Tom felt it should be him. He hated it that he had put out over two dozen Zep boots and Rick Gordon put out five and made ten times the money.

True, his own titles were seriously lacking in the sound quality department. They were mostly recorded from the audience, with cheap cassette players, but they were great shows that documented the history of the band. It was also true that before he started doing business Rick's way, he was slugging along, making barely enough to keep out of work and to keep up his Zep Collection. By signing on with Rick, he'd made enough money so that he wouldn't have to work for ten, maybe fifteen years.

But Rick shouldn't have put out the Zep board tapes without consulting him first. And he never should have put out Earl's Court. That tape was sacred. That show was the one that had shown him the way. He should have been able to lie in bed at night and listen to it with his headphones and enjoy. He couldn't enjoy it to the fullest knowing somebody else was enjoying it, too. The true collector lived to have a one of a kind thing. He should have been the only person in the world to be able to listen to that tape.

"When are we going to Disneyland, Dad?" his son, named after Led Zeppelin's famous guitarist, Jimmy Page Donovan asked from the back seat.

"Don't bother your father," Sylvia, Tom's new wife, said.

* * *

J.P. was glad to be with his father. It had been so long since he'd seen his dad. He couldn't believe it last week when he'd called his mom and asked if she would let him fly to L.A. and spend two weeks in Southern California, going to the beach, Disneyland, Magic Mountain and, of course, the Pasadena Meet. But he was surprised when his dad met him at the airport with a new wife. He wasn't sure how he should act around her or what he should call her. She seemed nice and he didn't want to not like her, just because she'd married his dad.

* * *

"It's okay, Sylvia," Tom said. Then, catching his son's eyes in the rearview mirror, he added, "Just as soon as I meet the guy at the meet and collect the tapes." He bet his son was the only eight-year-old in the world that knew the true value of a Zep board tape.

"Are we gonna listen to them on the way, Dad?"

"On the cassette player in this heap? You have got to be kidding. I'll bet the only time it ever had clean heads was when it was new, and it's not new now." If he had his way, they would go back to the motel straightaway after he got the tapes and spend the next forty-eight hours listening non-stop, but he had promised his wife a trip to Disneyland, and she would never forgive him if he put Led

Zeppelin ahead of Disneyland. It was a paradox to him that he loved and married a woman that hated the band.

When he received the letter, two weeks ago, with a sample song from the Montreal '76 show, he was euphoric. Whoever Sam Storm was, he was offering him a fortune for only a hundred dollars a show. Six shows, six hundred dollars.

"You're gonna miss your turn, Dad," J.P. said from the back.

"Good eye, J.P.," Tom said. He made a right turn into the college parking lot. The Pasadena Meet, as the Pasadena Record Swap Meet was called, was held on the third Sunday of every month at Pasadena City College, and for reasons that Tom didn't understand, was the best source in Southern California to buy bootlegs. What had probably started as a legitimate, once-a-month record collector's flea market, had rapidly turned into a bootleg free-for-all. Month after month, the same fifteen or sixteen bootleg retailers were interspersed among the ordinary record sellers, making between two and five thousand dollars each for a day's work.

Tom was usually apprehensive when he was in a place where bootlegs were sold openly, but not today. He was excited about the tapes, but he was worried about his son and that ghost dog thing that he was caught up in. Tom hoped it was just a phase. It was normal for kids to be afraid of things in the dark, but not his kid. J.P. had a head on his shoulders. He knew the value of a good Zep tape. How many other kids did?

"There's a spot, Dad." Again Tom had been brought out of his daydreams by his son.

"We don't have to go to Disneyland today if you wanna go back to the motel and listen to the tapes. I wouldn't mind."

"But I would," Sylvia said. "We planned on going to Disneyland today and we're going. There is no way we're going to sit in a hot motel and listen to Led Zeppelin all day." With that said, she crossed her arms firmly over her chest, her body language closing off any further discussion.

"Disneyland it is," Tom said.

"Yeah, Disneyland," echoed J.P., "but I wanna write a note to Mom first and send Dancer home." He'd brought Dark Dancer with him on the plane. He wanted his favorite bird to be a genuine five hundred miler and the only way to make him one was to release him five hundred miles away from home and have him return. He hoped Dancer wouldn't let him down.

"Is your bird going to be okay in that little cage?" Sylvia asked.

"Oh sure, he's used to it. Once Mom and I drove to San Francisco and let him go the next day. He was in the cage all night. He doesn't mind."

Tom put the Chevy in park, put on the emergency brake. "Time to find Mr. Sam Storm."

"Can I get a Coke and look around?" J.P. said.

"Meet us back here in forty-five minutes," Tom said.

"Should he go off by himself?" Sylvia said.

"He'll be fine. He loves it."

"Want me to take some money, Dad? In case I find something?"

Tom reached into his pocket and withdrew three twenties. There was always a chance the boy might stumble onto something worth having. "Here." He held out the money. "Bargain wisely."

J.P. grabbed the money and took off across the parking lot, dashing through a long corridor that lead to the other side of the campus, where the sellers were set up.

"I love that boy," Tom said to his wife.

"I know you do, but it wouldn't hurt if you taught him there is more to life than Led Zeppelin."

"He knows that."

"Why should he? You don't."

"Let's not fight about that now. We'll go to the cafeteria, meet Mr. Storm, collect J.P., and then go to Disneyland. Okay?"

"Okay."

* * *

J.P. dodged around a big man headed toward the cafeteria, where his dad was supposed to meet the guy with the Zep tapes. That must be Sam Storm, he figured. He looked familiar. J.P. stopped and started to yell at the big man walking away from him, but an inner voice told him not to. If his dad had wanted him to meet Mr. Storm, he would have told him to wait, and besides, he didn't want to talk to the man, because he might betray how much his dad wanted the tapes. Then Mr. Storm would ask for more money.

His dad had taught him to never betray how much you wanted something. "The number one rule a collector must always remember is to stay cool, play like you don't care. Otherwise you pay through the nose," his dad had said, so there was no way he was going to call out to Mr. Storm. He didn't want to be the one to ruin the chance at Zep board tapes.

His mind made up, he started to turn his eyes away from the big man's back, when the man stopped, turned quickly and locked his eyes onto J.P.'s. Then he dropped them to J.P.'s Robert Plant tee shirt.

"You like Led Zeppelin, son?" the man's gravel voice

boomed.

Without a thought, J.P. turned and ran. No way was he gonna talk to Mr. Storm and give anything away, no way. He ran down the corridor between the student union and the bookstore, emerging onto the grassy area where the record dealers were set up, not knowing that if he had stopped to talk to the big man, he would have already been twenty seconds dead.

* * *

Watching J.P. run down the corridor, framed by its circular columns, reminded Tom of Luke Skywalker maneuvering his starfighter between the walls of the Death Star. Like Luke, his boy was good and kind and honest. Thinking of Luke Skywalker brought Darth Vador to mind and then he saw the big man step into the corridor in front of J.P. He saw J.P. expertly dodge the man as only a boy could. He saw him stop, turn, then run away. Good boy, he thought, watching his son continue his run down the corridor. He didn't want to say anything to blow the deal or increase the price.

A feeling of unease grabbed Tom as the big man came closer. There was something about the way he carried himself. The way he moved his bulk with seemingly little effort. The strong strides. A confident man. Not the kind of man who spent his time with headphones clamped to his head listening to unreleased concerts. His tan gave him away. Tom had never met a Zep collector with a tan. Something wasn't right.

"Tom Donovan?" the man asked, approaching with his right hand extended.

"Sam Storm, I presume." Tom took the big man's hand. His grip was firm, but overpowering.

"That your boy I saw in the Robert Plant tee shirt just

now?"

"No, my son's in Toronto. Sylvia didn't want to take him out of school," Tom lied, with a nod indicating his wife. Throughout his bootleg career he had been used to deception. He often used different names as a matter of routine when dealing with his customers. A different name and a different background for each one, so the lie about J.P. rolled off his forked tongue with the ring of truth.

"I saw the shirt."

"The shirt?"

"The boy I saw, he had a Robert Plant tee shirt on."

"Black with a head shot of Plant?"

"Yeah, like that."

"Probably one of mine. I make and sell Zep tee shirts. That's mainly how I make my money. There are at least four dealers here that sell them." Tom had used the tee shirt cover story so many times to explain his income, that he said it naturally.

"That explains it." The big man laughed. "But I thought you also sold bootlegs."

"No, sir." Tom was put on his guard. Very few people knew about his connection to the boots. The fact that this man brought it up, told him that he might be more than just a collector with a few tapes to sell.

"One of the dealers last month said he traded you a few records."

"Oh, that," Tom said with some of the tension visibly leaving his body. "I'm a collector and I'm working on a book about the history of the band, so it's my business to know everything there is to know about Led Zeppelin. Bootlegs are a fact of life and an important part of the history of the band, and although some of them may sound terrible, you have to admit, they show what it was like to see Zep in their heyday."

"I suppose." The big man sounded less like a collector every second.

"Did you bring the tapes?" Tom asked.

"Right here." The big man tapped a coat pocket. "Gotta keep them out of sight. They're pretty valuable."

"Hold on, we agreed on the price."

"I know and I'm not going to back out of the deal. It's just that there's someone else who is also interested."

"I assumed this was going to be an exclusive deal."

"I never said that."

"But it was a valid assumption. If you sell the tapes to somebody else, how do I know he won't trade them around."

"I guess you don't."

"That would make them worthless."

"He's paying a whole lot more money than you are, so I don't think he's going to trade them. He'll want them for himself, like you do."

"That's good to know," Tom said, relieved. Then he asked, "Who is this person?"

"You wouldn't know him."

"Try me."

"A guy named Rick Gordon."

"Jesus Christ," Tom said through grinding teeth.

"Got a problem with that?"

"I'll say. You sell them to him and I don't want them."

"Why not?"

"He'll bootleg them faster than you can blink."

"I thought you didn't have anything to do with the bootlegs?"

"I don't, but that doesn't mean that I don't know who does."

"Well, I'll put your mind at rest, Mr. Gordon is retired. He doesn't make bootlegs anymore."

"Then why does he want the tapes?"

"Maybe he likes Led Zeppelin."

"Not a chance. The only thing he ever liked about the music business was the money it made him."

"There is something wrong with money?" the big man asked.

"There is if you make it on the backs of genuine collectors and fans who love the music for what it is."

"So what you're saying is, it's okay for you to make money on bootlegs, because you're a genuine fan and collector, but not okay for Gordon, because he only cares for the money."

"Exactly, every bootleg I ever made—"

"I thought you didn't make bootlegs," the big man interrupted.

"I don't. I might have. I mean I don't anymore."

"Like Gordon doesn't anymore?"

"That's not what I mean."

"What you mean is, you want my tapes to make bootlegs."

"What if I do?" Tom hated himself for being caught in his lie so easily.

"Then I think you'd better plan on paying a little more money."

"I didn't bring anymore with me."

"Are you going to bootleg them?"

"I think you already wormed that out of me."

"In that case, I think we need a few moments of private conversation."

"Whatever you have to say to me, you can say in front of my wife."

"Don't get me wrong, I'm sure she can be trusted and I don't mind if you tell her everything you and I talk about, but when discussing something of this nature, I prefer it to be on a one to one basis. That way if things should go sour in the future, it's my word against yours, not yours and your wife's. Do you understand?"

"Not really."

"It's okay, Tom. I left my purse in the car anyway," Sylvia said. Then turning to the big man she asked, "Ten minutes be enough for you, Mr. Storm?"

"More than enough."

Turning on her heels, Sylvia walked down the corridor, slapping the circular supporting columns as she passed them. The slaps echoed like gunfire down the empty corridor, each sound less loud than the one before.

Tom stole a quick glance to the big man standing next to him and felt a pang of jealousy when he saw those steel eyes glued to his wife's backside. Dirty old man, he thought, but then who wouldn't steal a look at Sylvia if given half a chance.

"If she's half as sharp as she looks, you are a lucky man."

"She's working on her Ph.D. in French Lit."

"Nice."

"She hates Led Zeppelin."

"Too bad," the big man said. Then without warning, he shoved Tom in the chest, slamming him into one of the columns that supported the covered corridor. Then Storm grabbed him by the neck and rapped his head against the column, stunning him. In seconds he had Tom's hands behind his back, arms around the column, hands handcuffed together.

Tom started to yell and the big man hit him in the stomach, winding him. Gasping for air, Tom's eyes bugged out and he barely saw Storm remove a roll of gray duct tape from a coat pocket. The big man grabbed him by the hair and pulled his head up until Tom was standing erect. Then he covered his mouth and started winding the tape, affixing his head to the column.

"If you could only see yourself," Storm said.

Tom moaned.

"Yeah, tell me about it."

Tom's eyes widened.

* * *

"Don't look at me like that. I didn't make you a bootlegger. You must have known that someday, someway, you'd have to pay for your crimes." Saying it made it sound just, but Storm knew it wasn't so. Since seeing Gordon in Tampico he had changed. Once a man who lived by the rules, he had turned into a man who lived by the gun. He'd become an old west sheriff bent on vengeance. Part of him reveled in the new Sam Storm, and part of him was repulsed, but he had gone too far to turn back now.

The new Sam Storm wanted the woman. He wanted her on the ground in front of her helpless husband. He wanted to feel the husband's fear and anguish as he saw his wife raped, then tortured. He wanted to taste her blood, smell her fear, swallow her terror, but alas it couldn't be, he was going to have to follow her out to the parking lot and do her there, after he finished with hubby. He had to kill the bootlegger and his wife and be gone, before they were discovered by a happy collector, looking for a safe place to do a line or smoke a joint.

As his helpless victim watched, Storm removed an ice pick from his coat pocket. Then he took a CD out of his shirt pocket. Tom started to squirm, fighting against the handcuffs as Storm inserted the point of the ice pick through the hole in the center of the CD.

"*Live on Blueberry Hill*," Storm said, indicating the

CD.

* * *

It wasn't fair, Tom thought, he was going to be killed and his favorite Zeppelin concert, the first Zeppelin bootleg, was going to be part of the murder weapon. It wasn't fair. It wasn't fair.

He felt a slight discomfort as the man inserted the ice pick into his left nostril, holding it with thumb and index finger below the shaft. Then he felt a brief stab of pain, when the man used the palm of his right hand to slam it into his brain. Then the lights went out for Tom Donovan.

CHAPTER
TWELVE

"IT'S NOT GOING TO BE THE SAME up here by myself."
Rick Gordon hefted Judy Donovan's suitcase into the
trunk of her old Dodge. He meant what he'd said, the
thought of being alone on the hill suddenly chilled him.

She stuck out her lower lip and blew the hair up from
her eyes, but it fell right back, so she pushed it back with
her hand. "I know," she said, "except for spending last
Christmas with Christina and the twins, I haven't been
out of this town for the last eighteen months."

"How's your arm?" He stood by the trunk, but he
didn't close it. It was almost like she couldn't leave as
long as he held it open. There was something about her

he was going to miss. She was different. Or maybe she wasn't, maybe she was the same, maybe he'd just never noticed before, but he was noticing now, and her leaving, even though it was for only a short time, tugged at him.

"Fine," she said. "Hey, you wanna autograph my cast?"

"Sure."

She took a pen out of her purse, "Write away." She offered the pen to him. She was trembling, just a little. He saw it in the slight shaking of the pen in her hand. He took the pen, feeling a slight tremor himself as he touched the writing instrument, then it was gone.

He reached out with his left hand, to steady the cast, and the tremor was back, the instant he touched her. Sort of a pleasant jolt of awareness, like he'd just woken from a good dream and he knew it was going to be a great day. Then the pen started to move in his hand, almost as if it had a life of its own.

"Friends forever. Longer than life," he said as he wrote, surprising himself.

"It's nice," she said, "but you didn't sign it."

"You know who it's from."

"But I'm not quite sure what it means."

"Neither am I," he said and they both laughed, but he sensed she was tingling inside, as was he.

Then she said, "You're sure you don't mind watching the birds? They can be a lot of trouble." And the spell was broken. The tingling stopped, but he still felt the aftermath, a pleasant feeling as he handed her back the pen.

"Not for me. I'll enjoy every minute of it." Then he picked up the second suitcase. "What do you have in here, lead?"

"Spent the day at Miles of Books. I intend to do a lot

of reading while I'm laying on that beach."

"Does Miles have anything left?"

"Nope, bought him out," she kidded. "Good thing too, because he's getting married, so he can probably use the money."

"Really, I thought he was a confirmed bachelor. Who's the unlucky woman?" He wasn't being flip. He thought Miles was sort of a dandy, the kind of man that would be more at home in upper crust London than small town Tampico. A stuck up snob, who acted like he was a cut above everybody else. He read a lot, knew a lot, and didn't mind letting you know it. Rick didn't like him very much, but it never stopped him from going into his store. It was the only bookstore in town and he liked to read.

"Sarah Sadler, she teaches at RFK elementary."

"That proves it, there's somebody for everybody," he said, hand on the trunk, resisting, not wanting to close it. He bit his lip and curled his toes in his shoes, trying to take his mind off these new feelings shooting up and down his spine. The tingling was back and he didn't know how to deal with it.

"If that's true, then there must be somebody for me." She moved around to the driver's side of the car, opened the door, but didn't get in. She just stood there, hand on the door, like he had his hand on the trunk.

"All of us, there's somebody for all of us," he said, thinking how stupid they probably looked, staring at each other like two teenagers. All of a sudden he felt awkward with her. Awkward like when he asked Ann out that first time so many years ago. He shuddered and closed the trunk.

She answered him with a smile. Then she slipped into the front seat, gently closing the door after herself. "See you in two weeks." Then as an afterthought she added,

"Is there anything you want me to bring back?"

"Only a suntan," he said.

She started the car and drove off, giving him a last wave, just before she made the first turn on the winding road down the hill.

He went over to his place, sat on the porch steps and watched the sun fade behind the pines. She was right in sending J.P. off to be with his father for awhile. As much as he missed him, he wasn't his father. The boy needed to spend time with Tom. And she was also right in taking two weeks to herself. Two weeks on the beach in Waikiki would do her good.

She needed to get her mind off of her problems and live a little. But he was going to miss her and it tugged at him. He was in love with Christina. At least he thought he was. He loved the twins, he knew that.

But Judy was only a few minutes gone and already he missed her. However, he was glad both she and J.P. were going to be out of town for awhile. Something was going on that wasn't right. If there was a wild dog on the prowl, then it was good they weren't going to be up here. And if it was something else, then it was also good that they were gone. If J.P. really had stuck three or four slugs into it, it was wounded and dangerous. If it was a dog? He wondered what else it could be.

His thoughts were interrupted by the phone ringing inside. He pushed himself up from the steps and went to answer it. He knew it was bad news the second his hand touched the phone. The tears were coming from far away and he felt them as soon as he cradled the instrument to his ear.

"Hello."

"Is that you Ricky?" he almost didn't recognize her golden voice. She was crying and she was the kind of person he couldn't imagine ever crying. Unless it was bad.

"It's me, Susan," he said.

"Danny's dead, Ricky. Somebody killed him on the river. I should have gone. I should have. But he said he needed time for himself. He lied, Ricky. He was with someone else, but I don't care, I just want him back. I can never ever see him again. We can never sing together again. It's all over."

"I'm so sorry. I don't know what to say. Can I do anything? Do you have anyone?"

"I'm at my mother's. I'll be okay. I just wanted you to know."

"I'll get a flight out today," he said.

"No, Ricky. That's not a good idea. I think you should go away for a while. Warn Tom and Christina. I have a bad feeling."

"What are you talking about?" His hand tensed on the phone and he had a queasy feeling in his stomach.

"Evan was murdered two days before Danny."

"Oh, no." He sighed, sitting down.

"It was the same man," she said.

"That's not possible," Rick said. "It has to be some kind of awful coincidence."

"They both had their heads cut off," she said. "Sherry's dead, too. I'm not even gonna stay for the funeral. I loved him, but I'm going to our place in Mexico till they catch whoever did it and lock him away for good."

"I don't know what to say. I'm just so sorry."

"They think you did it," she said. "The police found Evan's records. They know all about you guys and the boots. They think you're into more than the records. They think you're into organized crime, you know, like the Mafia. They know you were in New York. They think you left there after you killed Evan and came here and killed Danny."

"That's absurd," he said, but his hands were shaking. He could see how they'd think that. Bootlegs were against the law and they had been pretty organized. It had always been one of his fears, that the police would jump to a conclusion like that. But this was so much more. How could anyone think they'd harm each other. They were all friends. He could no more raise a hand against Tom or Evan than he could against J.P.

"I know it, but they're looking for you."

"Thanks for the warning and thanks for believing in me."

"Love you, Ricky. I gotta go. You take care."

"Love you, too," he said, then she broke the connection.

He cradled the phone and it rang again.

"Hello," Rick said as a hot flash zapped through him. He knew it was more bad news even before J.P. spoke.

"Someone killed my dad. They tied him to a post and cut his head off. There was tons of blood. Rick, you gotta help me. I'm really scared. I saw the man. It's him, I know it is. And I bet he has the knife. You gotta come. You gotta come now. I'm so scared."

"Calm down, J.P. Talk slower. Tell me slow."

"It's hard. I don't wanna cry, but I can't help it."

"Are you okay?"

"I'm across the street from the Record Meet in Pasadena, at Jumpin' Jimmy's. I couldn't hide in the bushes anymore. I had to go to the bathroom and I was real hungry. I saw the man."

"What man?" Rick said.

"It was the man from the bait shop the day those beggars were murdered. I saw him. At first I didn't recognize him, but I remembered. He killed my dad."

"Do you have any money?"

"Yeah, I got sixty dollars. My dad gave it to me to buy stuff, but when I remembered where I saw the man, I went back to tell my dad about how that guy was up in Tampico when you had to kill those bums and he was dead. Sylvia's dead, too."

"Who's Sylvia?"

"My dad's new wife."

"I'm sorry, J.P. I'll be down there on the first flight."

"What should I do till you get here?"

"You stay in the restaurant. Sit at the counter, talk to the cook, talk to the waitress, and don't talk to anyone else. I'm going to call Christina and have her come get you. Remember her?"

"Yeah, her and Torry and Swell."

"That's right. Don't leave the restaurant. And be very careful."

"So he doesn't get me, too?"

"Yes, so he doesn't get you, too."

He hung up and started dialing.

"Hello," Rick heard her voice coming down the wire.

"Hi, Chris."

"How come you didn't call like you said you would?" She was angry.

"Please don't talk, just listen."

His voice must have conveyed the urgency he felt because she said, "Okay."

"Susan just called. Evan and Danny are dead. Murdered. Sherry's dead, too. It looks like it might have been the same man. Susan thinks the killer may come after you and the girls. She's gone to Mexico."

"Oh, no," she said.

"Sorry to break it to you this way, but it can't be

helped. Do you know the Pasadena Meet?"

"Yes. I don't go, but I've been once or twice, just to look around."

"Tom and his new wife were murdered yesterday at the meet. J.P. has been hiding out there since yesterday. Right now he's sitting at the counter in Jumpin' Jimmy's. Do you know it?"

"Yes."

"He thinks he saw the man who killed his father. I want you and the girls to go and get him and then go check in to the Beach Inn on Ocean. Tell no one."

"But it's so close to here."

"Exactly, the best place to hide is where nobody would look. Nobody's going to look for you in a motel across the street."

"Gotcha, I'm leaving now. See you when you get here."

"Be careful."

"You got it. I'm out the door."

"No questions?"

"None."

"Good girl, and Christina?"

"Yeah?"

"I love you," he said.

"You always did a little," she said.

"See ya, take care."

"See ya," she said back. Then she hung up.

CHAPTER THIRTEEN

CHRISTINA PAGE STARTED DIALING as soon as Rick hung up. It took her three calls to find out the twins had gone to the movies with friends and wouldn't be back for a couple of hours. She couldn't find out which movie and she couldn't spend all night calling movie theaters. They were with a group of girls, in a crowded cinema, they'd be okay till she returned with J.P.

He must be so frightened, she thought. Sitting in that restaurant all alone. His father dead. It was all so hard to believe.

She thought about leaving a note for the girls, but she was only going to be gone a short time. They wouldn't worry and besides, she'd be back before they knew she had been gone.

She left the house and made her way to her car with her mind in a whirl. Rick's call, telling her that her friends were dead, tore at her heart, and the thought of J.P., afraid and alone, ripped at her mother's instincts. She fought to hold her feelings halfway between sorrow and rage.

She started the car and drove, mentally stabbing herself for agreeing to do what Rick asked. She should have called the police straightaway. She made up her mind to do so as soon as she picked up J.P. If he saw the man who killed his father, he should be telling the cops. They were the ones who should be handling this, not her.

Then she thought that whoever is doing this has been able to find some people who are very good at covering their tracks. There isn't exactly a who's who of bootleggers available in the local library. Danny, Evan and Tom had been living a sort of underground existence for the last twenty years. Like her, they had no credit cards, no bank accounts, no jobs, no listings in the phone book. They would be damned hard to find, unless you were a friend.

But someone found them, she thought.

Twenty minutes later she exited at Colorado. She'd made good time. Within an hour of Rick's phone call she was parking her car in the same parking lot where Tom Donovan's new wife had been murdered.

She looked both ways, then ran across the street against the light. J.P. saw her the second she came through the door and in an instant he was off his stool and into her arms, crying.

"It's going to be okay now, J.P.," she said, knowing it would never be okay for him again. Danny, Evan and

Tom, she thought, what had they gone and gotten themselves into? Who did they piss off?

"I'm glad you came." He had his arms wrapped around her, clutching as only a frightened child can.

"Come on, J.P. I'll take you home."

"Can we stop by the Holiday Inn and pick up my bird, cuz I gotta have Dark Dancer." He wiped the tears from his eyes.

"Sure we can, but you'll have to be careful when we get it home, the girls have a new kitten and we wouldn't want it to eat your bird."

"Oh, it wouldn't do that," he said. "Dancer's a tough pigeon. And besides, he's got a good cage."

Thirty minutes later Christina turned into the parking garage, ducking her head as she went down the circular ramp.

"That's silly," J.P. said. "You got lotsa room, besides you're in the car."

"It's an old habit, hard to break," she said.

"Wow, full up," J.P. said as they circled the first floor on their way down.

"There must be a convention in town."

"Lots of the record meet people stay here," J.P. said.

"This is a big hotel. I doubt that would fill it. There must be something else going on," she said as she passed through the second floor, heading on down to the third.

"Stop," J.P. yelled.

Christina slammed her foot on the brake.

"Sorry, ma'am," one of the men she'd almost run down said. "We should have used the stairs."

"What's going on?" she asked. Two of the men had open beer cans in their hands.

"Homicide convention," one of them said. "Homicide detectives from all over the world, swapping lies upstairs.

Right now this hotel is probably the safest place on the planet, must be over three thousand cops milling around."

"Not so safe for you three, I almost ran you over," she said. They laughed and waved as she drove on to search out a parking place on the lower level. The only parking spaces left were on the far side of the garage, away from the elevators.

"We're way out in left field," J.P. said.

"Not that far. Let's get your bird and go. I want to be back before the girls get home from the movies."

"I hope he's okay, he hasn't had any food or water for a whole day."

"I'm sure he'll be fine." They rode up to the sixth floor in silence, but when the doors opened, J.P. shot out of the elevator and ran down the hall. By the time she reached the room, J.P. had the door open and was inside.

"He's okay," J.P. said. "I'm gonna get him some water from the bathroom." He was back in a few seconds with a plastic cup. He poured some of the liquid into Dancer's water bottle and Christina watched while the bird drank.

"He looks big for a pigeon."

"He is, it's cuz he's a racing homer. They're bred to fly far and fast. He's got lots more muscles than commies."

"Commies?" she asked.

"Regular, everyday pigeons are called commies."

"Oh," she said. He started to pick up the cage and she asked, "Do you have any clothes?"

"Oh yeah." He set the bird back on the bureau, went to the closet and tugged out two suitcases.

"You don't travel very light," she said.

"I was gonna stay with my dad for awhile."

"I'm sorry." She looked around the room. "Where's your father's things?" She knew Tom always traveled with his tapes. She didn't want to leave them to cause unnecessary questions later.

"Next room." J.P. opened the connecting door. Apparently they went straight from checking into the hotel to the record meet, because they hadn't started to unpack. She found two suitcases at the foot of the bed. She opened one and seeing it full of female things, set it aside and opened the other.

"That's your dad," she said to J.P. One change of clothes and about a hundred tapes. "They can't all be Zep."

"Mostly," J.P. said "But he was into Pink Floyd too. Probably lots of Floyd there. We should take this with us. His customer list is in there." He pointed to a ledger wedged in among the tapes.

"I was thinking the same thing." She closed the suitcase and carried it into J.P.'s room. "Okay, time to go." She carried two suitcases. J.P. carried one and the bird cage and they made their way to the elevator.

She still felt like calling the police, but she was starting to think if she did, she might get Rick into trouble. If the boys were up to something, she didn't want to be responsible for getting Rick sent to jail.

It seemed like forever before the elevator showed and when it did, it wasn't empty. They rode down with two couples that had been drinking too much in the rooftop bar and a large black man who looked like he'd rather be wearing anything else then the new suit he had on.

"What kind of bird is that?" One of the men asked.

"Racing homer," J.P. said. "He's fast."

"I had racing homers when I was your age," the black man said.

"Really? Any five hundred milers?" J.P. asked.

"Some. You're going to let him go?"

"I was gonna but—"

Christina squeezed his shoulder and he bit back the sentence. She smiled at the black man, who got off on the third level.

"Gonna let him go and he's gonna fly away home," one of the women said. It didn't sound like a question and J.P. didn't answer. Christina didn't think those people should be driving, but she was a strong believer in minding her own business. She nodded at them when they acknowledged her, but when the elevator door opened, they were out of her mind.

"We'll leave the stuff here and go get the car." They set the suitcases and the birdcage by the elevator and they started toward her car, with Christina leading J.P. by the hand.

A can clattered across the garage, but Christina barely heard. She was in a hurry to get home to the twins, and once again she wondered what Danny, Evan and Tom had been up to. She didn't think it was drugs. She knew that Evan did coke, but Danny and Tom never touched the stuff. Tom didn't even smoke cigarettes. But whatever it was, it had to be big and there had to be a lot of money involved for someone to kill them all in such a way. She hoped Rick had no part of it, but she was afraid that maybe he did, otherwise why hadn't he told her to call the police right from the get go?

"Christina, look," J.P. said. She felt his hand tighten on hers as she followed his pointed finger.

"Shit!" She stooped to look at the front tire. "Someone cut it up good." She ran her hand along the slice. "Son-of-a-bitch!"

"And the back one too. Someone with a big knife." He was trembling. "The Ragged Man."

"The other side as well," she said, then asked, "What

Ragged Man?"

"He's a killer with a sharp knife, a Jim Bowie knife. I think he's the one who killed my dad. I—"

Tires screeched around the ramp, heading up, cutting off J.P. Words. The sound echoed in the underground garage. Christina wanted to call out, but it was too late, the two couples from the elevator were gone. She looked over the tops of the cars. The elevator was across the garage. It didn't seem like a short walk anymore.

"Listen," J.P. whispered.

"What?"

"No noise," he said. "No sound, it's like when the Ghost Dog walks in the woods. I gotta get Dancer." He started to tug away, but she closed her hand on his, holding him fast.

"What are you talking about?"

"The Ragged Man's dog," he squeezed her hand back. "The Ragged Man, you know, what I said, the man who killed my dad."

Somebody kicked another can and the rattling across the concrete electrified the silence.

"Down!" She pulled him to the floor behind the car. He was shaking and tense. She felt his sweaty, child hand in hers, and she started to get angry .

She let go of his hand and opened her purse. J.P. grinned when he saw the gun in her hand.

"We should be okay now. The Ragged Man doesn't have a gun."

"He could have bought one." Her whisper was forced and clipped. She didn't understand what the boy was talking about and this wasn't the time to be humoring him. They were in serious trouble and she needed all her concentration.

"I can't let him hurt Dancer."

"We can see the cage from here. If he gets anywhere near it I'll put his eyes out," she said.

"Does he look okay?"

"He's fine," she said.

A wine bottle came flying from out of nowhere and smashed on the wall behind them, exploding with a shattering sound that made her scream. This time J.P. did the hand squeezing and she calmed down.

She wanted to jump up and shoot the bastard, but there was nobody to shoot at. Maybe J.P. was right, she thought, maybe he didn't have a gun.

Then the lights went out.

"He knows where we are," she whispered into his ear. "We have to move." She shifted the gun to her left hand and gave him a reassuring squeeze with her right. "We can't take the elevator, we'd be too much of a target, so we'll use the stairs." The stairway leading up was adjacent to the elevator. "We're going to crawl along the cars. I'll go first, you stay right behind me." Without waiting for him to answer, she started crawling along the row of parked cars.

More glass shattered behind them. Another wine bottle, she thought. She was tempted to let loose a few rounds, but didn't. She didn't want to let whoever was out there know she had a gun, because despite what J.P. said, he might have one, too. The last thing she wanted was bullets flying in all directions.

Then the man started moving. His hard shoes ricocheted off the concrete floor, each step, a thunderclap in a hollow cave, and the steps were coming toward them. She reached back and grabbed J.P.'s hand and started crawling faster. The steps stopped and she did, too. He was listening. Trying to find them in the dark and now the dark was as much their ally as their enemy. If they remained quiet he'd never find them and sooner or later someone had to come.

A can clattered behind them and she stifled a scream. It was what he wanted. Another rolled off to their left, the noise reverberating throughout the garage, ripping through her nerves. Icicles scattered out from her spine and she tightened her hand on the gun as they continued creeping toward the stars.

A car door opened. She bit into her lip as the door slammed shut, a cannon to her heart, sending her pulse racing. Was he leaving? Was he not after them, after all? Why had he done this?

The elevator doors opened and standing in the middle of a box of light was the black man in the new suit. The man squinted into the dark garage. The light from the elevator casting a Twilight Zone glow into the dark and J.P. saw the cage.

A car started.

"I'm gonna get Dancer," J.P. twisted free from her hand and ran toward the bird.

Tires screeched.

"No!" Christina screamed, grabbing for him, but she was too late.

The black man saw the boy, heard the car and moved like an athlete. He darted for the boy as the headlights of the oncoming car captured him in their light, the boy's face shining whiter as the car closed on its prey.

The big man dove for the boy, catching him and dragging him out of the way as the car screeched by, circling up the driveway to the street above. The car was gone by the time her nerves stopped shaking.

"J.P.," she screamed from across the garage.

"He's all right, ma'am," the black man said.

"That man, he was after us," she said.

"Gonna kill my bird," J.P. said, clutching the cage to his chest.

"It's okay now, he's gone, but I got a good look at him and I never forget a face." He pushed the button for the elevator and the door opened wide, again shedding some light into the garage.

"I can't thank you enough," Christina said.

"You can put the gun away now. I'm a police officer," the man said. He led them into the elevator. He was reaching into his pocket for identification as the doors were closing and he handed it to her.

"Captain Hugh Washington," she read. "Long Beach."

"Yes, ma'am," he said as she handed it back. "I came back down because of the bird. When the boy said he wanted it to be a five hundred miler I got to thinking what's five hundred miles away from here and then it hit me."

"What?" she asked.

"Where I'd seen the boy before. Tampico."

"I remember you," J.P. said. "You were on the beach that day. You waved to me when I let Dancer loose."

"That's right," Washington said. "I heard about what happened that day. I should have stayed. I saw the homeless man on the beach, but I didn't think anything of it. I was sort of on leave when I was up there and my mind wasn't as open as it should have been."

"That man sliced my tires," Christina said.

"It's the times," Washington said. "We catch them and the courts put them back on the streets."

"I guess I'll have to get a taxi."

"What kind of car?"

"Toyota." She said.

"I think I can help there," he said and Christina and

J.P. found themselves escorted to the convention hall where Hugh Washington enlisted the aid of several homicide detectives from throughout the world. When Christina and J.P. left the underground parking garage they had four new tires and four rented Toyotas had slashed spares in their trunks.

And all the way home she wondered why she hadn't spilled her guts to Captain Washington. She was still wondering when she pulled into the driveway. It was dark, the lights weren't on and the girls were still out.

She looked over at J.P. He was asleep. He'd had a rough day, a terrible yesterday and faced an uncertain tomorrow. She felt sorry for him. Asleep, he looked so vulnerable, with his head leaning against the passenger window and his arms wrapped around the cage that held his favorite bird.

"Home again, home again, jig-a-de-jig," she said, opening the passenger door.

"My mom says that." J.P. blinked away the sleep.

"All moms say that, I think."

"Is Rick gonna come soon?"

"I think he'll be here in the morning." She took the caged bird from his lap and he followed her to the door. She wanted to take him by the hand, to hug him, but she was afraid any sign of affection would throw the boy into tears. He was trying so hard to be a little man and fighting hard to hold on to his sanity. He was trying to be strong and she didn't want to weaken him. There would be plenty of time for tears after the shock had worn off. She opened the door and J.P. followed her inside.

"Oh wow," he said, running across the living room and stooping to pick up a white kitten.

"She's only six weeks old. Swell brought her home yesterday."

"What's her name?" he asked, holding the kitten to his cheek and stroking her fur.

"We can't decide."

"Can I name it?"

"Sure."

"Can she sleep with me?"

"Of course."

She put J.P. to sleep in the downstairs den with his bird in its cage on the writing desk opposite the bed and the kitten locked in his arms. She sat in an antique rocker next to the bed, determined to stay with him till he fell asleep. She didn't have long to wait, he was asleep inside of five minutes and the kitten hopped off the bed and scurried into the kitchen in search of milk.

Christina rose from the rocker, went to the phone and called the motel, only to find they were full, but would have a vacancy in the morning. Then she saw the blinking light on the answer machine. It was a message from the girls, they were going to a friend's after the movie and would be home by midnight. They hadn't left a number. Well, there was nothing for it, but to wait till they got back.

So she locked up, then tried to read, then tried television. Sometime around 11:00 she wrote a note for the girls, telling them about J.P. being in the guest room and asking them to wake her when they got back. They'd be safe enough tonight, she thought, but when she went up to bed, she left her purse downstairs, the gun inside it too.

CHAPTER FOURTEEN

SAM STORM MOVED DOWN THE STREET with a cracked leather satchel clutched in his right hand. Walking with a panther's stealth, he mounted the front porch and tried the front door. It was locked, but he'd expected it would be. Even if she wasn't the cautious kind, she would have been after last night.

He was caught off guard when he saw her in the hotel and acted without thinking. Who would have thought there would be a police convention in the same hotel the bootleggers always stayed in. He should have continued with his checkout when he saw her walk across the lobby with the boy in the Robert Plant tee shirt, but instead he

followed them and tried to do them in a hotel full of cops.
Stupid.

And stupid again for not realizing right off the bat
that the boy was the son. But he'd make up for it now. He
looked down the street. The night was silent. The leaves
were still. He could hear waves lapping on the beach a
block away. He would make sure she didn't scream.

He walked around to the back, cupped his hand over
the gate latch to muffle the sound, and crept into the
backyard. He tried the back door, also locked. Then he
saw the curtains of a downstairs window, hanging still,
waiting for a breeze. The window was open. It was a hot
night. Like a midnight black cat, he ghosted in the
window. He was a big man and had always been clumsy.
He was still big, but lately he'd become agile. He felt
twenty years younger. He felt like an athlete.

He climbed into the dining room. Stairs came into
focus as his eyes adjusted to the dark. He took off his
shoes, left them on the second step. He felt the rail with
fingers that were alive, the oak crying out to him. He
wrapped his hand around it. Solid, hard, like his heart. He
started upward, a wraith in the night.

He eased the first door on the top of the stairs open
and stepped into the room. Eyes now adjusted, he saw the
woman. Her chest was rising and falling with the melodic
rhythm of sleep. She was helpless.

He stared at her face. Peaceful in sleep. The curtains
fluttered, an evening breeze coming from the sea. He
smelled the salt on it, felt the sea in it, he wanted to go.
He couldn't. He was helpless.

Pleasure coursed through him. Goosebumps peppered
his arms. He sighed with the chill of anticipation, touched
himself between the legs and suffered a pleasure greater
than any orgasm he'd ever known. He squeezed himself,

almost called out with the joy of it.

He was afraid to approach and afraid not to. How much delight could one man possibly feel. He started to back away and felt an ache in his testicles. A few steps back and the ache was a dull pain. A few more and they were hot. If he didn't go through with it, they'd burn. He had no choice.

He started back into the room and the joy returned. Standing above her, he reached into the satchel and removed a handkerchief and duct tape. He balled the handkerchief and cut off a piece of the gray tape. Then he grabbed the sleeping woman about the jaw, forcing it open with thumb and forefinger. He jammed the balled up cloth into her mouth and slapped on the tape.

The woman's eyes popped open, wide with fright. He felt her fear and shivered. She tried to sit, but he forced her back with the heel of his palm against her chest. She struggled against the cloth, holding her tongue to the bottom of her mouth and tried to scream. Storm grabbed her face, palm around her chin, pinching her nose with thumb and fore finger, forcing her into the pillow, cutting off her air supply.

"Be good," he said, "and I'll remove my hand. Do you understand?" Her face was hot on his hand and it made him hard. She started to buck, trying to throw him off and he shoved his other hand between her legs and forced her down into the mattress. Her sex scalded his hand and he quivered in ecstasy.

Her oxygen almost gone, she lay limp, and he removed his fingers from her nostrils, but not his hand from her mouth and not his other hand from her sex. He had her pinned to the bed and relished it. He'd never felt anything so soft, so fine, so tantalizing as the mound between her legs. And he could do anything he wanted with it. It was his.

"Cooperate and I'll leave your children alone. Deal?" he said.

She nodded.

"Good girl, don't fight it." He pulled his hand away from the bliss and flipped her over, onto her stomach. He bound her hands behind her with the tape, then flipped her around again, so she could see his eyes and he could see hers. Then he wrapped the tape around her feet.

"I like looking at you like this," he said. Then he took his knife out of the bag and cut off her night shirt and smiled when her breasts came into view. He bent forward and squeezed them both with a heavy, but gentle hand. They're mine too, he thought.

"Oh and about your daughters. I lied. I want you, but the girls go first. I'm going to use and abuse them, then I'll do you," he said, again rubbing himself between the legs. "Then you're all dead."

Her eyes opened wider.

"That's right, I'm going to kill you all."

She shook her head.

"I'm going to leave you here while I hog tie those little ones of yours," he grinned. "But first here's a little something to think about." He stepped up to the bed, jerked down his zipper, pulled out his semi-erect penis and urinated on her face, laughing while she shook her head, trying to avoid the steady yellow stream.

He backed away from her when he finished. "It won't take long." He held the knife up, so she could see it. Then without zipping his trousers, he walked out of the room.

* * *

Christina sat up the second he was through the door and

started working at the tape, twisting her wrists back and forth against it, working at it, stretching it. She folded her thumbs into her palms and elongated her fingers, so that she could slide out of the tape, like it was a bracelet.

But the tape was sticking and binding her wrists. Please, God, she thought, let it come off, let my girls be okay. She hated that she'd left the gun in her handbag, downstairs. She twisted and jerked her wrists, till they were raw. Then she hooked her left thumb under the tape binding her right hand and stretched at it, but she couldn't quite get it. She heard one of the girls scream and her heart pumped adrenaline, giving her the combined strength of motherhood and terror as she wrenched her hand free.

* * *

Leaving the woman, he moved on down the hallway. The next door was a bathroom. He spent a second and enjoyed the smell, lavender mixed with a dusky, woman odor. The joy rippled along his skin. The next door opened into a bedroom made over into an office. This was where she spent her time. He inhaled her presence and started to get hard. The fourth and final door was open. It was the twin's room. He felt like he was fifteen, a Friday night, his first payday, his first whore.

The twins were asleep in twin beds, separated by a nightstand. A nightlight plugged into a wall socket was on. The girl on the right was sleeping on her back. He bent over and clamped his hand over her mouth, and the one on the left screamed.

Throughout history there have been stories and tales about how twins feel each other's pain, hurt, joy. How they know what their twin is thinking, how they walk, talk and even think alike. Torry and Swell were like that.

The instant the big hand covered her sister's mouth, Swell woke with a scream. A blood-wrenching sound that gave her mother down the hall the strength to rip through the tape that bound her.

Storm shoved a handkerchief into Torry's mouth, slapping tape over it as he'd done her mother just a few minutes earlier. Then he rolled her onto her stomach. He started to bind her hands behind her back, when Swell pounced on him, digging her teeth into the back of his neck.

He screamed, but continued with the taping as the girl pummeled him and pulled at his hair. When he finished binding Torry, he reached a hand over his shoulder, grabbed Swell by the hair and flung her back onto her bed. With his fist balled in her hair, he shoved a third handkerchief into the kicking girl's mouth. Then he flipped her onto her stomach without taping it.

He had just finished binding her hands when Christina burst into the room, screaming. Storm turned in time to avoid a blow from a bedside lamp. He lunged for his knife as the lamp was slashing toward his head. He deflected the blow with his arm and slashed her across the stomach with the knife, but Christina was already pulling away and the cut wasn't deep.

She was a crazed mother running on pure adrenaline when she swung the lamp for the third time. He ducked out of the way and lashed out, missing her face by the smallest margin, then he was hit in the side and knocked down himself, by Swell.

He hadn't bound her feet. The girl rammed him with her head and kicked him while he was down, hard. She raised her foot to stomp on his face. He rolled, she missed and tripped. He smacked her, knocking her across the room. He rose, picked up the girl, threw her on the bed and turned to face Christina with the knife thrust out in front of him.

"Why?" Christina gurgled, spitting blood.

"Because I want," he said with a leer.

"Look at yourself," she hissed.

Sam Storm turned and looked in the mirror that hung over the girl's bureau, but Sam Storm didn't look back. Storm was staring into the face of Satan himself. Lucifer marched right out of the old testament to the present.

He met the reflection's gaze with his own and was lost in the bloodshot eyes, thirsty eyes, killer's eyes, dangerous eyes. They were his eyes.

My God, what had he become? What had he done? What was he doing? What was he going to do? Facing those awful eyes in the mirror, he screamed, for he was surely damned. Then he spun with the knife in his hand. He was about to lunge, about to finish it, but something stayed his hand. A little of piece of Sam Storm still survived. He wasn't going to kill these kids.

He screamed as pain racked his body and his eyes glowed red as the thing inside him willed him to attack, but he resisted, enduring the pain. Sam Storm had been no coward. He would not kill these children and he would harm their mother no more.

He fought the evil, turning away from the bloody, naked woman.

* * *

Christina saw a chance to attack, but something told her if she did, she'd die and her girls would die, too. She held back, gasping, filling her lungs with air, and watched as the battle raged inside of the man that had come to kill her.

"Take your children and go. Now," the man

whispered with his back to her. "Go and hide and don't come back. If I live, I'll find you." Then he put his cock back in his pants and left the room as Christina fainted.

* * *

J.P. heard the noise from upstairs. He didn't need a program to know what was happening. Someone was hurting Christina and the twins. Probably killing them. Probably the same man that killed his dad and Sylvia, the same man who had been after them in the garage last night. Then the man was going to come downstairs and get him. The Ragged Man.

He slipped out of bed and padded across the den to the closet. He opened the door and pushed aside the shoes. He knew from the two weeks he and his mom had spent with Christina over Christmas that there was a trap door in the closet that led under the house. He pushed aside old shoes and a vacuum cleaner and opened the trap door. Then he grabbed the cage holding Dark Dancer and entered the closet, closing the door after himself. In the dark, he slid through the square hole in the floor and pulled the trapdoor down over himself. Then he crawled on his belly across the cold dirt, pushing the cage in front, until he came to the foundation wall at the front of the house. He could see the street through a small mesh covered opening in the foundation. He hoped Rick would come soon.

* * *

Storm thudded down the stairs, stopped when he reached the bottom, turned and fought the urge to go back up and finish the job. The pain was intense, his skin was on fire, his insides were ice. He took a step up and felt the pain ease. The message was clear, kill the woman and her daughters and the pain would cease. He took another step up. The pain stopped and a ripple of pleasure ran through him. He turned amid a flash of boiling cold and hopped down to the floor.

He raised the knife, faced it inward and clasped it with both hands. There was one way to stop the pain, but before he could bring the knife down into his belly, the pain quit. Whatever wanted him to kill those little girls wanted him alive more.

Pleasure zapped through his body again, the woman and girls out of his mind, but he had to find the boy. Holding the knife in his right hand, picking up his shoes with his left, he made his way into the downstairs bedroom and discovered that the boy wasn't there.

Again the pain came and Storm dropped both shoes and knife and started to tear the room apart. He ripped out dresser drawers and emptied their contents onto the floor, then he smashed the drawers into the two bedside lamps, breaking them and breaking the lamps. Not satisfied, he put his fist into the dresser mirror, shattering the glass, cutting himself and showering the dresser top and everything he touched with blood.

* * *

It wasn't long before J.P. heard heavy footsteps overhead. Loud. He held his breath and shivered. He was aware of his own heartbeat. He was scared. The footsteps stopped directly above him. Then he heard the front door open and he heard the footsteps stomp across the wooden porch. He peeked through the mesh opening and watched a big man cross the street to an older car that was parked under a street light.

The man reached his car, turned and looked back at the house. He seemed to be looking directly into J.P.'s eyes. J.P. wanted to turn away from that stare, but he couldn't. The big man was the same man who he had seen at the record meet the day before yesterday. The man who had killed his dad. The Ragged Man. For a second he thought he was going to come back and kill him, too. Then the man turned away, opened the car door, got in and drove away.

* * *

"Mom, wake up."

Christina opened her eyes. She must have passed out. Swell was washing the blood off of her stomach and Torry was wiping the blood from her lip.

"We heard what the man said, we gotta get outta here."

"J.P.?" Christina said.

"He's gone. The room's a mess." Swell said, trembling. It's all covered in blood. We think the man killed him and took him away."

"J.P. might still be in the house," Christina said. "We have to look."

"No, he's not," Torry said. "We checked."

Five minutes later Christina and the girls quietly left the house by the back door. J.P. was gone and her heart ached about that, but she had her girls, her car and plenty of money. She'd be in Mexico by morning, sipping margaritas with Susan.

CHAPTER FIFTEEN

RICK'S PLANE LANDED about the same time Sam Storm was slipping in through Christina Page's dining room window.

He was the first one off the plane, his only luggage, a little over twenty thousand dollars. Ten thousand, in hundreds, in each hip pocket and a wad of twenties in the right front. He moved through the concourse with a stiff stride, trying to work out the kinks and get his blood circulating as he headed for the taxi rank outside.

He inhaled the night air as he passed the shuttle busses in favor of a more expensive, but much faster cab. It was a hot night and the jet and auto exhaust fumes made it seem all the more oppressive.

"Long Beach, The Beach Inn on Ocean. You know it?" he asked the first driver in the taxi rank, an elderly Vietnamese American.

"Like the back of your hand."

"You don't know the back of my hand."

"I don't know the way to the Beach Inn on Ocean either," he said, smiling.

"You know the way to the Long Beach airport?" Rick smiled back at him. He liked the man's sense of humor.

"Yes, sir."

"I'll direct you from there."

"You got it," the driver said. "Just settle back and relax."

Rick nodded and closed his eyes as the driver lurched the cab into the airport traffic. It wasn't long before he drifted off and found the sleep he couldn't get on the plane.

What seemed like scant seconds, but was thirty-five minutes later, the driver reached over and shook Rick awake.

"Okay, Mister, I need you to guide me."

Rick knocked the fog from his head and looked out into the dark.

"Go straight down Lakewood Boulevard to the Traffic Circle, follow it around to Pacific Coast Highway and then take the first right and follow it all the way to the beach."

They drove the next five minutes in silence, until the driver stopped the cab in front of the Beach Inn.

"What room is Christina Page in?" Rick asked the underage boy behind the counter.

"Just a sec." The kid punched keys as he stared at a computer screen. "Not here," he said after a few seconds.

"You sure?"

"The computer doesn't lie."

"She was supposed to check in this afternoon."

"That explains it. We're full up. Been that way for a couple days."

"Damn," Rick said. "Thanks." He left and walked down Ocean. He turned left on her street and walked the block to her house. He mounted the porch, rang the doorbell and waited. No answer. He tried the door and found it unlocked. He turned the knob and felt his stomach flutter. Something was wrong.

The living room was small and connected to the dining room. Only the change in ceiling texture told the division between the two. He made his way through the rooms toward the light switch.

He swore as he banged into a coffee table. He stepped around it, moving between the table and a sofa, toward the switch. He flicked it and the two rooms lit up. Calling out Christina's name, he went into the kitchen. He was worried. She wouldn't go out and leave the front door unlocked. In the kitchen, everything appeared to be in order. He opened the refrigerator and checked the vegetable bin where she kept a plastic head of lettuce, stuffed with a another kind of green. If she'd gone to ground, the hidy hole would be empty. It was.

He backed away from the refrigerator, glanced around the kitchen, looking for anything out of order and found nothing. He left the kitchen, moving toward the stairs. With trepidation he started up.

* * *

Oh, God, the killer's back, the thought rang through J.P. He lay on the cold dirt and covered his head with his hands. He heard footsteps overhead. Heard his heart beat.

He tried to make himself small. The footsteps went away and a few minutes later they came back, running. They moved around the house, the killer was looking for him. Then the footsteps ran across the living room, out the door, and down the porch steps. He looked through the mesh grill and saw Rick. It wasn't the killer, after all.

"Rick, it's me!" he shouted and Rick stopped. He shouted again and Rick turned and started back. "I'm down here, under the house."

"I'll get you out, J.P."

"I can do it." He scurried on his belly, soldier-fashion, with the bird cage in front, instead of a rifle. Rick met him in the bedroom. The boy handed the cage up to Rick,

"Did he kill them, Rick? Did he kill them?" he asked as he took in the blood-stained mess.

* * *

"We have to get out of here." Rick brushed damp dirt off the boy, then took him by the hand, led him through the house and out the front door. They walked quickly away from the house, not noticing the brown Ford Granada parked a half block down, on the other side of the street. They made a right at the corner. Rick looked over at the Beach Inn on the other side of the street, but kept going. If it was full a few minutes ago, it would be full now.

"Did he kill them?" J.P. asked again.

"I don't know. Both the twin's room upstairs and the downstairs bedroom were torn up and there was a lot of blood, but Christina and the girls were gone. Her money's gone and so is her car. I think they got away."

"But she wouldn't have left me."

"She would if she thought you were dead."

"Oh."

"We still have a big problem. Even if she got away, as

soon as the cops see the house torn up and all the blood, they're going to think I killed her and the girls."

"What are we gonna do?"

"First we have to find a place for the night."

"There." J.P. pointed.

Rick followed the boy's finger with his eyes to the red neon vacancy sign of the Ocean View Motel. Neither man nor boy noticed the brown Ford round the corner after them and park.

Crossing the threshold, Rick addressed the sleepy-eyed youth behind the counter.

"Can we have a room for the night?"

"Can have all you want, we're mostly empty," the boy was barely old enough to need a shave.

"They're full across the street," Rick nodded in the direction of the Beach Inn.

"They get the tour bus crowd."

"They don't come here?"

"We're not quite up to their standards, but don't tell the boss I said that."

"Not a chance. You got a room with two beds?"

"Sure, sign in here." The youth handed over a pen and the registration form. "You're in twenty-four, go out the door to your left, you can't miss it. TV works, we got cable, free coffee in the morning, you pay for the donuts." He handed Rick a key.

"Thanks." Rick took J.P. by the hand.

"The room is to the left, halfway down."

"We'll find it."

* * *

It was the moment Storm had been waiting for, the chance to go at Gordon. He clamped his left hand around the knife and started to open the door with his right and pain prickled his testicles. He let go of the door handle. Gordon wasn't going to be as easy as the others. He wouldn't be able to just walk in on him and attack him with his knife. Besides, he rationalized, he wanted him to suffer, to be humiliated, to know what it's like to be scorned. He was going to need help.

He started the car and went back to the woman's house. He ran water over his bloody hand in the downstairs bathroom, then wrapped the cuts with bandages he found in a medicine cabinet. Once he was satisfied his hand looked as good as he could make it, he combed back his hair, washed his face and straightened his clothes.

Time to get that help.

* * *

The first thing Rick noticed after entering the room, was the odor of mildew. No, not first class, he thought, as he watched a cricket dart across the carpet. He followed it to the bathroom and gave the room a cursory inspection. He checked the window and decided it was too small for him to squeeze through.

Turning, he faced the twin beds and studied the door that adjoined the next room. One of those doors that locked on each side. The cheap room had been designed so that it could be used as a two room suite. Mom and Dad in one, the kids in the other. When let as a single, the adjoining door remained locked.

Next he turned his attention to the closet and eased the sliding door open.

"What are you looking for?" J.P. asked.

"I didn't know till now, but I think found it."

"What?"

"Look here." He pointed to a trapdoor in the closet

ceiling. "With any luck this connects to the other rooms."

"Is that good?"

"Maybe, go bang on that door. I want to know if we have neighbors."

J.P. went over and knocked on the adjoining door.

"Again, louder this time."

J.P. knocked louder.

"Okay, we're going to assume the room next door is vacant. We're also going to assume there's a trapdoor inside that closet, like this one. Do you think if I boosted you up, you could crawl through to the next room?"

"Yeah, I crawled under the house, didn't I?"

"Good boy." Rick had to admire his pluck. His father had been killed only two days ago. Tonight he barely missed getting killed himself and he was still holding it together. Most men would be a basket case in similar circumstances.

"Ready?"

"Ready," J.P. responded.

Rick opened the trap, revealing a black hole in the ceiling above.

"It's dark up there," J.P. said.

"You gonna be okay?"

"Yeah," J.P. said.

Rick scooped the boy up and lifted him into the dark. "Can you see anything?"

* * *

"Kinda." J.P. peered into the darkness, there was just enough light coming through the open trapdoor from below to show him the way. "It's scary up here."

"Are you going to be okay?"

"I can do it."

J.P. squinted his eyes to try and see through the dark.

He smelled dust and he felt it as his hands clutched onto the ceiling beams. He was going to have to stay on the beams as he worked his way to the room next door, because he'd learned, when the contractors had added a room on their house in Toronto, back when his parent were still together and his dad was still alive, that the drywall might not hold his weight.

He balanced himself with his knees on adjacent beams and inched his way into the dark, toward the next room. He heard noises up ahead and stopped to listen. A rustling sound. He wanted to scurry backwards, but then he heard the chirping of baby birds and he sighed. There must be a hole in the roof, he thought, allowing the birds a way in to make their nests.

He scooted a little closer to his goal. His right hand slid through a sticky spider web. He felt the creature scamper across his hand and he resisted the urge to scream.

"There's spiders up here," he whispered back to Rick and he started creeping along the beams once again. "I found it." He pulled the trapdoor up through the ceiling.

"Good boy," Rick whispered through the dark attic. "Can you jump down?"

"Sure," J.P. whispered back. A few seconds later J.P. opened the connecting door with a smile on his face a block wide.

"Good work, J.P. You did good."

"What are we gonna do now?"

"We're going to move next door," Rick said.

"Why?"

"Just a precaution. If someone comes looking for us, we won't be here."

"You think the Ragged Man's gonna come?"

"No. I'm just being careful."

"I think the man who killed my dad is him."

"You mean the Ragged Man?"

"Yeah, him."

"It's just a story, J.P. Now come on."

Before entering the adjoining room, Rick went into the bath, took the clean towels off the rack and splashed water on them, before throwing them on the floor. Then he pulled down the bed covers on both beds and rumpled them to make it look as if they had been slept in.

"This way it'll look like we've been and gone."

Then the two of them, J.P. carrying the birdcage, entered their new room and Rick closed both doors.

"Okay, J.P., we have to leave the lights out, no TV, no talking."

"I understand. We're hiding, right?"

"Right."

They found their respective beds in the dark. They didn't undress. They lay on top of the covers, each lost in his own thoughts, staring at the dark ceiling.

J.P. thought about the big man and his steel gray stare. Then he thought about the Ghost Dog and he started to shiver. His shivering increased when he heard the rapping on the door of the room they had just vacated. He looked at Rick and saw that he held his index finger to his lips, telling him to be silent. He didn't need to be told, he knew who was next door.

"Police. Open up," they heard. Then they heard a key being inserted and a door opening. J.P. got up and moved over to Rick's bed and sat next to him.

"It's okay," Rick whispered. "They don't know we're here. They'll go away in a few minutes." It wasn't necessary to listen at the door, the paper thin walls offered no barrier against sound.

"I don't understand, they're not here." J.P. recognized

the motel clerk's voice.

"Did they have any luggage?" a fast-talking voice asked.

"The boy had a bird in a wire cage."

"That's them," a deep voice said.

"They only checked in two hours ago, it doesn't make any sense, them leaving like this," Deep Voice said.

"The bathroom's been used, the beds have been used, and the key is on the bureau. It looks like they just wanted a place to shower and rest awhile," Fast-Talker said.

"I didn't see them leave," the clerk said.

"Were you on the front desk the whole time since they checked in?" Fast-Talker said.

"Most of the time. I went across to the mini market for cigarettes about half an hour ago."

"Then if they left while you were across the street, you would have missed them?" Fast-Talker said.

"I guess so."

"Thanks for your help."

"Do you think they'll be back?" the clerk asked.

"No," Fast-Talker said, "I don't, and you can go."
J.P. heard the clerk leave the room.

"Okay, Mr. Storm, we tried," Fast-Talker said. "It looks like they flew the coup. Now, you want to tell me what's going on?"

"I told them when I called the station."

"Humor me."

"I'm a private investigator working for the RIAA. I was staking out the Page house, hoping Gordon would show. When he did, I decided to wait till morning and see if he would lead me to a warehouse full of bootlegs. I wanted to bust him real dirty."

"Did you know he was wanted for murder?" Fast-

Talker said.

"No, I didn't," Storm said.

"What happened next?"

"He came running out of there like a striped-ass ape, dragging the kid, and came straight here. It looked like they were here for the night, so I went back to the house to see if I could get the Page lady to tell me anything."

"Did you think she would?"

"I didn't know, but nothing ventured, nothing gained," Storm said.

"And that's when you found the house all torn up?"

"Not exactly. I knocked on the door and when I didn't get any answer, I went next door and woke the neighbors and got lucky. The neighbor lady had a key. She said she watches the house when the Pages are away."

"So the neighbor let you in?" Fast-Talker said.

"She came over with me. I waited outside while she checked the house."

"And you didn't go in with her?"

"I'm a private investigator. I got a license to protect. I don't go into anyone's home unless I'm invited."

"So the neighbor went in?"

"And came out a few seconds later, screaming her head off. I didn't have any choice, I went in, saw the house and dialed 911. You know the rest."

"Do you have any idea where Gordon will go next?"

"He'll go to Tampico."

"How can you be so sure?" Fast-Talker said.

"One, he has a house there, and two, he's sweet on the boy's mother."

"Do you think he'll harm the boy?"

"I don't know, but he has every reason to think he got away with what he did tonight. He'll go to Tampico. I'm sure of it."

"Well, he won't get there. If I remember right, there is only the one road into town from the Pacific Coast Highway. If that's where he's going, they'll get him by morning."

"I hope they do," Storm said.

"You want to come down to the station and write out what you told me?"

"Be glad to."

J.P. went to the window and peeked through the curtains as the men left. "Rick," he whispered, "come here quick. It's the man who killed my dad."

* * *

Rick looked out and got a clear view of the big man and the two policemen as they stood under a street lamp in the parking lot. They were too far away for him to hear what they were saying, but close enough that he recognized the big man as the man who went to get the sheriff and never returned that horrible day. The day Ann died.

However that day he hadn't said anything about the RIAA or bootlegs or given any indication that he knew who Rick was. Rick shook his head, he couldn't understand. Had the RIAA hired someone to kill the bootleggers? That made no sense, none at all. But there he was, the man who had killed J.P.'s father and he claimed that he worked for the RIAA.

Rick thought about calling out. He could tell the police who the killer was, that they were talking to him right now, but what if they didn't believe him? What if they arrested him? What would happen to J.P.? He decided to wait till morning and call Sheriff Sturgees in Tampico. At least he was a police officer who would listen to him.

He kept watch as the two policemen and the killer with the deep voice got into the police car and drove off.

"Okay, J.P., let's smooth up the beds. We don't want it to look like anybody's been here." With the boy helping, they had the beds looking like a motel maid had done the job in short order.

"Now what are we gonna do?"

"We're going back to our old room. It's the last place they'll look for us and with unmade beds and the dirty towels, they won't rent it again tonight."

"Does that mean I have to go up into the roof again?"

"Yeah, I'm afraid it does." Again Rick hoisted J.P. through a trapdoor into the dark attic and minutes later they were back in their original room, stretched out on their respective beds, staring at the ceiling. J.P. fell asleep first.

Rick thought about Christina. He prayed that she and the girls were safe and well. He blamed himself for what had happened tonight. If he hadn't taken off right away for Tampico, he would have been there to meet the killer. He had abandoned her and the twins and now they were running scared, or worse, dead. It was his fault and he felt like shit. He stayed awake for another two hours, but finally closed his eyes and fell asleep at around three in the morning.

He woke three hours later with his head in a fog. He'd been dreaming about Ann and didn't want to leave her, so he closed his eyes and tried to bring it back. He pictured her walking along the beach, yellow hair blowing in the wind. She turned to face him, smile shining, eyes sparkling. He never wanted to leave that place between sleep and not sleep. That perfect place, where happiness reigns supreme and nobody ever dies.

She had been the focus of his life, his reason for living,

his past, present and future. She laughed with him, talked with him, fought with him and loved him. When she died he was left adrift, a wandering sailor on a leaking raft. He ached for her and he fought to stay asleep.

He walked toward her and her smile faded, her eyes darkened. "You don't belong here," she said, and he was cut to the quick. He pleaded silently with his eyes and her eyes answered back and she said, "You can't stay, Flash. I love you. I'll always love you. I'll be with you soon and I'll never leave," she said, her smile returning, "but you have to go now," and she faded from his sight as he came awake.

He rolled out of bed, stumbled into the bathroom, where he closed the door. He didn't want to wake J.P. until he had to. The boy had been through a lot in the last three days and Rick wanted him to get as much sleep as possible, because they had a long day ahead of themselves.

He ran cold water into the wash basin, splashed his face, trying to wipe the sleep away. He looked in the mirror and winced at his reflection. The bags under his bloodshot eyes and the worry wrinkles on his forehead were like a flashing neon sign, saying that this man needs rest. He was bone tired. The few hours of restless sleep only seemed to exacerbate the problem. The cold water was no help.

He ran a hand over his face and mentally kicked himself for forgetting his shaving gear. He held a hand in front of his mouth, exhaled, then frowned. The toothbrush was in his bathroom up north, sitting next to his razor. He bent into the sink and took a mouthful of water, gargled and ran a finger over his teeth, a poor substitute. He felt lousy.

He stripped off the clothes he'd slept in and started

the shower. When the water was warm enough, he stepped in and stood under the spray. He thought about Christina and the twins and prayed again that they were away safe, alive and well.

* * *

The sound of the shower running woke J.P. He looked over at Rick's empty bed and rubbed his stomach. He was hungry. He reached into his pocket and grasped the money his father had given him. He was thinking about Ding Dongs and cold milk.

He pulled down the covers, slid to the side of the bed and put on his shoes. He figured he could go to the mini-market across the street and surprise Rick with breakfast. He tiptoed to the door, eased it open and stepped out into the morning. Stretching his arms, he met the day with a yawn and started across the parking lot. He thought about running across the street, there were no cars out this early, but he decided to cross at the light. It was a few feet out of the way and might take a few seconds longer, but his mother had taught him to never jay walk.

When he reached the crosswalk, he reached with an outstretched finger to push the cross button on the traffic signal, but someone clamped a beefy hand over his face and he felt himself being lifted off his feet.

* * *

Feeling better, Rick turned off the shower and stepped out of the tub. He toweled off, glancing at his ghostly reflection in the steamed mirror for only a second, before he dressed. It was time to wake J.P. and get on the road. He left the warmth of the bathroom and stopped, staring at J.P.'s bed. The boy was gone.

He ran his eyes around the room and saw J.P.'s shoes

just inside the door. They were sitting on a folded piece of paper. He pulled the paper out from under the shoes. It was note, someone had been in the room while he'd been in the shower. He unfolded the paper and read:

> I have the boy. He dies tomorrow Like the others — In Tampico at sunset. Tell anyone and I'll peel his skin off before sticking in the knife.
>
> I'll know if you call the police, so don't be stupid. If you're very lucky, maybe you can trade your life for his.
>
> I am damned but so are you.

It was unsigned.

CHAPTER SIXTEEN

J.P. WOKE TO PAIN IN HIS ARMS. He was lying on his back, his arms underneath his body. It was dark. It was hot. He was moving and he smelled gasoline. He tried to scream through his cotton dry mouth, but he couldn't move his jaw, and the sound he managed to get out couldn't be heard above the constant rumbling noise of rolling tires on pavement. Something was over his mouth, preventing him from calling for help, and something was holding his hands behind his back, causing maximum, huge pain.

Instinctively, he knew he was in the trunk of a moving car. His hands were tied behind his back and he was gagged, like a victim in the old black and white cowboy movies his mom liked to watch—and he was afraid. Afraid to kick out against the trunk lid and cry out for help, because the man who had grabbed him from behind and put him here was surely the man who had killed his father, and if that man was the one that answered the racket his kicking feet made, there was no telling what he would do. And he was afraid not to kick out against his metal coffin, because what if no one ever came and he was left in the hot trunk to die?

But somehow he didn't think no one would ever come. That man would come. The one who had done the horrible things to Christina and the twins. The one who had killed his father and Sylvia. The one who held him prisoner in this dirty, dark place. J.P. remembered well the story Rick had told and he remembered the Ghost Dog, and he knew who that man was.

When that man came, something bad would happen. J.P. was sure of that. But how bad, he asked himself? Real bad, he answered. He saw himself tied to a slow moving conveyer belt, a log in front and a log behind, heading toward a giant circular saw that would rip him in half, and nobody in white was coming to his rescue.

He felt the car go into a sharp right turn. Something fell and hit him on the head and he smelled the gas smell up close. From the bang the object made as it ricocheted off his forehead, he guessed it was a gas can. He tried not to gag on the fumes. It would not be good, he thought, to cough with his mouth taped shut.

The car made a sharp turn in the other direction, rolling him onto his side and something dug into his shoulder. He didn't know what it was, it only hurt for a second, but it was sharp. He was afraid that if he rolled onto it again, it would cut him. He was worried that he would roll back and forth, with every turn of the car, and the sharp thing would cut into him like the pendulum in his favorite scary story.

One of the rear tires picked up a rock and it made a steady click, click, click sound that shot through to his heart, sending him shivers and clarifying the image of the swinging pendulum from the scary story.

Something moved over his legs. He heard it squeal. He wasn't alone. He tried to lash out at the thing with his right foot and discovered that his feet were bound. Plus his shoes and socks were gone, he was barefoot. Now he was scared!

It moved again. There was no doubt in his mind about what it was. It had to be a rat. One of the rats from the pit. And the sharp thing was the sharp part of the pendulum. And every time the car turned, he was going to roll over the sharp thing, and it would cut him, and he would bleed, and the rat would smell the blood, and it would eat his blood, and it wouldn't be enough to make it full, so it would eat him till he was dead.

The car turned again. One of the rear wheels must have gone over a curb, because J.P. felt the shock as the tire slammed down onto the pavement. The gas can bounced again, making a loud ringing noise that scared the rat into screeching and scurrying around the trunk. It brushed against him and he rolled over the sharp thing in a effort to get away from it. He was lucky it was lying flat or it surely would have cut him.

He wanted to use his legs to push away from the sharp thing, but he was more afraid of the rat and he was having a hard time breathing. He lay still, catching his breath, scared, worried and anxious. He felt something move by his feet and he bent his legs, tucking his knees into his stomach.

He listened to the steady click, click, click and his ears told him the car was slowing. It must be a red light, he thought.

"Come on, Mister Rat, please move, so I'll know where you are," he whispered. The rat answered his prayers and crawled toward him. J.P. felt, more than heard, its advance. "Just a little closer," he said. He felt it with his bare feet. For a flash of a second, the thought that the evil man had stolen his shoes sent a flash of red anger along his spine, chasing away the fear. He lashed out with his legs.

He caught the furry beast under his feet as he straightened his legs, dragging it along the floor of the trunk, crushing its tiny ribs under his heels, and the trunk was filled with its scream. For a second he thought that it didn't sound the way the rats in the movies did, but he didn't wait to puzzle it out. Once his legs were straight and his knees were locked, he rolled onto his back, tightened his stomach, raised his legs, like his mother when she does her leg lifts, and brought them down hard onto the small beast, smashing the life out of it with his bare heels.

And as the life ran out of the little animal, J.P. knew that it was no rat. He started to cry as the light turned green and the car started to pick up speed. He had done a terrible, horrible thing. He was saddened like he'd never been saddened before. He felt worse than he did when his father had moved out. Worse than when his first pigeon had died. Worse than when Janis went missing and her parents were killed. And worse than he did the other day when his father was killed.

It wasn't right. He knew it wasn't right, but he couldn't help it. He didn't make his father leave. It wasn't his fault that the pigeon, or Janis, or her parents, or his father, or Sylvia were dead, but it was his fault that the little animal at his feet in the dark, smelly trunk was dead. If only it had been a rat, a big mean rat, a mean rat that was going to chew on his bloody side, a chewing rat that wouldn't stop chewing till he was dead, but it wasn't a rat, and he knew it wasn't a rat. It was Torry and Swell's cute, fluffy little kitten, and he hadn't even named it yet.

She wasn't going to eat him. She was probably as scared as he was—and he'd killed her. He wanted to get even with that mean, sleazy, lousy, punk of a man that scared him so much and tricked him into killing the little cat.

The car turned again in a wide arc. It felt like they were getting on a freeway as he slid toward the sharp thing and then he had an idea. Maybe it was sharp enough to cut the rope that was binding his hands behind his back.

He used his feet to push himself against the bottom of the trunk, moving the sharp thing from his upper to his lower back, so he could reach it with his hands. A small triumph. He felt the sharp thing and knew what it was. It wasn't part of a sharp pendulum at all. It was a knife and as he ran his hands along the blade he knew what kind of knife it was and he was scared. It was a Jim Bowie knife.

He turned it and started working the rope against the blade, cutting into the fibers. His heart picked up speed. He began breathing fast, through his nose. He tried to stop his frightened tears and he started sniffling as his nose filled with snot. He sawed harder against the rope as panic rose. He wasn't able to breathe. He tried to suck air through the tape that covered his mouth, but couldn't. He felt his lungs scream as they cried for air. He swallowed snot. He got light-headed. He saw stars, gagged and passed out.

As he came slowly awake through a sleep-fog haze, J.P.'s subconscious was feeding him the words. *Free the Dome Ring. Free the Dome Ring. Free the Dome Ring.* He used to worry all the time about the Dome Ring. He wondered what it was and why everybody sang about setting it free. He thought some terrorists had it and wouldn't let it go. Then on his fifth birthday he found out there was no Dome Ring. He felt foolish at first, but he'd grasped the idea of the Amazing Dome Ring held by evil bad guys and even if the real words in the song were *Let freedom ring*, he still saw in his mind's eye, a silver and gold magic ring, with a small diamond dome on it, where the magic power powder was kept.

He opened his eyes in the dark place and he tried not to breathe so hard. The snot in his nose had dried and hardened, leaving dust-filled boogers behind. He wanted to pick his nose more than anything, but his aching arms were still bound. He lay quiet and listened, wishing he had some of that magic power powder.

Click clack, click clack, click clack, the clicking rock had acquired a clacking cousin, or maybe it had been there all along and he just hadn't been able to hear it. He could hear it just fine now, though. His ears were wide awake, like they had never been awake before and his nose was sharp, too. He smelled the gas can, and an old dirty oil smell, and a cigarette smell, and they were all mixed with the dead cat smell, and it was hot.

His mind took him back to the black and white western and he saw himself tied on the railroad tracks. An old black steam engine, followed by a billowing, black-black cloud was bearing down on him, its wheels going, click clack, click clack, click clack. He had to stop himself from crying. If he cried his nose would make more snot. He would pass out again and maybe not wake up this time. He fought his terror and ripped his mind away from the TV western and the bearing down train.

He searched behind his back for the cold steel of the sharp Bowie knife. It wasn't there. He felt along the floor of the trunk, somehow the knife must have moved, he thought, then he felt it. The steel blade seemed to be calling to him and he answered with bone-aching fingers, running them along the smooth surface and thanking God.

He inched the blade toward his bonds, by clutching the hilt in his left hand and the blade between the thumb and forefinger of his right. He sawed on the ropes the way two lumber jacks move a giant saw through the base of a giant redwood. A smile crossed his pursed lips when he felt the knife slice through the first layer of rope, and the blood drained out of them and went straight to his tingling hands. Then he sliced through the second layer and his hands were free.

He started to remove the tape from his mouth, when he felt the car slowing down and he was caught up in indecision. If the bad man was stopping for gas, he could scream and maybe the gas station man would save him, but maybe the man would kill the gas station man, then kill him. But what if he wasn't stopping for gas? What if he was stopping because they were wherever the bad man wanted to take him? If he screamed then, the man would most surely kill him, like he had killed his dad.

The car stopped and he decided. He left the gag on and rolled onto his back, concealing the fact that he had freed his hands. He closed his eyes and pretended to be asleep. He heard the door open, then close. Then he heard footsteps walking on gravel. They were coming toward the trunk. He closed his eyes harder.

He felt the knife by his side and wondered if the

Ragged Man would use it to kill him. He didn't want to die and he was afraid like he'd never been afraid before. He tried to stop his jaw from quivering and his knees from shaking. He was hot, covered in sweat, dirty and he smelled as bad as the dead cat. His throat was parched dry and his hungry stomach ached for food, but he was determined not to cry, even though he couldn't get that Jim Bowie knife out of his mind.

He shuddered and almost shit his pants when a loud explosion roared through the trunk. Then it was followed by another and he did. His bowels relaxed and it oozed out, hot and wet, filling his pants with the shit stinking stuff. He fought not to gag, because with his mouth taped shut, to gag was to die.

Then his ears rang for a third time as the man beating on the trunk said in a purely evil voice, "Are you alive in there?"

He squeezed his eyes tight, trying to shut out the stink and the fear.

"Fee fi fo fum, I smell the blood of a spoiled little brat."

"These are the times that try men's souls," he mentally said, "when the summer soldier and the sunshine patriot will shrink from their duty." His father used to say that whenever times were hard, and times were hard right now, he thought, anxiously whispering the words, "These are the times that try men's souls. These are the times that try men's souls. These are the times that try men's souls. Oh God, please make him go away. Please, please make him go away."

But J.P. knew he wasn't going to go away. He just wasn't. The man was going to open the trunk and use the knife to cut him into pieces and it was going to hurt a lot and there was going to be an awful lot of his blood running all over his face and his body and his clothes. He wondered if the man would kill him in the trunk or if he was going to take him out. He hoped he would take him out. He didn't want to die in this dark place. He didn't want to die at all. He wanted the man to go away, but when he heard the horrible sound of the key sliding and clicking into the trunk lock, he bit into his lower lip, because he knew for sure the man wasn't going to go away.

He heard the key turn and peeked out of his eyes. He saw light begin to enter and chase out the dark. He closed his eyes back tight, but his ears felt the whoosh of cool air and heard the clunking noise as the trunk popped open. He clenched his fists against the fear.

"Shit, you stink," the deep voice said.

J.P. hoped the man would think he was asleep and maybe leave him alone.

"I know you're awake, so you might as well open your eyes."

J.P. closed them tighter.

"Shit your pants, did ya? Well, I suppose if I was in your place I'd be scared shitless myself." The man laughed.

J.P. felt the man brush his side as he reached for something in the trunk.

"Know what I have in my hand?"

J.P. knew.

CHAPTER SEVENTEEN

RICK'S FIRST IMPULSE was to pick up the phone and call
the police, but then he realized they wouldn't believe him.
They'd jail him without bail and J.P. would be killed.

It angered him that he'd allowed himself to be
followed from Christina's. His ruse last night may have
fooled the desk clerk and the police, but that investigator
either wasn't fooled or he'd figured it out later. Rick
thought he was better than that. He'd spent most of his
adult life looking over his shoulder, but if the kidnapper
had known where he was, why didn't he tell the police
and have him arrested for the murder of his friends?

He started to pick up the phone, to call Sheriff

Sturgees in Tampico. He was a man he could trust. But he stopped himself in mid-reach. If the kidnapper was the killer and he was working with the police, he might also have the Sheriff's confidence. No, he was on his own. He would have to figure out a way to save J.P. and catch or stop the killer himself, without help.

The first thing he had to do was to get out of the motel room. If the killer knew where he was, he was at his mercy. He could call the police at anytime and, if he was in custody, there was no way he could help J.P. He picked up the birdcage, then got an idea. He put the cage down and stepped out of the cheap motel room into the early morning mist, leaving the bird behind.

He crossed the street, making sure he wasn't being followed this time. He walked around the block, making doubly sure he was unobserved. When he returned to his starting place, he walked back into the motel office and to his great relief the pimply-faced youth from the night before had been replaced by an elderly woman engrossed in her knitting.

He told her he wanted a room for a week. When she handed him the registration form he thought of J.P., named after the Led Zeppelin guitarist Jimmy Page, and registered under the name John Bonham, Led Zeppelin's dead drummer. He paid cash in advance and wasn't surprised when the blue-haired woman didn't ask him for any identification or ask why he had no baggage.

After he had completed the formalities, he crossed the street to the mini market, bought a toothbrush, toothpaste, razor blades, razor and shaving cream. Then he returned to the room he'd slept in and picked up Dark Dancer, before going to his new room to brush his teeth, to shave and to think.

In the small bathroom, he sprayed shaving cream onto

his hand and shaved slowly, trying to concentrate on the nooks and crannies of his face, dragging the blade several times over the rough spot below his chin. When he reached the scarred area under his left ear, he gently shaved around it.

Finished, he washed off the remaining lather with hot water and brushed his teeth. He was marginally refreshed and had enjoyed the five minutes away from his problems, but now they were flooding back. He had to figure out a plan of action and act on it.

He had less than forty-eight hours to get to Tampico and stop whoever or whatever was bent on killing his friends. He couldn't call for help, without running the risk of going to jail. He couldn't drive, without running the risk of being picked up driving into town and he couldn't fly, because he was sure the airport would be staked out.

There seemed to be no way for him to get to Tampico, without running the risk of getting caught and yet if he didn't, J.P. would surely die. The killer had shown him, with daylight clarity, that he intended to continue tormenting him. And the killer had shown an amazing ability to ferret out his close friends and do away with them in a gruesome manner.

Evan and Sherry murdered in New York. Danny murdered on the river in Texas. Tom and his new wife, killed in broad daylight in Pasadena. Christina, Torry and Swell, vanished in the night. And if he didn't do something, J.P. would be next.

He left the bathroom, picked up the shirt he'd worn the day before and as he was putting it on a thought hit him. He could fly to Tampico in Christina's plane. It would be the last thing anybody would expect. But first he would have to get the keys. They were somewhere in her house and that meant he had to go back.

He did a few stretching exercises to get his blood moving and to calm his nerves. Then he went out into the day and headed toward her house. There were four police cars blocking the street, a crime lab van sitting in the front driveway and a crowd of gawking onlookers.

He joined the crowd, acting like another innocent bystander, and watched. After awhile two of the police cars left. Some of the crowd left. One of the remaining two police cars left. Two uniformed policemen draped a yellow banner across the front door bearing the words *Police Line Do Not Cross*. The last black and white left. More of the crowd left. The crime lab van stayed and Rick wandered away with the last of the crowd.

He felt so useless, with nowhere to turn, no one to turn to, no friend he could count on for help. He was truly alone, like he had never been before. Everybody he loved was either dead or gone and if he failed to get to Tampico in time, failed to find the boy once he got there, and failed to stop the killer, then J.P. would be dead, too. He didn't know how he would or could save the boy, much less get to Tampico. It all seemed so impossible.

And even if he was able to get the keys to the plane, he still had to get to the airport. He damn sure couldn't take a taxi. The last thing he needed was for an underpaid cabby to alert the police. He also couldn't rent a car, for if he was worried that the police had given his description or possibly his photo to the city's cabbies, then they also would have the rental companies covered, too.

And once he got to the airport, he had to fly the plane, something he hadn't done in over ten years. And he not only had to fly it, he had to fly it over five hundred miles, at night. And even if he accomplished that, he still had to land. Ten years was a long time, and landing an airplane, even a small Cessna, required experience and perfect precision.

He thought of Ann and how she had always encouraged him to try the impossible. She was the one who had pushed him to branch out into CDs, to learn to fly, to learn off road racing, to race, to travel to the most dangerous parts of the world. He imagined hearing her clear voice.

"Bury your doubts. The keys will be there. You will be able to fly the plane. You will get there in time. You will find J.P. and you will save him. Be positive, be strong, get mad, get even."

Hot anger burrowed into the river of blood running through his veins. It was now, more than ever, clear to him that J.P. had seen a Bowie knife on the porch the day Ann died, and that meant that the man who had J.P. was somehow, someway responsible for Ann's death. He had taken away the life of his love and Rick was going to make him pay.

He found himself wandering back toward Christina's, where he saw that the crime lab van was still there, but he hadn't really expected it to be gone. They would more than likely be there most of the day, he thought, and then he saw it, parked two houses away from Christina's. A beautiful 1956 Chevy Nomad.

An idea began to form, but it would mean some shopping. He smiled to himself, despite his desperate situation, because it felt good taking action, acting instead of reacting. He walked up to Second Street, the trendy shopping area of Long Beach's Belmont Shore District. McCain's Records was just opening and Elliot's Hardware next door already had customers inside and down the street was the small, but high priced Kornyphone Stereo Store next to Howdy's Candies. He'd be able to get everything he needed in just a few blocks and satisfy his sweet tooth as well.

At McCain's he bought *Brainwashed*, the George Harrison CD that came out shortly after his death. He bought a portable CD player to listen to it at Kornyphone's and at Elliot's he bought a claw hammer and a screwdriver. He decided to pass on the candy, instead buying a ham and cheese to go at the Toasted Deli and then he went back to the motel, where he ate his sandwich, then stretched out on the bed nearest the door and listened to the gentle Beatle till he fell asleep.

He didn't wake till well after dark.

* * *

He approached Christina's empty home with caution. It was a clear night. The neighborhood was quiet. The crime lab van was gone, but the yellow police warning tape was still pasted to the front door. He kept walking and turned the corner when he reached the end of the block. Less than a minute later he turned a second corner and approached the house from the alley behind.

When he came to her back gate, he ripped off the yellow banner, opened it and went into the backyard. He walked to the back door like he belonged. He stepped up to the porch, wrapped a wash cloth that he had lifted from the motel around the hammer's head and, like he'd done it a thousand times before, he tapped the laundry room window, sending shattering glass inside to cover the washer and dryer.

With his arm in the window, he was able to reach the security latch that helped keep the back door locked. He had no problem with the double deadbolt, he simply used the key Christina had given him over five years ago.

He didn't have to look long or hard for the keys. They were on a key hook next to the refrigerator. He pocketed the key ring, then left through the back door, going out the back gate.

He retraced his steps up the alley and around the block, till he was again in front of her house. He continued on, till he came to the '56 Nomad, where he again brought the washcloth covered hammer into play, swinging it against the driver's side windwing, sending shards of safety glass over the front seat as he had sent glass over the washer and dryer. And for the second time in a matter of minutes, his arm snaked in a window where it didn't belong to unlock a door.

He swept the glass from the seat. Then he took the screwdriver out of his back pocket and reached under the dash, pushing the metal end of the screwdriver into the ignition, making a connection between the positive and negative posts. The car started just as they all did during fifth period lunch when he had been in high school. He would not have been able to hotwire any car made in the last thirty years, but in the good old days, when everybody left their doors unlocked, any kid with a screwdriver or the tin foil from a pack of cigarettes could start a car.

He drove back to the motel, where he retrieved Dark Dancer. He left the key on the television, hopped back into the car and settled back for the short ride to the airport, listening to oldies but goodies on a push button radio that was just about a half a century old.

Fifteen minutes later he was standing in front of the red Cessna he'd sold to Christina so long ago, during better days.

He unlocked the door and climbed in. He set the caged bird in the back seat, removed the control wheel lock, checked to make sure the ignition switch was off and turned the master switch on. He visually checked the flaps by flipping the flap switch, raising and lowering them. He tried to think of what to do next. Then the folly of what he was attempting hit him. His hands started shaking. He started to sweat. He studied the controls. Did he pull the carburetor heat out or leave it in? What was the frequency for ground control? It had been too long. He had no business flying. It was a stupid thing he was doing. There was no way he was going to get to the runway, much less take off.

He flipped the master switch off. He needed help and there was nowhere he could turn. Then he thought of the Flight Room. A café with a bar across the street from the airport. Pilots used to hang out there. He bet they still did.

"Hang in there, Dancer," he said. "I'll be back."

Ten minutes later he took a seat at the only empty table on the café side of the Flight Room. The bar was through a red curtain, past the restrooms at the back of the café. He'd have no use for anybody over there. Any pilot worth his salt wouldn't fly tonight if he was already drinking.

"Can I help you?" The voice had a musical lilt to it. He looked up as the waitress handed him the menu. The Flight Room had been in the same location, serving pilots as long as he could remember. It hadn't changed. Even the smile on the aging waitress with the sweet voice was the same.

"I remember you," Rick said.

"And I remember you." The waitress smiled, blue eyes twinkling.

"Uh oh," Rick said.

"Why, uh oh?" she asked.

"It's been a long time and I didn't fly for that long. I got my license and maybe only flew for six months, before I sold the plane and stopped coming in here."

"You remembered me, why shouldn't I remember you?" She smoothed her skirt and gave a quick glance around the cafe to see if anybody needed anything.

"There were only two waitress here when I used to come in, easy for me to remember them, but you must see hundreds of customers," Rick said.

"You were different," she said.

"How so?"

"You flew every day, but you didn't fly."

"I could never really understand what made them stay up. In the back of my mind, I thought I could fall out of the sky at any second, so I wanted to be ready. I may not be the best pilot on the planet, but I can put a Cessna 172 down on a postage stamp in a hurricane."

"I believe it," the waitress said, still smiling, then adding, "My name's Katherine Spencer."

"No relation to Susan Spencer up in Tampico?"

"My sister, you know her?"

"I live up there now," Rick said, thinking, wondering if he could ask this woman for help. "Susan's one of my best friends."

"You know how she used to work in the diner, saved up her money, then bought it?"

"Yeah," Rick said.

"Well, this is my place. I own the Flight Room now," she said.

"Really."

"You're in trouble, Rick Gordon. They're saying some pretty awful things about you on the radio."

"I can imagine," he said. "Why didn't you get on the phone and call the police the second I walked in?"

"Because Susan called right after I'd heard it." She slid into the booth opposite him. "I remembered you and I brought it up. She said it had to be hogwash. She said she knew you and that it absolutely wasn't true."

"And you believe her," Rick said, wary.

"We're twins, not identical, fraternal, but we're close. We think alike, no, not alike, the same, identical. What I experience, what I see, what I believe, what I feel, all that I am, she knows. Like I know about her. We talk everyday. We may live over five hundred miles apart, but we're as close as two humans can possibly be. If Susan says it's hogwash, it's hogwash. I'd sooner doubt the sun was coming up in the morning than doubt her word. Now, how can I help you?"

"I need to get to Tampico, yesterday. I have my old plane, but I can't fly it. It's been too long. I need someone to fly me up.

"I'll ask around. Meanwhile you look like you need a hearty meal. Meatloaf's the special tonight. I can have it on your plate before you can blink. It's on the house." She slid out of the booth and true to her word, Rick was tucking into meatloaf, mashed potatoes and gravy in no time at all.

He was halfway through the meal when she returned. She slid into the booth like they were old friends, while he swallowed a delicious bite of her meatloaf.

"I found someone," she said. "I told him you were supposed to meet a pilot here to take your plane up to Palma-Tampico. He's only going as far as Bakersfield, but it's a start and it's in the right direction. He'll fly your plane for free, seems he got here a little too late to meet his ride. He thinks you're a godsend."

"Sounds like a match made in heaven. Where is he?"

"Finishing his dinner in the bar."

"Has he been drinking?"

"No, he's a regular, Bob Mitchel. Flew B-29s in World War II. Been flying out of here ever since. Teaches flying at Condor Aviation. He doesn't drink, he just prefers the atmosphere in the bar."

"Hey Katy, that the guy?" a deep base voice boomed across the restaurant. Katherine waved as Rick turned his head. A big man, with penetrating blue eyes and a shocking silver mane, waved back as he approached the table. Rick started to get up. "No, don't get up on my account," the man said, hand out.

"Rick Gordon." Rick shook his hand as he sat down next to Katherine and for a second he felt like kicking himself. How could he have been so stupid as to give his real name. What if the guy had seen the news.

"Katy tells me you want someone to fly your plane up north."

"That's right," Rick said.

"You the same Rick Gordon that used to fly One-Six-Tango in the pattern every morning, before Christina Page bought it out from under you?"

"The same." Rick thought he was about to be busted. "How do you know about that?"

"Worked the control tower for twenty years. I'll never forget you taking off and landing, taking off and landing, touch and go, touch and go, but it was the power off, side slip, practice emergency landings I remember best. You'd dump the power halfway through the downwind, go into the slip and drop like a rock, then straighten out at the last possible instant and set it down, squeaking the wheels on the numbers every time. It was beautiful to watch. She sell you the plane back?"

"Yeah," Rick lied, relieved that the man apparently wasn't aware of his present problems. "She wants to buy something a little bigger and a little faster and I kind of missed flying, so it worked out all the way around."

"So what do you need a pilot for?"

"I haven't flown in ten years."

"Shame."

"I really need to get up to Palma-Tampico."

"Don't suppose you have your log book handy?"

"You're kidding, I haven't seen it in years."

"But you have your license? They're good for life."

"In my wallet." Rick wondered why the man was asking.

"Anybody that flies a plane the way you did should be able to get it back by the time we get to Bakersfield. I'll grab a blank log book, by the time we put down, we'll have gone through all the basics. I'll sign you off and you'll be legal again. Then you can fly the rest of the way by yourself."

"That'd be great," Rick said, genuinely grateful.

"Rick Gordon, that you?" Rick turned. "Just the guy I want to see," Harrison Harpine, Palma Chief of Police said.

Rick's heart sank.

CHAPTER EIGHTEEN

"I FELL IN LOVE with the wide blade that day in Tampico. So shiny, so sharp, so right for what I want to do," the Ragged Man said.

J.P. braced himself for the pain that was going to come, but instead felt only a small pin sticking sensation below his chin.

"Open your eyes or I'll shove it up into your brain."

J.P. refused, keeping his eyes closed with all his might.

"I'm not kidding!"

J.P. felt the knife break skin and he felt a gooey wet tickling as small droplets of blood dripped down over both sides of his neck.

"Open them!"

J.P. opened his eyes wide.

"That's better. You see we can get along, you and me."

J.P. stared into the man's steel eyes and saw nothing there. He thought of the under-the-bed monster that had caused him so many sleepless nights shortly after his father had left them. Nothing, he had thought, was worse than that thing that lived under the bed, but he was wrong, there was something worse and that something worse was staring into his soul, holding a gleaming Jim Bowie knife that was dripping his very own blood.

His eyes must have held a question, because the big man reached out and ripped the tape off his mouth. The tearing, ripping sound of the tape was worse than the stinging pain.

"What?" the man asked.

"Are you the Ragged Man?"

"Not so ragged, I don't think." The big man stepped back and looked down at his clothes. "Hmm, maybe I haven't changed in a few days." He rubbed his chin. "Or shaved. Maybe I am pretty ragged." He seemed to be talking to himself.

"Then you are the Ragged Man," J.P. said, his hoarse voice traveling through a parched throat.

"What the fuck are you talking about?"

J.P. didn't answer

"Don't make me mad, boy. I can be nasty when I get mad."

"The Ragged Man can't die. He kills and kills and he can't die."

"Everybody dies."

"Not the Ragged Man. If he dies he takes over another body."

Sam Storm dropped the knife and J.P. heard it thud against the ground. For a second J.P. thought he saw a glimmer of something in the man's eyes. Then for a another second, he saw the big man's crooked frown change into a smile, but it didn't last.

"How?" he asked through bone white lips.

"He's a demon from Australia and he can't die. He takes over people and makes 'em kill, and now he has you."

"You're full of it, nobody has me. I should peel off your skin, but you stink. The last thing I want is your shit on my hands."

J.P. watched as the big man turned and left his sight. He heard footsteps walk away. He heard the car door open, then heard heavy footsteps coming back. The man had a roll of gray duct tape in his hands.

"Gonna tape your mouth shut again."

"I won't make any noise," J.P. promised.

"Not when I'm through with you, you won't." He raised J.P. by the neck and started winding the tape around the boy's head, covering his mouth, cheeks, chin, ears, the back of his neck and with the last wrap his nose. J.P. saw it coming and sucked in a deep breath through his nostrils before the stubble faced man closed off his air and slammed the trunk down, again encasing him in the dark.

"Sweet dreams," the man said with a bang on the trunk that hurt his ears.

J.P.'s hands were leaving their hiding place behind his back and going to his face even before the trunk slammed shut and the light was gone. His fingers met his cheeks below the eyes and he ran them down along his nose, digging them under the tape. He tugged it down, pulling with all his strength. His lungs were bursting with the need to breathe and the tape didn't want to give.

He inched his fingers down further under the tape and jerked out, pulling the tape from his nose. Then he pulled down again and the mummy wrapping slid over his nose and he filled his lungs with air. After a few breaths, he tried to dig his fingers under the several layers that covered his mouth, but he couldn't do it. He pulled his fingers out and started working the tape down, pawing at it over and over, until, after several attempts, he had it sliding down over his upper lip. He opened his mouth wide and took in several breaths of the stink-filled-air. No air in all his young life had ever tasted so sweet.

Now, able to breathe, he felt around his head and found the place where the tape ended and began to peel it off. The first couple of layers peeled off without difficulty, but the last layer hurt as it pulled hair from his head, but he had been through too much to be put off by a little pain. He ripped it off with the same speed a doctor uses to remove a bandage, quickly done and quickly over with.

With the tape off, he rolled onto his side and bent his body at the waist, stretching his arms, grasping the rope that bound his feet. He tried to untie it, but his small hands were no job for the masterful way the big man had tied the knots. He tried to wiggle his feet out of the rope, but he couldn't get it over his heels.

He wished the Ragged Man would have left the Jim Bowie knife, but he hadn't.

There had to be another way. He began a thorough search of the trunk. Above his head, he felt the tire jack bolted onto the center of the spare tire. He ran his hands over and behind the tire and grasped what could only be battery cables.

He pulled the cables from behind the tire, grasped one of the ends in his hands. He opened and closed the clamp.

He ran his fingers along the sharp teeth of the clamp's jaws and had an idea. If he could break the clamp in half, he could use the copper teeth as a saw.

He grabbed one end of the clamp in each hand, twisted and twisted again, working the clamp back and forth like he would a metal coat hanger he was trying to break in half. The bottom and top of the jaws separated a little further from each other with each twist, till he managed to twist the clamp enough that the jaws came apart. Again he ran his fingers along the teeth and thought they would be sharp enough to saw through the rope.

He was wrong. After repeated attempts at sawing on it and making no progress, he gave up. The rope was stronger than his makeshift saw. He would have to find something else.

He found the battery cables behind the spare tire, maybe there was something else there, too. He shimmied back over to the spare and reached over it. Nothing. He ran his hands into the well under the front part of the tire. Nothing! He searched the rear area and bingo, wedged between the tire and the well, he found a flash light.

He pulled the light to his breast like a mother would a baby. He was almost afraid to turn it on for fear it wouldn't light. He counted to ten then flicked it on, sighing as the beam of light illuminated the cramped space, and to his absolute relief, on the other side of the trunk, up against the wall, the light landed on a bright red tool box.

His shaking hands caused him to lower the beam, and he fought tears as it landed on the dead form of the poor little kitten. He scooted around, carefully moved the white kitten's bloody body out of his way, without noticing the sticky blood that stuck to his hands. Then he opened the tool box.

He hovered over the metal box, like a pirate over treasure, and went through its contents. He removed the top tray and its assorted nails and screws, then he rummaged through the tools—wrenches, screw drivers, a tape measure and a hammer—not quite sure what he was looking for, then he found it, a metal gray utility knife.

He took the utility knife out of the tool box, handling it as if it were Spanish Doubloons. His prayers had been answered, this was his magic ticket. He caressed the smooth metal tool with his thumb, then used that same thumb to flick out the razor sharp blade.

Boy, he thought, if that Ragged Man came back now he would be in for it. One slash and no more eyes Mister Ragged Man. A second slash and no more throat. Let's see how brave you are now, he angrily thought. And then common sense took over and he began to think. If the Ragged Man came back, he, not the Ragged Man, would be the one in deep shit.

He slashed through the rope that bound his legs, wincing as blood started free flowing to his bare feet. He lay still through the pain and tingling, waiting for normal feeling to return.

He played the light over the top of the trunk, then directed the beam to the lock. He could see there was no way he could open the lid, but he had to give it a try. He felt around the lock, hoping that maybe there was a cable or something he could pull on to open it. There wasn't.

From the lock, he sent the light back over the tools and saw no help there, unless he wanted to use the hammer to beat on the metal sides of his coffin-like enclosure to draw help. But what if his captor was the only one outside? He would be in for it then.

Moving the beam, he rested it on the gas can. Its

fumes, suppressed by the combination smell of his fouled pants and the dead cat, were no longer noticeable. He jiggled the can. There was gas in it. Moving the light more, he checked out the spare tire, the tire iron and jack, oily rags, the battery cables, the dead cat and lastly he pointed the beam on the back of the back seat.

Then he lay very still and listened.

No sound. No sound from inside and no sound from outside. He tried to think. How long had it been since the Ragged Man had slammed the trunk shut? Five minutes, ten, maybe fifteen? When he came back, would he check the trunk? If he did, he would be mighty mad that he was still alive and not dead like a mummy.

But if the Ragged Man was up front, sleeping or maybe reading, and he tried to get out of the trunk by kicking his way through the back seat, he would be in just as much trouble as if the Ragged Man found him alive in the trunk.

He had to make a decision. He decided to go for it.

He squirmed around so that he was laying on his back, feet facing the back seat, head facing the back of the car, and using his bare feet, he pushed against the seat. It gave a little. He saw hope and pushed harder. He could feel the seat want to give way, but something was holding it in place.

He drew his legs back by bending his knees to his chest and kicked. Pain racked his feet as they hit metal and he felt no give, only resistance. He was not going to be able to kick his way through with his bare feet.

He wormed his way around to study the situation. From the top right end of the seat to the bottom left end was a metal brace and from the top left to the bottom right was its opposite twin. The pair of braces formed a large metal X. When he had pushed and felt the seat give, he was pushing on the seat. When he kicked and met resistance, his feet, both of them had hit the braces. Even if he was able to push the seat out, he wouldn't be able to squeeze between the supporting bands.

The metal X blocked his way, so it would have to go.

He pulled the tool box closer, took out a claw hammer. He worked the claw end between the body of the car and the top part of the brace that started on the right side of the seat. Using the end of the hammer as a lever, he pulled up and out. To his amazement the spot weld gave and the metal brace sprang free.

He pulled the metal strip away from the seat, saw that if he managed to kick the seat out, he would have room enough to squirm through.

He had to think. The back of the seat was covered with springs. If he kicked against them, they would cut into his feet and he would never be able to get out of the trunk. Then a light bulb went off in his head. He needed shoes and he had none, but what did shoes do? They protected his feet. He needed to protect his feet.

He emptied the tool box, careful to set the tools well out of his way. Then he took the oil rags and stuffed them into the metal box. This had to work. He wiggled back around into position to kick against the seat. He drew his knees back against his chest and stuffed his feet into the tool box with the rags between his feet and the metal bottom to cushion them. Then using the box as a battering ram, he kicked out against the seat. He felt it give as a metal bracket, that held the seat in place, popped.

He lay back and listened. If the Ragged Man was up front, now was the time he would come for him, but he heard only silence.

He reared back with his tool box covered feet and

kicked again. Then again. Another bracket popped and he needed to kick no more. The seat had given way. There was room for him to squeeze through. He was tired, exhausted and red-blood angry. He wanted out and he wanted to get even.

He removed the tool box shoe from his feet and set it next to the gas can. Then he picked up the can and shoved it through the opening into the back seat. It was time for his escape.

He thrust his head through the opening and learned that it was going to be a tight fit. Tight but possible. Arms first, he squeezed through, scraping chest and back, but he'd been through so much he was immune to the pain, as the rough metal cut through his tee shirt and into his skin. Once the top half of his body was through, his waist, legs and feet followed easily.

Out of the trunk, he pushed the top half of the seat back into place and climbed over into the front. He opened the glove compartment, looking for matches and smiled when he found several packs. The Ragged Man was a smoker. He took a pack out, then reached into the back for the gas can.

He poured gasoline over the front and back seat, then stepped out of the car into the cool evening. With a start, he realized he was in the woods, at the end of a dirt road he knew well. If he followed it back the way the car had come, he'd wind up on the twisting winding road that led up the hill to home, but he had no intention of going that way. If he went on into the woods he would find an animal trail that he had played on often. He could follow that around and up the hill and maybe get home without running into the Ragged Man coming back to his car.

He took off his Levi's and soiled underwear. He put the jeans back on, tossed the underwear onto the front seat and struck a match. There was no breeze. The match lit easily and stayed lit. He tossed it onto the front seat, and the interior of the old brown Ford Granada burst into flames. He turned away from the fire and jogged into the familiar darkening woods—heading home.

He was free. He had freed himself, and he had done it without the Dome Ring and its magic power powder.

CHAPTER NINETEEN

"IT'S ME, HARRISON," Rick said, shoulders slumped. It was out of his hands now. He'd tell Harrison about J.P. The FBI would be alerted. They'd do things by the book. He hoped it would be enough, but he was afraid it wouldn't be. The man who kidnapped J.P. had killed before, he wasn't about to stop now.

"I've been wanting to talk to you for the last six or seven months, so it sure is a lucky coincidence, me running into you here tonight, so far from home," Harrison Harpine drawled, his florid face grinning wide.

"What for?" Rick asked, shoulders picking up. Whatever it was, it wasn't anything that was going to land him in jail, not if he'd been looking for him for that long, and not with that grin.

"I hear you gave a thousand dollars to Sturgees' re-election campaign last time around," Harrison said. He was wearing a red, white and orange plaid sportcoat that he couldn't quite get buttoned over his beer belly and didn't match his dark blue slacks.

"I didn't know that was public knowledge, but so what?" True enough, he'd given the money, but it wasn't because he'd liked Sheriff Sturgees, he just couldn't stomach Ozzie Oxlade. Ozzie and his brother Seymour ran the used car dealership across the way in Palma. A pair of sleezeballs to the nth degree.

"Oh, yeah, anybody can find out who gives. They gotta post a list. It's the law," he said, looking down at the three of them sitting in the booth. Rick didn't move. Katherine scooted over and Bob Mitchel followed her lead, giving Harrison room to sit.

"I didn't know that, but it doesn't make any difference. Why should it interest you?" Rick said, but he could guess.

"You gonna pass some of your money around Palma way?" He folded his hands on the table.

"Chief, you don't run for election. You're appointed."

"Yeah, but the mayor's not. He needs all the help he can get. It'd be a big feather in my cap, if I could say I talked to you and persuaded you to give to his campaign."

"He won't face the voters for another year yet."

"Let's face it, Mr. Gordon. He's been in office a long time. Some people are already talking about a change. We're just trying to get all our ducks lined up in a row, so to speak. Can we count on your support?"

"I'd be glad to help out." Rick didn't particularly like Chief Harpine and he didn't like Mayor Clifton Wood at all, but he wanted to keep Harrison Harpine happy tonight. If that meant he had to shell out a thousand dollars to help Wood get elected, then so be it. If he survived the next few days without winding up in prison, he'd be more than happy to contribute.

"That's great, just great." Harpine beamed.

"What are you doing here anyway?" Rick asked.

"I was supposed to get a flight to Frisco, but they were overbooked, so I get to wait till morning.

"You going up to Palma-Tampico?" Bob Mitchel asked.

"Yep, just came down for a homicide convention. We don't get many murders up in our neck of the woods, but I like to keep up. Also I get to meet cops from all over the country, you never know when that'll come in handy."

"You go to a lot of conventions?" Rick asked.

"Every chance I get," Harpine said.

"So you know a lot of cops."

"Bet I know someone on every force in America" Harpine said. "I got a computer database full of contacts."

"We're going up in my plane. You want to hitch a ride?" Rick said. He didn't want Chief Harpine on the plane with him, but more than that, he didn't want the man sitting in a lonely motel room watching the news, then calling up some of his many contacts.

"When you leaving?"

"That's up to Mr. Mitchel. He's the pilot for the first leg."

"I'll go by the flight school and pick up that logbook," Mitchel said. "Then I'll grab a few things and meet you at the plane."

"You know where it is?" Rick asked.

"Old One-Six-Tango, yeah I know were she is. Heck, I know where every plane on this field is."

"Bob spends his life at the airport," Katherine said.

"Yeah, some nights I even sleep on the couch in the back room at the school. Since the wife died, doesn't seem much reason for going home."

"Hey, what's with the bird?" Chief Harpine said twenty minutes later as he climbed into the back of the plane.

"A racing pigeon I picked up for J.P. Donovan," Rick lied, not wanting to explain.

"There's a rumor going around that you're sweet on his mama," Harpine said.

"Just a rumor, Chief," Rick said, but he wondered if that wasn't a lie, too. He brushed the thought from his mind as he walked around the plane, checking the flaps, oil level, rudder, ailerons and the fuel, making sure there was no condensation in it.

"You seem to know your way around a plane," Mitchel said.

"Yeah, well, I've preflighted this one enough, I could do it in my sleep."

"I'll bet you could fly it in your sleep, too. You just need a little confidence."

"Checking it over and taking it off are two different things," Rick said, feeling a slight tingle at the base of his spine.

"Don't worry about it, you'll be fine," Mitchel said, climbing in the right side of the plane. Rick heard the older man grunt as he pulled himself in. "These old bones don't do anything anymore without aching and hurting," he said.

"I've got a few aches and pains of my own." Rick strapped himself into the pilot's seat, turned the master switch on, visually checked the flaps from the inside of the plane, like he'd done earlier, by flipping the flap switch up and down. He rotated the yoke, checking the ailerons, moved the foot pedals, checking the rudder, then he looked at Mitchel.

"Mixture," Mitchel said.

Rick set it for full rich.

"Carb heat off," he said.

Rick set the carburetor heat.

"Fuel gauges."

Rick checked them, saw that both tanks were full. He gave a silent thanks to Christina.

"Prime the engine."

Rick pushed and pulled on the throttle, a strong, quick three times.

"Ignition."

Rick started the plane.

"Oil pressure."

Rick checked it and saw it climb into the green arc.

"Brakes on and bring it to about a thousand RPM."

Rick tapped the brakes and pulled out the fuel control knob till the tach needle climbed up and settled at a thousand RPM.

"I already checked the weather," Mitchel said, "clear with about five knots coming out of the west."

Rick looked at the wind sock, sure enough a slight wind was blowing right down the runway.

"All right," Mitchel said, "we'll fly directly over Los Angeles International, through the VFR corridor, at fifteen hundred feet."

"What's that?" Harrison Harpine asked from the back seat. Rick thought he sounded tense.

"According to VFR, that's Visual Flight Rules, private pilots and their small planes are allowed to over fly the airport northbound at that altitude. We'll be too high to interfere with traffic landing and taking off and too low to interfere with commercial traffic passing overhead," Mitchel said.

"So we're going right over LAX? I'll be right on top of the big jets?" Harpine said.

"Yes, sir, right on top of them," Mitchel said.

"Hot damn, wait till I tell the boys." He didn't sound tense anymore, more like a child going for ice cream.

"I'm going to dial in the Gormon VOR." Mitchel bent forward, turned the knob on the VOR radio. "We'll fly that fix as soon as we're over LAX. All you have to do is keep the needle centered and it'll guide you safely through the pass in the mountains and out of the L.A. Basin. I've got all the frequencies for the stations all the way to Bakersfield, but they're really not necessary, because we can fly the highway." Interstate 5, a road straight as an edge, cut through California from L.A. through Bakersfield to Sacramento and beyond.

Five minutes later they were through with ground control, through with the runup, through with the controller in the tower. The engine was purring, the prop was turning, the plane ahead had just lifted off and then Rick was facing down the four thousand feet of runway, trying to slow his rapid heartbeat.

"Everything seem familiar?" Mitchel asked.

"Yeah," Rick said.

"Nothing out of order?"

Rick ran his eyes over the controls, made a last check of flaps and rudder. "Nothing."

"Then you're ready."

"Hey, wait a cotton pickin' minute. What's going on around here?" Harpine piped up.

"Calm down, Mr. Harpine, we're getting ready to take off."

"Does he know how to fly this thing or what?"

"Not now, Mr. Harpine," Mitchel said.

"No! Now's the time. Turn this thing off. I want out!" The smooth syrup was gone from his voice. He was shrill now.

Rick stomped on the brakes, pulled the throttle all the way out.

"No, I want out!" Harpine shouted.

Rick released the brakes and the plane responded, shooting down the runway like a horse given its head.

"Stop!" Harrison Harpine screamed.

"Shut up, Mr. Harpine!" Mitchel screamed louder. Then to Rick, "Start your roll at about seventy or seventy-five."

Rick kept his concentration on the long runway. In an instant it would be too late to abort. He looked at the airspeed indicator. Forty, forty-five.

"Let me out of here!"

Fifty, fifty-five.

"Sweet Mother of God, I'm going to die!"

Sixty, sixty-five and he started to ease back on the yoke.

"Shit, shit, shit, stop it!"

Seventy, and he pulled back a touch harder.

"You're both under arrest. Stop this now! You are under arrest! This is an order!"

Seventy-five and Rick felt the wheels start to leave the ground as he pulled back a little harder.

"Now, motherfucker! Shut it down!"

Eighty, eighty-five and he pulled back more. They were well past the point of no return.

"Noooo!" Harpine screamed as they left the ground.

Tense, Rick smiled as he kept the back pressure on the yoke, the familiar tingling sensation shooting through him.

"Feel the rush?" Mitchel said.

"Yeah," Rick answered.

"Some people were just born to fly. You're one of 'em. Every time you leave the ground that rush will get to ya. Like a runner's high, like drugs. Makes no difference the type of plane—jet, helicopter or single-engine-land. It'll even attack you in tourist class on a 747."

"Yeah," Rick said, again. He knew exactly what the man was talking about. He relaxed the pressure on the yoke a bit, guiding the plane, flying the plane.

"Wanna do a touch and go?"

"What's a touch and go?" Harpine squeaked from the back.

"Can we?" Rick said.

"If I'm gonna sign your ticket, I'll have to see at least one."

"What's a touch and go?" Chief Harpine squeaked again.

"Make your climbing turn to the right and level off at a thousand," Mitchel said.

"I remember," Rick said.

"Mr. Harpine," Mitchel turned toward the back, "what's the problem?"

"I heard you telling him what to do. Maybe it took me a bit to figure it out, but now I got it figured. He don't know how to fly a plane. You didn't tell me that."

"Let me assure you, Mr. Gordon is an excellent pilot. But we have rules. If you haven't flown in a year, you have to have a licensed instructor sign you off to stay legal. Since I'm licensed, we decided to kill two birds with one stone. Mr. Gordon will fly us up to Bakersfield and I'll sign off his log book and he'll be legal again."

"That's it? You're not shitting me?"

"No, I'm not shitting you. Other than a practice

landing and a few maneuvers in the air, that's it. By the time we land in Bakersfield, Mr. Gordon will be as qualified as he ever was."

"Serious?"

"Serious. You can just sit back and take in the view. Enjoy the flight. I brought a thermos of coffee along. As soon as we get the touch and go out of the way, we'll sit back and relax. How's that sound?" Mitchel's voice was soothing and smooth.

"Fine. Sorry I got excited," Harpine said.

"Okay, Rick, we're at seven-fifty," Mitchel said, "climbing at a hundred and fifty a minute, that's fine, make your turn to your downwind."

Rick turned the aircraft, then leveled off at a thousand feet.

"You want to make one of your famous side slip landings?" Mitchel asked.

"I've never done it after dark."

"Plane flies the same." Mitchel picked up the mike. "Long Beach tower this is Cessna One-Six-Tango in a right downwind for Two-Five Right, requesting permission for a touch and go."

"Sorry, One-Six-Tango, we have noise abatement here. No touch and goes after dark."

"Come on you piece of toe scum, give us a break. Just one, I wanna sign off a ticket tonight."

"That you Mitchel, you slimy piece of weasel droppings?"

"It's me, Jimmy."

"Okay, Bobby, Just one. Hope I don't get my you know what in a ringer, never know who's listening."

"You don't have to worry," Mitchel said into the mike. "We're going to cut power now and slip it in so quiet, the neighbors won't even know we're here. We'll land at the halfway point and be outta here quieter than a soft rain."

"This I gotta see. Permission granted."

Rick shoved the power in, turning the Cessna into a glider.

"What?" Harpine said.

"It'll be all right, Harrison. Trust me," Rick said.

Rick shoved his left foot forward, giving it full left rudder as he cranked the ailerons to the right, cross controlling the aircraft, keeping it in control as he went into the slip, dropping fast.

"I don't like this," Harpine said.

Rick kept the nose pointed to the right, toward the runway. They were dropping at two hundred and fifty feet a minute. Rick stayed in the slip, keeping the plane pointed toward the runway.

"Going down a little fast," Mitchel said.

"It'll be fine." Rick pushed down on the yoke a bit, increasing the rate of descent even more.

"Shit!" Harpine said.

"Shit!" Mitchel said.

Rick pushed down some more on the yoke.

"Fuck a duck," Harpine said, loud.

"You sure you have it?" Mitchel said, louder. The ground was coming up fast.

"I have it." Rick pushed the nose down more and the cross controlled plane turned forty-five degrees to the runway.

Mitchel started to reach for the yoke on his side of the plane.

"Keep your hands off the controls!" Rick said, voice firm, but calm.

Mitchel pulled his hands back like they'd been burnt.

Two hundred feet from the ground and Rick started

to ease off the left rudder.

A hundred and fifty, the plane was almost all the way around, and he released the left rudder altogether. A hundred feet and he added a little right rudder and eased off the pressure on the ailerons, straightening them a little.

"Oh, fuck!" Harpine, squealed.

"Shit, shit, shit!" Mitchel said.

Fifty feet from the ground and Rick eased off the right rudder and straightened the ailerons. He was flying straight and level, only a hair's breath to the right of the runway. He eased the plane to the left and at ten feet he was over the center line. At five feet he started his flare, squeaking it in smack in the center of the four thousand foot runway.

"Motherfucker!" Harpine said.

"I'll sign your ticket right now!" Mitchel yelped as Rick added full power and started his takeoff roll.

Four and a half hours later Harpine was dozing in the back seat as they were lined up for a straight in to Bakersfield.

"For a man who wanted out of the plane like there was no tomorrow, your friend sure 'nuff settled himself in," Mitchel said.

"Harrison can sleep anywhere," Rick said.

"Guess that's what makes him such a good chief of police."

"You're underestimating him. Many a man's found out it doesn't pay to underestimate Harrison Harpine."

"You're right, I don't know him."

"He's a good man," Rick said, conscious of the fact that Harpine was probably listening.

"Okay, 'nuff said. I've written down all the frequencies you need to get up to Palma-Tampico. All you gotta do is keep putting them in and keep the arrow centered. Piece of cake. Child could do it." Mitchel stretched, then yawned. "I've signed your logbook so now you're legal."

"Thanks," Rick said.

"Mind if I bring it in?" Mitchel asked.

"No problem." Rick released the controls, sat back and relaxed as Mitchel landed the plane and drove it off the runway to the terminal.

"Again, thanks for everything." Rick shook hands with Mitchel on the ground. Then he was back in the plane, with Harpine in the right hand seat, taxiing to the runway.

"I appreciate what you said about me, back before we landed," Harpine said. As Rick had suspected the wily police chief had been listening.

"Only spoke the truth," Rick said.

"Well, I appreciate it," Harpine said.

"Here we go," Rick said, then he was shooting down the runway, then into his takeoff roll. This time he was the pilot in command. There was one to help him if he screwed up. When he'd owned the plane all those years ago, he'd spent countless hours in the pattern, practicing all kinds of landings, but he'd very rarely gone anywhere. He'd fooled Mitchel and Harpine with that power off landing. He set the frequency into the VHF radio, hoping the weather held. The last thing he needed was any surprises.

And he didn't get any till daybreak. Harpine was waking up with the sun. It promised to be a gorgeous day. The wind was rushing away from the mountains on the right, toward the sea, when all of a sudden they were caught in turbulence and Rick lost control of the airplane.

CHAPTER TWENTY

WHEN J.P. LEFT THE CAR he knew exactly where he was, the end of Old Luke's Road. Where the road ended, the hiking trail started, winding through the pines for several minutes till it met Bear Clearing, a man-made meadow where two or three times a year the boy scouts came to set up their tents and camp. The younger kids sometimes played there during the day and the high school kids sometimes lit campfires and drank beer during the early evening. Tampico was a small town and the young people had to make their own entertainment.

The path picked up on the far side of Bear Clearing and continued on for ten minutes at a brisk walk, snaking into Lover's Hideaway, a small natural clearing, where the high schoolers went to make out and sometimes do a little more. From Lover's Hideaway the path twisted its way to Prospector's Donkey Road and a five minute walk down the dirt road would find him on Mountain Sea Road and only ten minutes from home.

He walked fast, away from the burning car, wanting to put as much distance from it as possible. When the Ragged Man came back he wanted to be long gone. He wanted to run, but his feet hurt and they were swelling up, forcing him to hobble along like an old man. He wanted to stop and rest, but he forced himself to go on.

"Ow!" He stubbed his toe on a baseball sized rock. He looked down to inspect the damage. His right big toe was pouring blood and the toenail was broken. The front half of the nail stuck up ninety degrees, hinged on only by a flap of skin. It bobbed and flapped as he moved his foot, reminding him of a raw piece of meat, and it hurt like all get out.

His old man's hobble was slowed to an older man's limping stumble. He wanted to quit, to rest, but he remembered something his dad used to say. "Winners never quit and quitters never win." He didn't want to be a quitter. And besides, when the Ragged Man came and found out what he'd done to his car, he was going to be really, really mad. So J.P. stumbled on toward Bear Clearing.

Then the forest went quiet, like it did that day the Ghost Dog chased his mom and tried to get his birds. J.P. stopped and listened.

Nothing. No sound.

This is bad, he thought. He turned his slow stumble back into a faster hobble, then into a slow run. His feet no longer hurt and he picked up his pace, bursting into Bear

Clearing at a fast run.

He stopped in the middle of the clearing, dead out of breath.

The sun was going down in a sea of orange haze. The shadows were getting darker.

He looked around the clearing.

"I'm not a quitter," he said, panting, "I just need a minute to rest." His bloody foot was throbbing and his sides ached where he had scraped against the rough metal, getting out of the trunk. Gingerly, he felt a bruised side and was shocked to find his hand covered in blood. He checked and found that both sides of his chest, under his arm pits and the insides of both arms were bruised, scraped and bleeding. His feet, battered against the rocky path, fared no better. He needed to rest.

He walked over to one of the two fire pits. The charcoal remains were surrounded by tree stump stools, empty beer cans and junk food wrappers. He bent over and picked up a Ding Dong wrapper. It's Ding Dongs that got me into this, he thought, and if I ever get home, I'll never eat another one as long as I live.

He sat on one of the tree stumps and tried to imagine what it would be like in front of the campfire, safe, with lots of friends. He closed his eyes, his head fell forward. He jerked it back. A quitter would fall asleep. He just wanted a few minutes rest.

He roamed his eyes around the clearing. The ground was covered with leaves and pine needles. The circling trees offered a wall against the outside world and the open sky allowed the setting sun to work its shadow magic on the trees, giving the clearing a ghostly, vampire feeling.

He wished he was home with his mother, but wishing wouldn't make it so. He had to get there himself, without help, without wishes, so only marginally rested, he got up from his stool and limped through the clearing to the path on the other side. He was tired, hurt, bruised and scared, but he wasn't a quitter. He was going home, no matter how rough the going was.

He heard a noise at the edge of the clearing, a movement through the brush, or the wind through the trees. He stopped, afraid to turn. A low rumbling growl froze him in place. The growl turned into the sound of deep breathing, then into the purr of a big cat, like the tigers in the San Diego Zoo. He wanted to run, but he couldn't. He had to see. No matter how dumb it was, and he knew it was dumb, he had to see.

He turned his head and followed it with his body, swinging around, pivoting in place like a slow motion kung fu fighter. His skin was on fire and he felt his hair trying to stand. His mouth, dry from several hours of no liquid, got dryer and his hungry stomach churned. His feet, sides and arms screamed with pain and his mind said run, but he had to see.

And he saw.

Across the clearing, standing on the opposite side of the path, where he had entered it only a short while ago, stood the Ghost Dog. Only it was no dog. The red eyes bore into him and he met its cat-like stare head on, as curious as he was afraid. He knew what he was seeing, and it was no dog. No dingo dog like Rick told about in his story. No wolf. No bear. It was big, black and it was a saber-toothed tiger.

Its long white tusks gleamed in the setting sunlight and its glaring claws dug into the hard earth like it was Jell-O. Its smooth black fur glistened with sweat and its powerful looking legs resembled slick, black-oiled, muscle covered tree stumps. It was tiger-big, tiger-dangerous and it growled a tiger-growl. It didn't take a genius to know that it was tiger-mean. It snorted misty smoke from its nostrils and J.P. hoped that it wasn't hungry.

For a full minute that felt like a full day, they stared at each other, eyes locked in a deep soul grip and J.P. knew what had happened to his cousin Janis. Like the whale that swallowed Jonah, this thing had swallowed Janis, only she wasn't coming back. The saber-toothed Ghost Dog had eaten her, ripped her flesh apart and eaten her, then it drank her blood and all she was now was saber-tooth, Ghost Dog, tiger shit somewhere in the woods. And if he wasn't very, very careful and very, very lucky, that's what was going to happen to him, too.

Slowly he started to back up, neck hairs curled as he inched away. Any second he expected the black demon to pounce, and it looked powerful enough to clear the clearing like Superman, in a single bound.

Maybe the thing could jump like Superman, J.P. thought. But he was fast as the Flash. If only he could get a head start, maybe he could get away.

He backed up another inch and the satisfying purr of a cat that had the mouse turned to an irritated growl. The animal perked up its ears and J.P. stopped his retreat.

He waited but the black demon animal didn't move. J.P. moved back another slow inch. Then another, then another. The Ghost Dog lowered its ears flat against its head and J.P. thought it was going to jump. He had to do something. So he did the first thing that came to his mind.

"Stay!" he commanded.

The animal stopped its growl, perking its ears back up.

"Oh God, make it stay," he pleaded as he inched further into the woods. He moved cautiously, carefully, inch by inch, then foot by foot, never taking his eyes from the beast. As soon as the path angled and the animal was out of sight, he turned and ran, paying no attention to his bleeding feet, starving thirst or the heart pumping pain that pierced his lungs.

He didn't hear the animal give chase, but he knew it would.

He dodged through the brush, pumping his arms like a sprinter, picking his bare feet up and laying them down on the dirt path like he was wearing track shoes and running on cinder. His raw feet were unable to send the messages of pain to his stressed out brain, because it was too frightened to listen.

He sensed, rather than heard, the black beast somewhere behind. He tried to pump his arms harder, knowing that his fleeing feet would keep pace, but his young body had been battered, abused, bruised, deprived of food and water and now he was losing blood. It was unable to answer the mind's call.

He was running toward Lover's Hideaway, on the verge of collapse, when he heard a woman's voice crying out for more. There was help ahead. If only he could go on just a little longer. The hope of help sent a second wind soaring through his lungs and he was able to force himself to continue on, picking them up and laying them down.

He hoped that whoever was up ahead would be able to deal with the Ghost Dog, but down deep he knew that nobody could deal with a saber-toothed tiger. Not and live, but he wasn't going to give up. He wasn't going to be a quitter. Even if he couldn't go on much longer, he wasn't going to quit. Quitters never win.

A scream that could have come straight from the African bush roared through the night, sending arrows of fear running up J.P.'s back, causing his body to pump out whatever remaining adrenaline it had left in a quick short blast. J.P. burst into Lover's Hideaway Clearing, a screaming banshee wraith of a boy, covered with blood, sweat and dirt, looking like he had run straight out of hell.

He saw Stacy Sturgees, the Sheriff's daughter, naked, sitting atop Deputy Terrenova and lightning quick he knew they were having sex. She was screaming, "More, more, more," and somewhere back in his mind he knew she was enjoying herself, but he doubted she would be enjoying herself much longer.

He ran toward the couple, jumped over them and continued on without looking back, darting onto the path on the other side of Lover's Hideaway, chugging like a dead-tired fox fleeing from the hounds. He shot along the familiar snaking path, grabbing for air and ducking low branches, like he'd done so many times when playing tag with his friends, only now it wasn't a game. If he lost, he really lost.

He rounded the last curve before the path ended at Prospector's Donkey Road and he saw the police car. He poured on speed, like a long distance runner, running for the tape. Please God, let it be unlocked, he silently prayed as he ran toward the driver's door.

He pulled on the door and cried out. It was locked, but he had come too far and been through too much to quit. He tried the back door. Locked. He ran around to the passenger side and pulled the door open. Thank you God, thank you God, he thought as he piled into the car, shutting and locking the door after himself.

He was safe. At least for now. He lay back on the seat with his heart sending blood pounding to his brain. He fought for breath, but he failed to get and keep enough air to remain conscious. He passed out as the shooting started with one thought in his head. He hadn't quit.

* * *

Jesse Terrenova was wide eyed, watching Stacy's breasts bob and weave, twin melons of sexual excitement, as she slid her cute ass back and forth, pumping like a jack hammer. She screamed for more as the orgasm hit her.

He reached up and grabbed a melon in each hand. Their sexual softness sent shivers through his body and he squeezed and held on as his own pleasure began to build to a rising peak. "Oh my god," he moaned, "I'm going to come again."

She kept pumping through her own orgasm screaming, "Come for me baby. Come for me baby. Come for me baby."

He was so excited, so worked up, so lost in the moment that he imagined he heard a jungle cat roaring in the forest. His second orgasm was so close and her fever rapid body was sending pricks of pleasure through him that were small precursors of the total rapture that he was about to experience.

He felt it building. He picked up his rhythm to accommodate hers. They moved as one. He was about to blast his way to heaven on earth when J.P., looking like he'd been put through a meat grinder, jumped right over them and continued on through the clearing. Stacy, her eyes closed in pleasure and abandonment, wasn't even aware her privacy had been invaded.

He started slamming his seed into her when a deafening roar ripped through the clearing, drowning out Stacy's orgasmic screams and all of a sudden a large-toothed, black panther-like animal roared into view. With a great leap it sprang upon Stacy, sinking its tusk-like teeth into her breasts, yanking her pumping, fucking body off his stiff hardness, leaving him to ejaculate into the cool evening breeze.

Still shooting his sperm, he instinctively rolled toward his service revolver, keeping his eyes on the huge animal. By the time he'd reached his weapon, the animal had ripped Stacy's breasts from her body and blood was shooting from the screaming woman's chest. He raised the forty-five automatic as the beast devoured her breasts and began shooting as it clamped its jaws on her once beautiful head, ripping it from her body, leaving the headless, breastless body squirming in the dirt.

The first shot hit the animal in the left shoulder as the black beast continued its grisly meal. The second and third went wild as the beast crushed Stacy's head with cat like speed. He sank the fourth and fifth into its flank as it swallowed the bloody mess. The sixth and seventh hit the animal in the chest as it charged. The eighth and final shot followed the first into the left shoulder, but the beast kept coming.

* * *

J.P. had to go to the bathroom, and his sides hurt, but it was his feet that were the big problem. They were black and blue, swollen to almost twice their normal size. Getting out of the car to pee was going to hurt. He didn't have to go all that bad, he thought, so he decided to wait.

Inspecting the inside of the cruiser, he found Jesse's thermos and was reminded of how thirsty he was. He spun the top off, unscrewed the rubber cork. He had only tried coffee once, when his mother wasn't looking, and had quickly decided he didn't like it, but Jesse Terrenova's lukewarm coffee was the sweetest tasting drink that had ever crossed his parched dry lips. He downed the coffee, chug-a-lugging, like a drunk in a bar does a pitcher of beer, spilling as much down his chest as he swallowed.

With his thirst satisfied, he popped open the glove compartment and took out the box of granola bars that he knew he would find there. Like every boy in town, he'd spent plenty of time riding in Jesse's cop car. Jesse coached Little League, ran the weekend crafts at the park, taught Bible school and did a myriad other things that caused him to give the kids in town a lift in the black and white, not to mention taking them on patrol with him. There wasn't much about Jesse or his car that J.P. didn't know.

The box of ten was half-empty, and he greedily scarfed down the remaining five, in a hurry to blunt the aching in his stomach.

Feeling a little better, with two of his three basic urges taken care of, he decided to concentrate on the third. There was no way he was going to get out of the car to pee. Reason number one, what if the black, saber-toothed Ghost Dog was still out there, and reason number two, he didn't think he could walk on his battered feet. But he darn sure didn't want to wet his pants.

He thought for a second, decided he could take the risk of opening the door. If he saw the Ghost Dog, he could close it quickly enough, but he wouldn't get out of the car. He'd pee out from inside.

He rolled the window down and listened. The woods were making their normal noises. Birds were chirping, the morning breeze was rustling through the trees. They sounded alive and safe. He opened the passenger door, knelt on the front seat, unbuttoned his fly and pissed a strong yellow stream out into the wind. When he finished, he reached out, closed the door and rolled the window back up.

Then he checked the ignition and realized that he was going to have to get out of the car anyway. He needed the ignition on to use the radio and Jesse had taken his keys with him when he left the car, but fortunately J.P., like everyone else in town, knew he was always locking himself out of the car and that he kept a hide-away-key under the front bumper.

Again he rolled down the window and listened. Then he opened the door and gingerly stepped out of the car, onto his bruised, hurting feet. It was like walking on shards of glass or through hot coals. And as swiftly as he could, he made his way to the front of the car, leaning on it for support. He reached under the bumper, pulled out the magnetic box and painfully returned back to the safety of the car.

Once the door was closed again, and locked, he put the key into the ignition and turned it to the accessory position. Now that the radio had juice he picked up the mike, holding the push to talk button down with his thumb as he'd seen Jesse do.

"Is anyone listening out there?" he said, lips inches from the mike.

Ten minutes later, J.P. sat secure behind locked doors and watched as Deputy Lincoln Hewett's police car drove up the dirt road and parked alongside. Not until the Deputy was out of the car, did he unlock the door.

"Well, J.P., I'm sure you have quite a story," Lincoln said.

J.P. had always like Lincoln, but he wished the sheriff had come instead.

"Come on, J.P., what's going on?"

J.P. told him about how his father and Sylvia were murdered. How he was kidnapped and held in the trunk. How he got away. How he saw the saber-toothed Ghost

Dog. How it chased him. How he saw Jesse and Stacy, naked, making love. And how he got safely into the police car.

"Stacy and Jesse were up at Lover's Hideaway?" the deputy asked, pointing up the dirt path.

"Yes, sir."

"Show me!"

"I can't walk too good and besides, I don't think it's a good idea to go up there."

"Nonsense. I'll carry you." Lincoln pulled J.P. out of the car, hefting him up to his shoulders the way his dad used to when he was younger.

"I don't wanna go there."

"It'll be fine."

J.P. kicked against Lincoln's chest.

"Stop that." Lincoln squeezed his leg, hard.

"You're gonna be sorry."

"Just calm down."

"This is a bad idea." But it was no use, because now they were in the clearing and Lincoln set J.P. down.

The dead leaves, pine needles and the dirt throughout the center of the small clearing were covered in wet blood. The couple's clothes lay in a heap, near the clearing's center, undisturbed.

The deputy bent to pick up Stacy's frilly blouse.

"The Ghost Dog did it," J.P. said. "It killed 'em, then it ate 'em."

"There is no Ghost Dog," Lincoln said.

"Yes there is. I saw it. It chased me."

"He fired his weapon," Lincoln said, talking to himself. He bent over and picked up a shell casing. He found the forty-five near a pool of blood, picked it up. "My God," he said, "he emptied it. Whatever did this is one bad son of a bitch."

When they reached the end of the clearing, J.P. heard a low growl and wailed, "Oh, no, not again," as the black beast slammed into Lincoln Hewett.

He had a front row view as the Ragged Man stepped from the bushes and slit Lincoln's throat with his Jim Bowie knife.

J.P. wanted to run, but he was frozen in place as the Ragged Man stepped away from the dead deputy and the Ghost Dog moved back in, clamping its powerful jaws around Lincoln's neck and closing them with a sharp snap, severing his head and sending it rolling toward J.P. like a soccer ball kicked out of play.

J.P. passed out.

CHAPTER TWENTY-ONE

HE WAS TOO LOW AND TOO CLOSE to the cliffs. The plane slid out of his control, reminding him of the time when a rogue wave grabbed his board and ripped it from him, leaving him to be tossed about at the ocean's mercy, his board a deadly weapon lashed to his feet. He kept his head and toughed it out then, he'd keep his head and tough it out now.

"We're gonna crash!" Harpine shouted

Rick grabbed a quick look at the man. His florid face had darkened from its usual drinker's pink and he was drenched in sweat.

"Can you get us out of this?"

"Hope so." Rick shoved in the left rudder as he pulled back on the throttle, and like that time when he had to slip loose from the board and claw his way from the sea, the plane clawed its way away from the cliffs. He nosed down toward the ocean, to try and free the plane from the turbulence. He couldn't abandon the plane like he had the surfboard.

"Oh, sweet Mother of God, we're going down! Hail Mary full of grace, forgive us at the hour of our deaths."

"That's not how it goes," Rick said.

"Who the fuck cares how it goes! Oh, Lord we're going in the ocean. I'll be good, God. I'll be good!"

Rick tried to tune Harpine out and gradually added power as they closed in on the water.

"Oh, sweet Jesus, forgive me. We're gonna die!"

Rick stared to get the plane back at three hundred feet and regained full control at a hundred and fifty. He leveled off at a hundred feet and flew over the rough sea. He spotted a lone surfer below.

"Thank you, Lord. Oh, thank you," Harpine said. Then to Rick. "What the fuck was that all about?"

"Turbulence off the cliffs. Much more than I expected. Took me by surprise."

"You gonna have any more surprises like that?"

"Hope not," Rick lied, because he knew he'd have one grand surprise for him. No way could he put it down at the airport. There was a good chance that Mitchel had seen a news broadcast. If so, Sheriff Sturgees might be waiting for him.

He brought the plane back up to five hundred feet, then leveled off.

"Higher, we should be higher."

"It's okay now, Chief. Trust me."

"That's what you said before and look what

happened."

"You're still breathing."

"Barely. It's a miracle my heart's still beating."

"All right, I'll take it up to a thousand." Rick pulled back slightly on the yoke, starting a slow climb. Fifteen minutes later he leveled off and they flew in silence for about twenty minutes. Then he eased in the throttle and they started a gradual descent.

"What now?" Harpine said.

"Palma dead ahead," Rick said, "about ten miles." He turned in, toward the coast and was at five hundred feet when he flew over the beach, headed inland.

"What are you doing?"

"We have to go inland, then make a wide left, to make a straight in landing on runway two-seven," Rick lied. He'd never flown out of Palma-Tampico, never been to the airport, didn't have a clue what the runway numbers were, and he had no intention of getting anywhere near the airport today. Two miles inland he saw a place were he might be able to land, a straight stretch of dirt road that ran from the twisted highway through the pines to a log cabin-like house.

If he was able to make it through the trees without clipping the wings, if there were no large potholes in the road to throw them into the trees once they touched down and, if there was a headwind and not a tailwind, they had a chance. But if his timing wasn't right on, they could wind up in somebody's living room.

He was preparing to fly over the dirt track and check it out when the plane sputtered. Shit, he thought, out of gas, he wasn't even going to have to fake it with Harpine. He'd only get one chance. He wasn't lined up. He was too high. He was going too fast.

"What's wrong?" Harpine asked, agitated.

"Out of gas," Rick said.

Harpine spun his head around, fixing Rick with a cold stare. "You're shitting me!"

"No."

"What are you going to do about it?" Harpine looked out the window, scanning the land below.

"First we're going to slow her down." Rick pulled back on the yoke, but not enough to stall out, then added full flaps. The plane slowed, like a reined in horse, from just over a hundred to eighty.

"Shit," Harpine said.

"You can say that again." Rick shoved in left the rudder, turned the ailerons to the right and put the Cessna into a side slip.

"Mother fuck!" Harpine said as the plane, losing lift, lost altitude.

"It'll be okay." Rick kept the nose pointed to the place where the dirt track intersected the road, with one eye on the spot where he planned on touching down, the other on the altimeter.

"You gonna land it on the dirt road?"

"Yeah." They were still in the slip, dropping fast.

"You can do it. I got faith," Harpine said, voice gone quiet.

"Where'd that come from?"

"What, my faith in your flying? I admit I mighta been doubting you before, but I believe in you now."

"That's good to know," Rick said.

"Well, I don't have much choice, consider the alternative."

"Very reassuring, Chief." Rick edged the plane a little to the right, keeping it lined up with where he wanted to put it down.

"Just trying to be honest. I don't wanna cause you to

fuck up here."

"We're gonna be fine," Rick said with a confidence he didn't feel.

"Getting low," Harpine said.

"Yeah, were at a hundred feet. I'm leveling off," Rick said, for his benefit as well as Harpine's. He looked at the airspeed indicator. "Seventy-five miles an hour, too fast."

"Don't seem that fast." Harpine seemed calm now.

"We must be headed into the wind, that's good." Rick took the plane out of the slip, then pulled back slightly on the yoke. "Forty-feet, thirty-five, Thirty, Twenty." He pulled back some more, pulling it into the landing flare.

"Fifteen feet, Ten, Five," this time it was Harrison Harpine calling out the numbers.

"Grab your socks!" Rick yelled out.

"And kiss your ass goodbye!" Harpine shouted.

They touched down with a teeth chattering thump. Rick stiffened his legs, fighting to keep the plane headed in a straight line. He stood on the brakes, then released the pressure, then stood on them again. The cabin was closing fast. He wasn't going to make it.

He looked up in time to see an excited couple coming out of the house. He pulled his left foot off the peddles and pushed hard with his right. The plane spun right, into the trees, with a tearing sound and a sudden stop. Somehow he'd managed to stick the nose between two of the tall pines. The trees grabbed at the wings, ripping them off and stopping the plane. He didn't have to shut down the engine, he had landed on vapor. They were alive but the plane was finished.

"Holy Mother of God, we made it!" Harpine whooped.

"Are you okay?" the throaty voice belonged to an old

man who had pulled Rick's door open.

"I think so."

"You two better get out of there."

"What time is it?" Rick asked.

"Seven in the AM," the man said.

"My door's stuck," Harpine said, surprisingly calm.

Rick unbuckled and jumped to the ground.

"I need some help getting out of here!" Harpine wailed, the calm gone.

"You hurt in there mister?" the old man said.

"I just want out!" Harpine said.

Rick moved around to Harpine's side of the plane. The old man followed.

"I'll push and you pull," Harpine said, voice gaining an octave.

Rick grabbed onto the handle, turned it and pulled. The door popped. Rick and the old man jumped back as Harrison Harpine came tumbling out, landing on his side on the wet, early morning earth. Rick offered him a hand up. Harpine grabbed it in a Viking grip and Rick pulled him from the dew damp ground.

"We are a pair of lucky, sons-of-bitches!" Harpine said, relief flooding through his voice.

"Okay, Chief, you're alive, now I gotta go," Rick said. Then to the old man. "I have thirty minutes to get to the pier."

"Mister, why didn't you put down at the airport?"

"I'll give you five hundred dollars if you get me to the *Seawolf* before it sails."

"I'll get the car."

"Nate, don't you want to know why he put down here and why he's in such a hurry?" the woman asked. She'd been standing behind the man when he'd opened Rick's door. She was thin and frail, with gray flecked auburn hair and crystal green eyes. It was easy to see that she'd been a looker in her time.

"Nope. Five hundred dollars is all I need to know." Nate was thin, too, but wiry, with muscles that hadn't gone to seed. His eyes were as green as hers and just as penetrating.

"I wanna know," Harpine said.

"You got a gun, Chief?" Rick asked.

"No, I don't carry when I fly, too much of a hassle."

"What about your plane?" the woman asked, ignoring Harpine.

"I'll give you another five hundred for the inconvenience and I'll come back in a couple of days and take care of getting it removed."

"Get the car, Nate!" the woman said and the man limped around the house to the garage in back.

"No one's going anywhere," Harpine said.

Nate ignored him, continuing on toward the garage.

"You have to understand," she told Rick after her husband was out of earshot, "we live off of Nate's Social Security. We don't get any other money. If his brother didn't let us live in this cabin, I don't know what we'd do. A thousand dollars is a lot of money to us."

"It's a lot of money to me, too."

"What's so important about getting to the fishing boat?" Harpine asked.

"It's personal." Rick turned back to the plane, reached across his seat and took out the caged bird.

"What do you have there?" the woman asked.

"A bird that's going to carry a very important message." He fished into a side pocket on the pilot's door and pulled out Christina's log book. Looked around in the pocket some more and pulled out a couple of charts. He tossed them on the seat, reached in the pocket again, coming out with a short stub of a pencil. He ripped part of a page out of the log, held it against the plane and wrote:

Judy,

J.P. kidnapped. Am coming with the Wolf. Phone may be tapped. Meet me. Bring the GUN.

Rick

"What's that all about?" Harpine asked, reading over his shoulder.

"Not now, Chief," Rick said and something in his voice held Harpine in check for a few seconds while Rick tore off the top of the page containing the message and rolled it into a tight ball. He took the racing homer out of the cage and opened the capsule that was affixed to the bird's leg and inserted the message.

"Go home, Dancer." He released his grip on the bird.

He looked up with his left hand, shielding his eyes and watched Dancer fly into the sun and start a great circle, but before completing the three-sixty the bird got his bearing and took off in the direction of Tampico. Somehow he knew Judy would be at home. Somehow he knew that she'd cancelled her trip to Hawaii. The thought danced as true through his mind as Dancer's flight path toward Tampico.

"Now all I have to do is get to the boat in time."

"This sounds like police business to me," Harpine said.

"Sorry, Chief, this is private."

"I can stop you."

"Or you can come along?" Rick said, not wanting Harrison to come, but not wanting him to stay behind, suspicious enough to make any phone calls, either.

"With you? After what you just put me through? I'd sooner eat dog shit. Besides, I fuck with you too much, you might forget that campaign promise. Tell me about the boy," Harpine said.

Rick sensed that Harpine was looking for a face saving way of not going with him, of not getting involved. He gave it to him. "It's a custody battle. J.P.'s father has the boy," Rick lied. "He plans on threatening Judy with a nasty court battle she can't afford. The gun's just to scare the chicken-shit son of a bitch." Tough words, words Chief Harrison Harpine could understand.

"The last thing I want is to be a party to murder, two thousand dollar campaign contribution or no." Rick noticed Harpine had doubled the amount.

"I thought I'd promised three," Rick said, winking.

"Oh, yeah, I forgot." Harpine winked back.

"Nate will get you there," the woman said, interrupting them and then was interrupted herself by the sound of the car as it backed out of the garage. "It might be old," she said of the battered pickup, "but it runs fine. It'll get you there."

"Hop in," old Nate said, "time's a wastin'."

Rick opened the door, slid into the passenger seat, cranked the window as the man backed the car around, so that it was facing down the dirt track, away from the house. Then he threw it into first and put his foot to the floor. The old man knew how to drive. "We'll make it in time, son, don't you worry none."

The pickup kicked up dust as the tires bit into the dirt and the taste of it on his teeth reminded Rick of the race in Australia. Somehow, in some weird way, all of this,

everything that had happened since he had returned—
Judy's encounter on the beach, the Donovan's murder, the
Bootleg murders, J.P.'s kidnapping and perhaps Ann's
death—were all connected with something that happened
there.

"Hold on son," the man shouted above the engine's
roar.

Rick snapped to attention in time to brace himself as
Nate expertly applied brake pressure into the turn off the
dirt road and onto the highway. Three quarters of the way
into the turn and he had the throttle to the floor. Nate
knew how to drive.

"I'll have to slow down when we reach the bend. That
shithead Malloy sits there with his new toy."

Rick didn't know what he was talking about but
found out as they approached a bend in the road and Nate
hit the brakes, slowing to a respectable fifty-five. When
they rounded the curve, they saw a Palma City Trooper
sitting on his Harley with a radar gun pointed at them.

"Little shit really gets off with that thing," Nate said.

As they passed the trooper, Nate picked up the speed.

"Aren't you afraid he'll come after us?"

"Naw. He's too stupid to turn around."

Minutes later, doing fifty in a twenty-five, Nate spun
onto Main Street, speeding through the center of town
like he was on the freeway.

"I'll have you there in less than a minute." And true to
his word, the old man was slamming on the brakes, laying
rubber onto the pavement, bringing the truck to a stop
where the Palma Pier met the land.

"I got you here with twenty minutes to spare. Not
bad for an old man."

"And I appreciate it" Rick pulled a banded wad of bills
out of a hip pocket.

"That's a pile of money."

"And it's yours. There's ten thousand dollars here." He handed the banded bills to the old man.

"You don't have to give me all this. We had a deal."

"If I save the boy, it was worth it and if I don't, I won't need it."

"Well, we can use the money. That's a fact."

"One more thing,"

"What's that?"

"I probably won't be coming back for the plane."

"Don't worry, I'll handle it."

"I gotta go," Rick said, and the two men shook hands.

"You be careful, son."

"Yeah." Rick got out of the car and jogged down the pier toward the *Seawolf*.

CHAPTER TWENTY-TWO

RICK HEARD THE HUM OF THE MOTOR drop a key as its RPM was lowered. He spent the thirty minute trip from Palma to Tampico below, on one of the top bunks, pretending to be asleep. He counted himself lucky that he was able to buy a ticket, get on board and get below without running into Wolfe Stewart.

He didn't know if Wolfe knew the police were looking for him and, as much as he wanted the man's help, he couldn't afford to take the chance. It was better, he reasoned, to err on the side of caution.

He felt the boat slow to a stop and then reverse. Shortly, he heard the sounds of the crew above, tying the

Seawolf to the pier. And when he heard the sounds of the Tampico anglers boarding, he jumped out of the bunk and climbed the stairs into the morning sun. He glanced quickly around the boat and satisfied himself that Wolfe was still on the bridge. Then with a head-down-straight-arrow walk, he left the boat, passing the boarding anglers on the gangway. Nobody gave him a second glance .

Off the boat, he looked down the pier, toward town, half expecting to see an army of police with high-powered rifles trained on him. He was pleased to see instead, Judy Donovan running in his direction.

He jogged toward her, meeting her halfway. He put his arm around her waist and led her back toward town.

"I don't want anybody to know I'm back." He held her close, managing to hide his face from at least half of the people on the pier.

"I didn't tell anyone I was meeting you." Then she asked, "how did you know my phone was tapped?"

"Maybe it's not. I'm just a little paranoid. But when someone is running around killing off your friends and the police are trying to pin the murders on you, maybe being a little paranoid isn't such a bad thing."

"J.P.'s okay," she said.

"What?"

"Sheriff Sturgees called a little while ago. J.P. somehow wound up in Jesse Terrenova's police car out at Donkey Road and called for help. He sent Lincoln Hewett, one of his new, young deputies, out to get him."

"What about Jesse?" Rick asked.

"Probably goofing off somewhere with Stacy."

Rick shook his head. When they reached the end of the pier, she led him to the parking lot and a new Mitsubishi Montero.

"We can talk in the car." She unlocked the passenger

door. He climbed into the four-wheel-drive vehicle, stretched over and unlocked the driver's door for her and she climbed behind the wheel.

"New car?" he asked.

"I was on the way to the airport, when a sudden urge took me into the dealership. Before I knew what happened, I was driving out in a sporty, new four-wheel-drive SUV and I'd cancelled the Hawaiian vacation."

"When will J.P. be home?" he asked, watching as she ran her hands over the steering wheel. She'd put on his old, leather, wheel cover, the one Ann had given him so long ago.

"Maybe now," she said. "Sheriff Sturgees said that they would question him for about fifteen minutes, then bring him straight home."

"Aren't you in a hurry to see him?"

"By now he's with the sheriff, he'll be okay. Besides, I wanted to see you. And anyway, your note said you needed the gun." She handed him a leather overnight bag. "It's wrapped in a beach towel."

"Thanks." He wondered about the wheel cover. Why had she taken it off his Jeep?

"Come here, Flash." She pulled him close, reached out with a hand, brushed his hair aside as she ran her tongue along the length of the scar behind his left ear, sending shivers of temporary pleasure from the scar to his spine. "Does that still drive you crazy?

He pulled away shocked, trying to wipe what just happened from his mind. He didn't have time to think about it.

"I need you to do something for me," he said.

"Anything."

"Get Wolfe Stewart to hold the boat till I get back."

"How long will you be?"

"I don't know, an hour, maybe two, maybe longer. You'll have to get him to cancel his fishing trip. Tell him it's a matter of life and death. Tell him someone kidnapped J.P. Tell him Ann was murdered. And tell him when I come back to the boat, I'll have that son-of-a-bitch in tow."

"He'll hold the boat."

"You're sure?"

"That man would move heaven and earth for J.P. He'll hold the boat."

"And have him send the crew away. Just him and you on the boat. Nobody else. Will he do it?"

"He'll do it."

"Good. Now I need your car."

"I figured you would," she said, getting out.

He got out too, met her halfway to the driver's side and they embraced.

"Be careful," she said.

He kissed her briefly on the lips, "I'll be careful." He broke the embrace, climbed into the car and drove off. He saw her walking down the pier toward the boat in the rearview and smiled as she held her arm up high and waved. She knew he was looking.

He drove half a block down the street, then pulled over and parked. Making sure that nobody was looking, he fished into the bag and withdrew the thirty-eight. A quick inspection told him that Judy had reloaded. Then a strong feeling attacked, like an inner voice, and it was telling him that he needed a bigger gun.

He put the revolver back into the overnight bag, checked the rearview to make sure he was still unobserved, got out of the car and started down Seaview Avenue toward Jaspinder Singh's Mini Market and Bait Shop.

So many questions. Why had his friends been murdered? Why had J.P. been kidnapped? How had he gotten away? What had he done to cause it all? And now, why had Judy kissed him like that, running her tongue along his scar and why had she called him Flash? He decided to put it all out of his mind and focus on the one thing he could do, and that was find the man who was responsible, and stop him.

"Rick Gordon, I am truly glad to see you," Jaspinder Singh said, the golden bells announcing Rick's arrival as he entered the bait and convenience store.

"I'm in a little trouble and I need a favor."

"The sheriff has been telling me about your troubles. They are really looking for you. But I am believing none of it."

"I was hoping I could count on you."

"If you could be counting on nobody else on this God-forsaken planet, you could be counting on me."

"You know why they're looking for me?"

"They think you are a murderer."

"I think the real murderer killed Ann and he's going to come after me sometime today."

"How can I be helping?"

"Six months ago you had a very big gun behind your cash register. Do you still have it?

Jaspinder Singh reached down to the shelf under the register and brought out an automatic pistol. He laid it on the counter in front of Rick.

"Yeah, that's a big gun." Rick said.

"It's a Para Ordinance forty-five automatic, made in Canada. It carries five more rounds than the Colt, thirteen in the magazine, one in the chamber. It is fully loaded with Starfire PMC Eldorado hollow points for maximum penetration and expansion. They will stop anything short of an elephant."

"You keep a round chambered?"

"And the safety off. When I am wanting to use it, I am wanting it ready. Take it." He pushed the gun toward Rick.

Rick took it, clicked on the safety and shoved the gun between his Levi's and his skin. His loose shirt easily concealed the weapon. Then he reached into his back pocket and withdrew the other packet of bills. "There's ten thousand dollars here, if anything happens to me, I want you to use it to get Judy Donovan and J.P. as far away from here as possible."

"You are afraid that they will wind up like Mr. Donovan and his family?"

"Yes."

"I will do as you ask." Singh took the money.

"Thank you, Mr. Singh."

"Good luck, Rick." in their relationship, both professional and personal, it was the first time he had addressed him by his first name. "Oh, yes, this might be helping." Singh reached back to the shelf under the register. "You might be needing an extra magazine."

Rick took it and slipped it into the bag, then he stuck his hand out and Jaspinder Singh shook it.

"If you don't hear from me by this evening, get them out of town tomorrow." Then he turned and opened the door, setting off the three golden bells as he left.

On his way back to the car, Rick cleared his mind of everything, but the moment. The sun was rising, changing from orange to yellow, and brightening the day. The soft breeze carrying the scent of the sea came in from the ocean and the gentle sound of lapping waves competed with the occasional passing car. Any other time he would have taken in the air and enjoyed the morning to its fullest, but today he tried to clear even the sunrise and ocean air from his mind.

And, as he forced everything out, he felt one thought sticking and he concentrated on it till it screamed and he knew where the big man was. He had come to Tampico to humiliate him one last time, before sticking in the knife, and the best place to find him was at home. The man with the gravel voice was most likely sitting in his living room, waiting to jump him as soon as he walked in the front door.

But before confronting the killer, he wanted to go up to Prospector's Donkey Road and make sure J.P. was okay.

Five minutes later, he turned from Mountain Sea onto the dirt track, slowing the car when he left the pavement. He drove up and parked behind one of the two police cars and felt a pang in his chest when he saw they were both empty. There was no sign of the deputies or of J.P. He feared the worst.

With the forty-five auto in hand, he got out of Judy's new SUV and started toward the path. He clicked the safety off and kept his finger on the trigger. He couldn't help feeling like he was walking into an ambush.

He heard a rustling in the brush off to his left and stopped, pointing the gun in the general direction of the sound.

"J.P., Lincoln, Jesse!" he called out. The rustling stopped. "It's Rick Gordon." He waited for a long twenty seconds and getting no answer, continued on toward Lover's Hideaway.

A low growl stopped him in his tracks. He crouched low and waited. There was something out there. His mind raced back to the day Judy had been chased by the bear and how J.P. had insisted that he'd fired the revolver at the Ghost Dog, not a bear.

He waited a few more seconds and hearing no further sound, got up and continued. Then he tripped over something. He threw his hands out in front of himself to break his fall. He hit hard, twisting his arm, spraining his wrist and losing the pistol.

"Damn!" He turned and started to get up and came face to face with Lincoln Hewett's bloody head. "Shit!" He scrambled back.

The horrible head, eyes screaming wide, stared into the sky with an unfathomable fear frozen onto its face, daring Rick to go further, but he no choice, he had to know what had happened to J.P.

He looked around for the gun, trying not to look at Lincoln's staring eyes. He couldn't find it. He stepped back and saw why. It was lying next to the dead deputy's head, with blood on the grip. When he dropped the gun it must have landed on the head and bounced off. He grit his teeth, picked it up, wiped the blood off on his Levi's.

He was stepping around the head when he heard the low growl. Something was on the path behind him. He turned and pointed the gun down the path, but there was nothing there except silence.

He turned back toward Lover's Hideaway, moving as quickly as possible, rapid heartbeat, tense nerves and clammy skin betraying his fear. When he plunged into the clearing, his horror at the bloody sight sent him reeling backwards and he had to fight to keep from running away.

He turned away from Lincoln's headless body. He didn't need to inspect it to know he had been maimed and killed by a big animal. He picked up a khaki shirt and dropped it. He saw Jesse Terrenova's automatic and picked it up. It was empty. He tossed it aside, and with pain in his heart, he saw J.P.'s Levi's and the striped shirt that he'd been wearing yesterday.

He sank to his knees.

"Not J.P., too," he cried. Grief overcame him. He loved that boy. It was like his own son had been ripped from his breast by starving wolves. He had been dealt deep wounds, piled on, one after another until now he began to believe what the killer had said in his note.

He was damned.

His friends and lovers were being torn from him in the most brutal of ways and he was unable to stop it. Now he was going to have to face Judy and tell her that her son was dead. He didn't know if he could do it.

He felt eyes on him.

He looked up through his tears and saw what could only be both J.P.'s Ghost Dog and Ann's beautiful, horrible animal. It was a long way from Australia. The animal stared at him, unmoving, and Rick took the time to study it.

The beautiful black coat that Ann had told him about was now matted with blood. Rick assumed that the deputy had gotten off some good shots. The beast was wounded, but still very much a threat.

Rick tightened his grip on the forty-five as the animal stepped into the clearing and lowered itself, ears back, onto its haunches, like it was going to leap. He raised the gun and started firing. He missed, but the animal turned and fled, vanishing in a hail of bullets pinging in the earth behind it and slapping into the bushes and trees over its shoulders.

Rick kept firing into the brush until the gun was empty, hoping that he might have gotten in a lucky hit, then he jammed the hot gun back in his pants and scooted over to where Lincoln's headless body lay and tore the thirty-eight police special from its holster. It wouldn't do the damage of a forty-five, but it could kill just as deadly.

He remained still and listened for the animal's deep breathing and, hearing nothing, he made his way to the path. He wanted to get back to the car. He moved swiftly with the thirty-eight clutched tightly in his right hand. If he fell again, he was determined not to lose the gun.

Halfway back to the car, he heard a heart stopping roar coming from the direction of the clearing. He heard the beast as it started down the path after him. He stopped, crouched and waited.

He didn't have to wait long, within what seemed fractions of a second the beast was in sight charging down the path. Rick started firing, hitting the animal several times, not only stopping it but forcing it to turn and flee again. And Rick fled also, continuing his dash toward the car.

Running full tilt with not far to go, he heard the beast crashing through the brush, parallel to him and overtaking him. He fired two rapid shots, without slowing, in the direction of the crashing sounds. They were panic shots, serving only to quicken his already frantic pace, but the beast beat him to the cars. When he reached the end of the path, it was standing by the Montero, its black coat covered in wet blood and it was foaming at the mouth.

It roared into the morning, then started for him.

Rick fired on the move, but the hammer fell on an empty cylinder. The weapon was empty. He dashed for one of the police cruisers, grabbed the door, dove in and slammed it shut.

The beast pounced, smashing its head into the safety glass of the passenger window. The glass cracked into hundreds of small bloody pieces, held together by only the safety film, but it held. The black beast bounced off and readied itself for another charge. Rick knew the glass wouldn't stop it a second time.

He ripped the riot gun from its rack, clicked off the safety, pumped a round into the chamber and fired as the beast's head hit the glass for a second time, deafening him and shattering the glass outward, turning the black beast's head into bloody mush.

He didn't wait to see what it would do next. He jumped out on the driver's side, pumped a second round into the chamber, dashed around the car, fired again into the bloody pulp that was the beast's head. He emptied the remaining three rounds into its chest at point blank range.

And then he collapsed, fighting for breath. The Ghost Dog was dead.

CHAPTER TWENTY-THREE

J.P. WOKE SITTING UP. He tried to move, but it hurt his neck. He opened his eyes to a glaring light and studied his surroundings in a way that wouldn't have occurred to him just forty-eight hours ago.

He was in Rick Gordon's upstairs bathroom, in the bathtub and he was naked. His hands were again tied behind his back and his bruised feet were lashed together in the same manner as they were when he had been held captive in the trunk.

He was horribly thirsty and the tub was full of warm water, but he was unable to drink. He couldn't move his head. His neck was in a noose and tied to the hot and cold water handles. The water to quench his thirst was so close and yet so far.

He tried to scream and discovered that again his mouth was taped. He inhaled through his nose, trying to calm himself, as he studied the bathroom in search of something that could aid in his escape. He found nothing. Then in the soap dish, his eyes locked on a small compact mirror sitting on top of a well used bar of soap. He wondered if it was Ann's and he wondered if he could break it and use a piece of the sharp glass to cut his way through the ropes.

Maybe, if he pulled his knees into his stomach, he could straighten his legs, and maybe, just maybe, if he was lucky, he could knock the mirror off its perch, and it would fall into the tub.

He moved back, pressing his back up against the faucet, tucking in his knees. The faucet dug into his back, but he forced himself to ignore the pain. He straightened his legs and rocked on his behind, thrusting his foot toward the soap dish.

He missed, but not by much.

He was getting ready to try again, when he heard the heavy steps coming up the hardwood stairs. He didn't have to play twenty questions to know who was coming. He lay his legs back down and braced himself for the worst. Then he realized that the Ragged Man was going to see him naked.

But of course he had already seen him without his clothes on, otherwise how did he get to be tied up naked in the tub. He didn't like the idea at all. Why did he have to be naked? He didn't like people to see him naked. He hated it when his mother came into the bathroom when he was in the tub. He always covered himself with a washcloth and pleaded with her to leave. It wasn't funny, but she always laughed.

He hoped the Ragged Man wasn't going to laugh. He hoped the Ragged Man wasn't going to do anything at all.

He heard the footsteps as they left the stairs and made their way down the hall, coming toward the bathroom, coming toward him. He heard the doorknob turn and click, sending his heart through his throat. The door opened, a squeaky hinge screeching like chalk on a blackboard, sending shivers of fear along his spine. He wanted to shrink inside of himself, to make himself invisible, to vanish like a ghost in the woodwork, but he couldn't. All he could do was wait in the tub, naked, and face his fear.

He stared up at the man as he entered the bathroom. He wanted to close his eyes, but the last time he did that, it made the man mad and that was the last thing he wanted to do.

"So, you're awake." The man walked over to the washbasin and studied himself in the mirror. Then he turned to look at J.P. "You know how it is, children should be seen and not heard. And I can see an awful lot of you."

J.P. turned red.

"Ah, embarrassed, are we? What's the matter? Don't like showing off your little pecker?" He bent over, so that J.P. could smell his foul breath, and shoved his hand under the water, flicking his finger against J.P.'s limp penis.

J.P. jumped and squirmed against the noose.

"Relax, I'm not a baby raper. I might slit your throat and peel off your skin, but I'll leave your little peepee alone." He laughed, a raspy, insincere sound that chalked his spine worse than the squeaky hinge.

"I'll bet you want to know what I have in store for

you. Well, you're about to find out."

The man left the bathroom and J.P. heard him go down the stairs and fumble around down there. He felt nothing but dread when he heard the footsteps coming back again. J.P. had no idea what the man had in mind, but he knew it was bad.

"What I have here," the man said, "Is your basic digital timer. I'm setting it to go off at, oh what's a good time, how about noon, that sound good to you? It sounds good to me." He plugged the timer into the wall with the bright red read-out facing the tub.

"Now, I'm going to plug the extension into the back of the timer." J.P. watched him do it. "And now, I'm going to plug the radio into the extension cord." J.P. watched him do it. "And now, the fun part, I turn the radio on." J.P. watched him do it. "But oh, no," the man said, feigning surprise, "the radio didn't come on. Oh, yeah, it won't come on till high noon, when the timer goes off. Can you guess what I'm going to do with the radio?"

J.P. opened his eyes wide, telling the man how frightened he was.

"Smart boy, I'm gonna put the radio in the tub."

J.P. watched him as he set the radio in the tub, two feet from his feet.

"At twelve, when the timer clicks on, you can kiss your naked ass goodbye." the Ragged Man laughed.

J.P. squirmed, but the noose held him firmly in place.

"Who knows. You're a clever lad. You got away last time, maybe you'll get lucky."

The big man clomped out of the bathroom, closing the door on his way out. J.P. heard him thud down the hallway and down the stairs. He heard the front door slam a few seconds later. He was alone with the radio.

He wondered what station it was tuned to. Would he be electrocuted by The Rolling Stones, Weezer, The Black Crowes or by Rush Limbaugh? No, probably during the news, then later he would be the news. "Naked boy electrocuted in bathtub, film at eleven."

"Naked," would be the highlight. They would make it a big deal that he was naked. Policemen, reporters, his mother, strangers, maybe friends, maybe even girls, would all see him naked. He didn't want to be found naked.

He didn't want his friends at school to laugh after he was dead. And he especially didn't want his teacher to know that he died naked. It was bad enough that he had to die, but it was so embarrassing to be tied up without his clothes on, and he was so humiliated, because that big ugly man had touched him down there, between his legs. Nobody should be able to do that. It was wrong, and he started to cry.

He was so tired. Nobody could blame him if he just gave up. He was thirsty again and the water in the tub only served to tell him how dry his throat could get. He was hungry and he felt like he was starting to get sick, like the time when he had the two day flu.

A quick note of terror struck his heart. He threw up when he had the flu. He threw up a lot. If he threw up with his mouth taped, he would die, drowned in his own vomit. Well, he didn't throw up in the trunk and he'd try not to throw up now. But he wondered, if he was sick, if he had the two day flu, would he be able not to throw up? He was more scared than ever.

But everything wasn't as bad as it could have been. The warm water felt good against his aching sides and his cut and bruised feet.

And the soothing warm water called to him to close his eyes and relax. Maybe Rick would come home in time.

Maybe he'd fight and kill the Ragged Man and come upstairs and save him before noon, but maybe he wouldn't. Maybe the timer wouldn't work, but it probably would. Maybe he should lay back in the warm water and give up, but maybe he shouldn't.

He didn't want to be found naked.

He looked down at the radio and stretched his feet toward it till the noose was digging into his neck, choking him. There was no way. The closest he could get was still a foot away, twelve big inches.

He decided to try for the mirror again. He scooted back, easing the noose and brought his knees to his chest again, rocked on his butt and smashed his feet into the wall. Better luck. His foot banged the wall just under the soap dish, as searing pain splashed up his leg.

He screamed against the tape, then clenched his teeth. A winner never quits. He pulled his knees back till they almost touched his nose, straightened his legs, bent his foot back, rocked his body and this time, instead of smashing his battered feet into the wall, he faced it, with his foot on the wall above the soap dish. Then he inched it down till his bent back foot was resting on the top of it.

He closed his eyes and jerked his foot down, managing to just touch the mirror, before the stretching pain caused him to relax and his legs fall back into the tub. He was downhearted. He had given it his best, his very best effort. Now there truly was no hope. He was destined to die in the bathtub, alone and naked. It wasn't fair, he thought, to have a means of escape so close. It wasn't fair. It wasn't fair. It wasn't fair. Then he looked at the soap dish and gave a quick gasp of surprise.

It was empty.

He had succeeded after all. He started to feel around the tub for the mirror. It didn't take long for him to discover that it had fallen out of the reach of his bound hands. If he lay his legs out flat against the tub he could feel it between the white porcelain and the back of his right knee. Too far to reach by hand and too close for him to use his feet to pull it toward him.

But he had come too far to give up. He raised his legs and scooted down as far as the noose would let him. Then he lowered his legs onto the small mirror. This time it was sitting a little higher under his leg and when he scooted back, letting the faucet dig into his back, he dragged the mirror a little closer to his hands.

He repeated the process, raising his legs, scooting toward the radio, lowering his legs, scooting back toward the faucet two more times, and after the third effort he was able to reach and grasp the mirror.

He closed his eyes and tensed up as he smashed it against the porcelain, breaking it into several pieces and cutting a deep gash into his right thumb. The stabbing pain and immediate red coloration of the water sent thunderclaps of terror through him. He had seen a movie once where a woman had slashed her wrists and bled to death in a bathtub. The red tinged water in the movie bathtub looked just like the red tinged water in the real bathtub.

Frantically, he felt around for a piece of glass big enough to saw through the rope and discovered to his horror that there were several tiny, very sharp slivers of glass covering the bottom of the tub and every movement he made sent one of the slivers stinging into his skin, but there were no pieces large enough. He had expended the effort to get the mirror and cut himself for nothing.

All for nothing.

* * *

Sam Storm went down the stairs with heavy feet and dark thoughts, head bent in sadness. The Black Beauty was dead. When its spirit left its body, Storm felt a sense of loss that killed much of his resolve, and he began to feel uneasy. He had done terrible things, foul unspeakable deeds, things against the laws of God and Man, things that violated his very nature, but they were things he had enjoyed doing, wrong as they were, God help him, he had enjoyed it. Part of him wanted to quit, but he had to go through with what he had started. There was no other way.

Downstairs, he went to the coffee table in the living room, opened his satchel and took out the Bowie knife. He ran his thumb along the blade as if testing the sharp edge, but a force he didn't understand made him apply too much pressure and the knife sliced through to the bone, sending a wakeup call of sharp pain from the sharp blade.

The sight of his own blood snapped him back to his purpose. He wrapped his bloody hand around the hilt and walked through the kitchen, out the back door and down the landing, stomping on every step as he headed toward the pigeon cage.

The birds quieted their billing and cooing as he left the landing and stopped completely as he neared the cage. By the time he was standing in front of the loft, they were cautiously eyeing him, silent sentinels alert at their posts.

What was there about him, he asked himself, that made the birds eye him so suspiciously.

"I'm not going to hurt you," he lied.

The birds responded by cocking their heads, as if listening intently.

"I just want a look." He wondered what it was about pigeons that could fascinate a young boy. When he was a child his parents hadn't allowed pets and he hadn't missed them. Not until the Black Beauty had come into his life. The black animal had been the first pet, if he could call it a pet, that he'd ever had. He had been able to understand the animal as he'd never been able to understand a human. The animal had been more friend than any he had ever known, and he missed it.

Then something bucked up his courage, or rather reinforced whatever it was that caused him to do the horrible things. He eased the door of the loft open and slid into the cage, making sure none of the birds got out.

With a methodical and mercenary deliberation, he systematically slaughtered all twenty-six of J.P. Donovan's pigeons, by using the knife, like a giant sword, against their tiny heads. The birds, frozen in place, sat like ducks in a shooting gallery with the motor off, waiting for the blade to fall.

Then, with the bodies of the headless birds and their heads strewn about the sandy bottom of the loft and his feet covered in their blood, Sam Storm stood and contemplated what he had done and what he was about to do. He had killed so many and part of him wanted to go on killing, but another part wanted to stop, to fade into the sunset. Jamaica maybe, or the south of France. But before he could do any fading, he had to finish Rick Gordon.

He stepped through the bloody mess and exited the loft, not bothering to close the door, and stalked back into the house, leaving blood-red footprints in his wake. There was plenty of the red stuff left on his shoes for the carpet to soak up when he entered the dining room on his way to the stairs.

On the second floor, he poked his head into the bathroom to check on the boy. He smiled as the frightened youth looked up at him from bloody bath water with his eyes wide in horror.

"I killed your birds," he said. Then he went back downstairs to wait for Rick Gordon.

* * *

Rick Gordon pulled up the driveway. He wanted to kick the front door down and go in like Bob Dylan's John Wesley Harding, with a gun in every hand, all of them blazing, but he knew that would be stupid.

He shut the engine off, looked at the house and listened. It was too quiet. He got out of the car, keeping his eyes locked on the front door, went around to the passenger side, took out the forty-five, ejected the spent magazine, reloading with the fresh one, before shoving it between his Levi's and the small of his back. He picked up Lincoln Hewett's thirty-eight and reloaded from a box of shells he'd found in Lincoln's glovebox, then he stuffed it into a back pocket. Next he picked up the riot gun and jacked five shells into it, also found in Lincoln's glovebox. Then clutching the shotgun, he started toward the house.

He approached the front door, alert and cautious, taking the steps up to the porch, like a soldier walking into an ambush. He turned the knob slowly, threw the door open when the latch clicked and leapt into the living room, diving onto the carpet and rolling toward the coffee table.

He met no resistance. He got up, trying to shake some of the fear. Maybe he had been wrong and there was no killer at home. He started to relax, when he heard a crashing noise from behind, near the fireplace.

He turned and blasted two rounds out of the pump gun, one into the mirror above the fireplace and one through the adjoining window, blowing the glass out. He jumped back as a small, black kitten darted past and ran through the dining room into the kitchen. The crashing noise had been caused by the cat knocking a soapstone sculpture off the mantle above the fireplace.

A scraping noise from somewhere in back of him sent a warning tingling up his spine. He turned and pumped a round into Ann's antique rocker, blowing a twelve inch hole through the straight wooden back, sending splinters and pellets into the wall behind.

Someone had been in the house. When he left, he had locked it tight. There was no possible way that cat could have gotten in by itself. He turned toward the fireplace, heard a loud tortured cat-kitten scream from behind and once again he whirled around, pumping the shotgun, shooting from the hip.

The first shell smashed into the dining room table and the second blew apart the television, exploding it in a hail of sound and glass, causing him to pump and dry fire. The riot gun was empty.

The cat darted across the room and he threw the shotgun at it, missing by five or six feet. He cursed. Somehow the kitten had caused him to empty the riot gun, depriving him of his best weapon.

The kitten dashed into the kitchen. Rick decided to follow. He drew the forty-five and moved across the carpet toward the dining room. He stepped past the damaged rocker and the destroyed television, stepping around broken glass. In the dining room, he smiled at the crystal vase sitting on the center of the badly mauled table. Ann bought the vase in Prague, and during her life, had kept it full of flowers. By some miracle it survived the shotgun blast to the table and he took it as a sign that he would survive, too.

He skirted the table, eyes on the vase, and something

hard, soft, sticky and wet slammed into the side of his face with gale force.

He jumped back from the headless pigeon as he emptied all thirteen shots from the forty-five into the empty kitchen, screaming louder than the deadly roar of the bucking pistol. When he was out of ammunition and silence again reigned, he realized the kitchen was empty. Whoever threw the bird had used his pitching arm from the back landing, sending the headless Dark Dancer flying in through the back door, through the kitchen, into the dining room.

He dropped the forty-five onto the carpet and withdrew the thirty-eight from his hip pocket and warily entered the kitchen to find that he had killed both the microwave and the blender and had severely wounded the refrigerator.

* * *

J.P. heard a car pull into the drive downstairs and felt a surge of short-lived relief. His first thought was that his mother had come to save him, but his second thought quickly pushed the first aside. If his mother came into Rick's house the Ragged Man would get her, and who could tell what horrible things he would do to her. He hoped she would back the car out of the drive and go away. His heart sank when he heard the engine cut off.

Only moments ago he thought things couldn't get worse. He sat in the water that wasn't warm anymore, looking at the digital clock, frozen in fright. At 8:44 the Ragged Man poked his head in the door, stinging him with a quick penetrating stare that scared the living shit out of him, and now his mother had arrived just in time to be the Ragged Man's next victim.

He sat in the water and listened to the silence. If there

was only a way out. Again he looked around the bathroom. There had to be something. There had to be. He figured a way out of the trunk against impossible odds and anybody that could figure their way out of that, could figure their way out of this. In the trunk he had only minutes to act. Here he had till noon, but maybe not that long. Maybe the Ragged Man had lied and was going to kill him sooner. And maybe he was going to kill his mom now.

His heart screamed as he struggled, trying to slip his hands through the ropes, but they wouldn't give.

He started to get an idea and a glimmer of hope began to inspire him. Then he heard two loud explosions. He stopped his struggle, confused and scared. Had the Ragged Man killed his mother or had his mother killed the Ragged Man? He screamed against the tape, but he knew the weak sound wasn't able to penetrate the bathroom walls.

Another explosion followed by a loud screech and two more explosions. It sounded like a battle was going on downstairs. It wasn't his mother down there. It was Rick. Rick had come to save him. Rick was fighting the Ragged Man. He hoped that the Ragged Man was losing and losing big time.

He checked the clock. 8:47. A lot had happened in just three minutes, he thought, and he was beginning to hope that maybe he would be saved after all, when he heard several rapid gunshots, followed by more silence.

CHAPTER
TWENTY-FOUR

RICK, THIRTY-EIGHT IN HAND, ran through the kitchen to the back landing. Panting, he studied the landscape and saw nothing out of the ordinary, and again he thought it was too quiet, but he couldn't put his mind on what was wrong.

He ran his eyes over the edge of his property to the woods beyond, and then he trained them on the Donovan house. Judy's back door was open.

He had the killer on the run, but why didn't the killer blow him away when he drove up the drive, or when he entered the house, or when he stood in the living room and emptied the shotgun into windows and walls? And why challenge him with a dead pigeon when a bullet would have been much more effective?

At first Rick thought the killer was toying with him, playing a deadly game of cat and mouse, but then the truth flashed before him. The killer didn't have a gun.

All of the murders had been committed with a knife. Maybe the killer had an aversion to guns or maybe he just plain enjoyed using the Bowie knife. In either case, the end result was the same. He was facing a clever killer who had managed to sucker him into firing at air and now his big guns, the riot gun and forty-five were useless.

Staring at Judy's back door, he was reminded of the kiss and the unanswered questions that it posed. How had she known to run her tongue along his scar and why had she called him Flash? Ann, and only Ann, would have done those things. Ann, and only Ann, he thought.

He needed to see Judy again. He needed to ask her about the kiss. He needed to ask her about Ann. But first he needed to deal with the Ragged Man. And now he had no doubt, the killer was the Ragged Man.

He took the steps from his landing to the ground below, one hand on the rail, the other holding the thirty-eight, but he kept his finger off the trigger. He had been suckered into using up his starting offense and he didn't plan on throwing away his last quarterback.

On the ground, he made his way to the loft, then he knew what had bothered him earlier. He had become used to the billing and cooing of J.P.'s pigeons. It took him awhile to miss the sound of the birds, but he missed it now.

When he got closer to the cage, he saw why. The bastard had killed them all.

He tightened his hand on the butt of the gun as he passed the cage, making sure he took in the horrible sight.

He didn't want to forget it. When he caught the son-of-a-bitch, he wanted to make him pay. Pay for the birds. Pay for J.P. Pay for Ann. Pay for his friends. He wanted the bastard to pay and pay and pay, and then he wanted him to pay some more.

He went up Judy's landing, the way he'd gone down his, one hand on the rail the other holding the gun out in front of himself, finger next to the trigger, but not on it. He would be hard to fool this time.

He cautiously peered into the laundry room and recoiled. The washing machine and dryer were covered in blood and feathers. The walls had been smeared in the stuff and the remains of several mangled, headless bird bodies covered the floor.

Clenching his teeth, he waded into the laundry room, avoiding the rent and torn bodies. He moved as quickly as he could, without slipping on the blood-greased tile. In the kitchen, he saw red footprints going into the dining room and he followed, inserting his finger inside the trigger guard. He didn't want to be fooled again, but he didn't want to be caught off guard either.

In the dining room, he saw that the carpet had soaked the blood from the Ragged Man's shoes as it was soaking the blood off his. The footprints vanished by the time he reached the living room. He checked the front door and saw that it was locked with the latch thrown from the inside. The Ragged Man was still in the house.

He checked the downstairs den and the room Judy used as an office. Both empty with no signs of having been disturbed. The man had to be upstairs.

Again he grabbed onto a rail with the gun out in front. He was nervous, tense and excited. Every fiber of his being was awake and taut. He was ready to kill and he was ready to die. Either way, it made no difference.

At the top of the stairs, he checked J.P.'s bedroom, the bathroom, the guest bedroom, and last on his list, Judy's bedroom. He took in the room as he made his way to the closet. He opened the door and eyed her clothes. This was a woman's private place, with a woman's private things, and he had no business spending any time longer than necessary.

He started toward Judy's private bath, then stopped. An uneasy feeling crept up his spine and niggled at his mind. He hadn't checked the downstairs bath. He turned and hurried through the bedroom and down the stairs. When he reached the bottom, he knew that the Ragged Man had been hiding in the bathroom, for scrawled in blood on the living room wall were two words:

OUTSIDE MOTHERFUCKER

* * *

Sam Storm looked between the kitchen blinds and couldn't believe his eyes. Gordon had another gun. Where did the son of a bitch keep getting them? He tried to study the man's face. He wished he was close enough so that he could see his eyes. He wasn't sure, but the man didn't seem afraid.

He watched as Gordon made his way to the loft and inspected the scene inside. It seemed like he spent too much time studying the slaughter and it seemed like it didn't frighten him as it was designed to. When Gordon turned away from the loft and continued toward the house, Storm saw the determined set of his jaw, and when he closed the distance, he was able to see the cold-green hate radiating from his eyes, and Sam Storm was afraid.

He didn't mind killing, but he didn't want to die. Not now, not ever, and he didn't want Gordon to win this battle. Caution was called for, so when he heard Gordon's steps on the back landing, he jumped into the half-bath that adjoined the kitchen and hid in the small shower, drawing the curtains.

He hated the fact that he was cowering like a girl, but there was something about Gordon that he hadn't counted on. A fierce determination. Somehow the man had gotten past the police roadblocks and into town. Somehow he'd managed to acquire an awesome amount of firepower. And somehow he'd had managed to turn Sam Storm's spine into jelly.

He had become convinced there was nothing left, alive or dead, that could frighten him, and the thought that he was frightened of Gordon threatened to loosen his bowels.

He felt more than heard Gordon enter the house and pass by his hiding place. He shivered, unable to move. He leaned back against the tile wall and wished the man would go away, but he knew he wouldn't.

After what seemed forever, he heard footsteps overhead and he knew Gordon was upstairs. He left the shower covered in sweat and a foul odor and, not wanting to seem the complete coward, he went to the service porch and wiped his hand in the blood. Then he went to the living room and wrote his message on the wall. A challenge he didn't intend to keep.

Let Gordon search outside to his heart's content. He wouldn't find him, because Sam Storm was going to be long gone.

He hastily left the house out the back way, starting toward the woods, when something caught his eye.

Movement by the loft.

A baby black cat was in the loft, feasting on the carnage. Storm studied the scene and drew comfort from it. For a moment he forgot about Gordon upstairs as he approached the loft to watch. The small animal stopped its gorging as Storm approached and locked its baby black eyes onto Storm, and for a darting instant, they flashed red and Storm knew he wasn't alone anymore, and he knew he wasn't going to run away from Rick Gordon.

* * *

Rick looked away from the gruesome message and started toward the kitchen. He took in the new set of footprints and saw where the Ragged Man had smeared his hand in the pigeon blood. Without a thought, he crossed through the bloody mess, this time ignoring it, and stepped out onto the back landing.

This time there was no hesitation on his part and he didn't grab the rail as he jumped down the steps. He moved in a crouch to the center of the clearing, studying both houses and the loft. Seeing no sign of life, he made his way to the clearing's edge and started to walk the perimeter, looking for a sign.

He didn't have to look hard. The Ragged Man had marked the spot with one of the remaining birds. The dead pigeon was laying on the ground with its wings spread and a severed head six inches from the body, acting as a pointer, pointing to the path Judy took every morning to the beach.

Rick noticed that the red-check head didn't match the blue-bar body and he felt a second's sorrow for the two dead animals as he passed their remains and stepped onto the path.

He moved quickly down it, figuring that the Ragged Man was making his way to the beach. He felt eyes upon him. He turned, a turn that saved his life. Something slammed into him, knocking him down and sending the gun flying. He felt cold steel slice into his shoulder, where an instant ago his neck had been.

He rolled away from his assailant, tried to get up, but the Ragged Man grabbed him by the foot with his left hand and sliced into his leg with his right. Rick kicked at the hand holding his bleeding leg with his free leg. The Ragged Man jumped back, screaming, and both men scrambled to their feet. Rick darted his eyes around the clearing searching for the gun and found it, but the big man blocked his path. Both men were panting hard and Rick was losing blood.

The Ragged Man lunged for him, swinging the knife. Rick dodged back and, standing on his good leg, kicked the big man in the balls. The Ragged Man grunted, stepping back, temporarily disabled, staggering. Rick was too weak to deliver much force behind the kick.

The man fell, moaning, and Rick started to move in to finish him, but stopped his attack when he saw why the man had gone down. He was feigning injury to distract Rick. He had fallen toward the gun, was reaching for it as Rick turned and left the path, thrashing into the woods seconds before a bullet whizzed over his head.

The man didn't fire a second time, because in his frenzy to put distance between him and the armed man, Rick had vanished into the thick woods.

"I've got the gun now!" the man boomed into the forest.

Rick didn't answer.

"It's only a matter of time before I get you."

Rick still didn't answer.

"I spent two years in Vietnam tracking VC. You're no match for me!" the Ragged Man shouted.

Rick took off his shirt and checked his shoulder. He had been lucky, the cut wasn't deep and the blood was light, not dark. His leg was a different matter. He was pumping too much blood out of the injury for it to be a mere flesh wound. He tore the shirt into two strips and knotted them together. Then he tied it around his leg as tightly as he dared.

With the makeshift tourniquet in place, he started through the woods, not sure of his direction, but hoping he was circling back toward the clearing and away from the Ragged Man. He was going to have to live to fight another day.

"I see you!"

A bullet slammed into a tree six inches from his head. Rick turned into the woods with renewed energy.

After two minutes of desperate flight with brush and branch whipping against his bare skin, he stopped to listen. The man didn't appear to be following, and if what the man had said about Vietnam was true, it didn't make any sense, because he was leaving a trail a blind man could follow.

"I still see you."

Rick was moving before the two quick shots were fired. He didn't know where they landed and he didn't turn to look. He just moved, tearing through the growth.

Another minute of full-bore flight and he stopped to rest again, grabbing a few deep breaths, then he started breaking trail. The son-of-a-bitch was going to have to be in excellent shape to keep up with him.

And as he ran, he thought, three shots fired, three shots left. Maybe two could play the game. Maybe he could get the man to use all his ammunition. New hope coursed through him as he pushed on through the woods. He was lost, but not down, and not out. He heard a car pass by and he knew the road was up ahead. He continued on, struggling through the pines, until he was on the pavement, about a quarter mile below his house.

Without stopping to rest, he started up the road. In a few minutes he would be home. He could take the Montero and drive to town, where he figured he could buy a shotgun at the sporting goods store and enough shells to finish the job. Three minutes to the car, five minutes to town, five minutes to buy the gun, five minutes back. Eighteen minutes and he would be ready to do battle again.

He was halfway home when he heard the big man's booming laughter and a bullet slammed into his already sliced shoulder, knocking him down. He rolled and pushed himself up, fighting the pain, and made like a jack rabbit, sprinting toward home.

As he came into the driveway, he heard another shot and a distant part of his mind said, One bullet left, only one bullet left.

He reached the Montero, grabbed onto the door latch, pulled the driver's door open. He fumbled in his pockets for the keys, found them, bent over the steering wheel, and with a hand steadier than it had a right to be, inserted the key into the ignition, but before he could crank it over a bullet flew through the front passenger's window, slicing into his right shoulder, lancing along his back to his left, leaving a foot and a half graze along his back before it smashed out the driver's window and lodge into the front porch.

And a lightning thought flashed through the haze. He had another gun. He reached into the bag Judy had given him and withdrew her thirty-eight. Then he opened the driver's door and fell like a dead man onto the driveway, clutching the gun to his chest.

He lay, playing possum, for a half-minute that seemed like half a lifetime, before he heard the sound of the

Ragged Man's hard shoes scraping against the pavement. He waited until he felt the big man's shadow cover his body.

"Fuck you!" He rolled onto his back as he fired the pistol into the man's right thigh.

The big man screamed and fell back, landing on his ass.

Rick forced himself up and staggered over to the man who had done so much killing.

"I should kill you now, but I'm more afraid of you dead than alive." Rick saw the quizzical look on the man's face. "You don't understand, do you?"

The man didn't answer.

"My plan is to take you out to sea, about a mile or so, and to toss you in while you're still breathing. By the time you die, I'll be long gone and you'll be all alone. All alone with nobody around, nobody to possess. You'll die a final death and then you'll be nothing but shark bait."

The man's eyes lit up.

Rick lowered the pistol and blew off the man's left knee cap.

The Ragged Man rolled on the ground, screaming in pain until Rick brought the butt of the pistol down on his head, knocking him out.

He checked his pulse and, satisfied the man was still alive, dragged him to the rear of the Montero. Breathing heavily, he opened the back and put up the back seat. Then calling on all of his reserves, he picked up the Ragged Man like a sack of stones and stuffed him into the back, closing the door on him with no more regard than he'd have for dead fish.

Then he drove down the hill toward the pier.

* * *

J.P. heard the car start and felt a lump build in his throat. Was Rick dead or was he leaving without him? No matter which, it wasn't fair. He had been through too much to die naked in a bathtub.

He looked at the clock, 9:50. He had two hours and ten minutes to figure a way out of the mess he was in and he had to do it himself, all by himself, because he was alone, all alone.

He tried twisting his wrists against the rope to no avail. The Ragged Man had tied it too tight. With all his might he struggled to pull his right hand loose, but only succeeded in further bruising his already bruised and cut hands.

Then he tried stretching to see if he could reach the radio. It was a no go. He was still an easy foot shy. In frustration, he raised his bound legs and brought them down in the tub, splashing water, and he splashed again and again and again, sending the red tinged water splattering through out the bathroom. Tired, he dropped his legs and his right foot hit something in the tub.

The soap.

If he could get the soap he could use it to slicken up his hands, and maybe then he could slide them through the ropes.

He used his feet to drag the soap up to where he could stretch and reach it with his hands. Then he raised his hands out of the water and started spreading the soap around. On his hands, on his wrists and on the rope. He rubbed until he had a good lather and then, clenching his teeth against the pain, forced his right thumb under the palm of his hand, till it was pushed firmly against the little finger, and he slowly and firmly pulled.

He felt the rope pulling and scraping against him and it hurt like someone was scraping hot chunks of glass across his skin, but he kept up the pressure and he felt his hand start to slide loose. He pulled harder, sucking his lower lip between his teeth, biting down on it till he tasted blood. His effort paid off. His hand slid through.

He jerked the free hand to his mouth, ripped off the tape and spit blood. He took a deep breath, spit more blood. He untied his other hand. He untied his feet. Then he tried to untie the noose that held his neck back against the hot and cold water faucets and couldn't.

He struggled with his hands behind his head, against the knot, but it wouldn't give. Either it was too tight or it was the kind of knot that couldn't be untied, like the kind he used to get in his shoelaces. When he got that kind of knot the only way to undo it was with a scissors.

He needed a rest.

He looked at the clock.

It was 10:15.

CHAPTER
TWENTY-FIVE

RICK GORDON TURNED the Montero off Mountain Sea and onto the pier, ignoring the *No Vehicles on the Pier* sign.

He hit the horn and kept it blaring for the length of the pier, scattering tourists and locals from his path. When he got to the boat, Captain Stewart and Judy Donovan were waiting. He jumped out of the car, causing the waiting couple to jump back at his bloody appearance.

"My God," Judy gasped, "what happened to you?"

"I've been shot."

"We need to get you to a doctor!"

"Later. First we have to dump some human garbage out at sea."

"No. We have to get you to a doctor!" Wolfe Stewart echoed Judy.

"We have a much more important thing to take care of." Rick went to the back of the Montero, opened the rear door.

"Is he alive?" Wolfe asked.

"Not for long, we're going to dump him at sea and leave him for the sharks."

"No, we're not!" Wolfe Stewart said. "We're not taking the law into our hands. We'll call the sheriff,"

"He killed J.P."

"Load him on the boat," Wolfe Stewart said.

"I was afraid of that." Judy turned ashen, her voice cracking.

"I'm sorry. I tried, but I was too late."

Wolfe started for the unconscious man when Judy said, holding back her tears, "I know that man."

Rick Gordon and Wolfe Stewart stopped.

"He took me to dinner."

"He won't be taking anyone else to dinner," Rick said. Then to Wolfe Stewart, "Let's get him on the boat."

Wolfe took Storm under the arms, Rick grabbed the legs and they hauled him out of the back of the car and up onto the deck.

Wolfe went up to the bridge and started the engines. Judy released the lines and Rick went to the galley and gulped water from the faucet.

Judy hopped on board as the boat started to pull away from the pier and stood over the unconscious Sam Storm, eyeing the man, more out of curiosity than anger.

"I would have expected tears," Rick said, coming up from behind.

"She will have time to cry later, after we dispose of Mr. Storm," Judy said.

"She?" Rick leaned against the rail for support.

"Haven't you wondered about all this? Haven't you asked yourself, why? Why you?"

"Yes."

"And?"

"And I think this is the galka that Ann was afraid of. I think he can't be killed, or is damn hard to kill."

"Go on," she said.

"I think that when he dies, he moves into another body, someone close by."

"That's why you want to dump him at sea? Alive?"

"Yes."

"So he'll be alone in death?"

"Yes."

"How far away do we have to be when he goes?"

"I don't know."

"What if we're not far enough?"

"I don't know."

"What if we're not far enough and he tries to take over you?"

"I don't think he can."

"Or me?"

"I don't know."

"He can't take me."

"Why not?"

She moved in close and kissed him on the lips, then she ran her tongue along the scar under his ear. "This is why not. It's you and me Flash, just like it always was."

"Ann?"

"I'm here, Flash."

"What are you talking about?"

"I'm here, inside, with Judy. That's why I came to you instead of waiting for J.P. You were in trouble and we thought, in error, that J.P. wasn't."

"This can't be happening."

"We are Marangit, you and I. We are the sum of everything and everyone that made up those old Aborigines. I am the sum of all the old woman's lives plus Judy's, or put another way, she is the sum of all the old woman's lives plus mine. Either way, I'm here."

"I don't believe it."

"Believe it, Flash." She kissed him again as only Ann had been able to kiss him and once again she ran her tongue over the scar. "Believe it."

"Why don't I feel any different?"

"Usually it takes a while before one realizes he is Marangit. Sometimes one never knows, but usually when the Marangit are called upon to fight the Galka, one knows, or is made to know. When that happens, the strongest personality, or the most capable, takes over the living body."

"And you have taken over Judy?"

"Not exactly. We've decided to share, to merge ourselves. My memories are Judy's and Judy's are mine. I'm not Ann and I'm not Judy."

"You kiss like Ann. You know about the scar, and only Ann would know that. You called me Flash, and only Ann did that. But I'm finding this hard to buy into."

"You bought into the galka concept. You're taking a barely alive man out to sea to die far away from any potential victim."

"I'm not sure I believe in God, but if I was going down for the third time, I'd pray."

"You're doing this, just in case?"

"No, I guess not. He's evil. He is what you were afraid of. He is the Ragged Man."

"And me?"

"You're Judianne."

"A nice name for us, because now we are one." She paused for a second, then said, "Say it."

"Judianne."

"Say it, and kiss me."

"Judianne." He took her in his arms and kissed her.

She broke the embrace and said. "We still have a problem."

"We have lots of problems."

"No, we have an immediate problem. The galka can't take you and it can't take me, but what about Wolfe?"

"Did I hear my name?" the bearded sea captain said, walking toward them, holding a well-worn flannel shirt.

"We were just wondering," Judianne said, "if you'll get into any trouble for helping us."

"I'll take my chances." Then he added, "And I think right now it would be a good idea, Judy, if you took Mr. Gordon into the galley and cleaned him up some. Then he can get into this," he offered the shirt. "It might be cool, but you can burn just as well on a cool day at sea as you can a hot one."

Judianne took Rick by the arm and said, "Lean on me. The captain's right, you need to clean up, and that shoulder needs looking at." She started to lead him away.

They heard a grunt of surprise as they moved away from the captain. They turned to see Sam Storm grab Wolfe Stewart from behind the left knee and jerk him to the ground. With rattlesnake speed he grabbed Stewart's Bowie knife from its scabbard and slit his throat, all the while staring at them with death defying eyes. He put the knife to his mouth and licked off the captain's still-dripping blood.

"I heard what you said." Blood dripped from his chin as Rick and Judianne stood spellbound. "I enjoyed the killing. It's like I have a bad side. It wanted me to kill, but

I picked the victims."

"You didn't try to fight it?" Rick asked.

"I didn't want to. I'd been beaten down all my life, a nobody man in a nobody job. I had a chance to shine when the RIAA hired me to track you and your bootlegger pals down, but I couldn't even do that. Then, all of sudden, in that bait store, when you killed that man with the bottle of wine, I was somebody. I was supreme, above anyone, above the law, above fear, till I tried to fuck her." He pointed at Judianne with knife. "Then I knew I was in for a fight, but I won't die easy and I'll win in the end."

"Bootlegs? You did all this because of the records?" Rick couldn't believe what he'd just heard. "That doesn't make any sense."

"And what about any of this does?" He looked at the knife, turned it, as if he were fascinated with it. "And one more thing," he said, "the boy is alive. He's in your upstairs bathroom, tied with a noose around his neck, sharing a tub full of water with a radio on a timer set to go off at noon. Pretty quick the boy fries." He brought the sharp edge of the blade to his lips again and licked off the remaining blood.

Judianne reacted with a combination of Ann's determination and Judy's youth. She screamed and charged the wounded man, kicking him in the face, driving the blade of the Bowie knife through his mouth to the back of his head. Then she whirled, building momentum, and slammed her foot into his blood gushing mouth with full force, splattering blood and brains on the deck.

She looked down at what she had wrought and said, "He was wrong, he died easy."

* * *

After he caught his breath and allowed his thumping heart to cool down, J.P. wanted a drink. He looked at the blood tinged water and the thought of drinking that made him gag. He reached his right hand behind his back, stretched and managed to turn on the cold water. He set the tap at a dribble. Then he cupped his hand, grabbing a lap of water and brought it to his lips. Repeating the gesture several times he was able to satisfy his thirst.

When his parched throat no longer screamed, he looked at the clock and frowned, 11:15. He had forty-five minutes left.

He wanted out of the tub. He wanted clothes. He wanted his mother. And he knew that help was probably not coming. He was on his own.

His hands were free, so things that were out of reach, when they were tied up, might now be within grasp. With a renewed eye, he studied the bathroom. The bathroom sink, next to the tub was off limits. Too high. But the drawers below were not. He stretched against the noose, reached for a drawer. He was able to ease a it open and using his hand like an eel, he snaked it into the drawer and felt around.

A few small bottles, emery boards, a larger bottle, then pay dirt, a pair of nail clippers. He could snip away at the rope and get free. He latched onto the clippers and pulled his hand out, banging it on the top of the drawer, dropping the clippers on the wet floor, where they bounced and slid out of reach.

"It's not fair," he said, but he wouldn't give up.

He sat in the tub with the noose pulling at his neck and thought, and he realized there was something nagging at him, like in school when the teacher calls on you and you know you know the answer, but can't remember it. It's on the tip of your tongue, but your tongue is frozen.

There was a way, he was sure. He just had to reason it out.

* * *

Without talking, they dragged Storm's body to the rail, Judianne at the shoulders, Rick at the feet. They lifted the lifeless form and hoisted him over the side. Then Judianne made a quick trip to the galley and returned with a painter's tarp that covered the grill when it wasn't in use and draped it over Wolfe Stewart's body.

"Can you drive this thing?" she asked.

"How hard can it be?" he answered.

She helped him up to the bridge.

"Where are we and where is back?" She looked around, seeing only fog, mist and blue ocean.

"We're on a heading of two-seventy," he said, looking at the compass, "so in theory, if we swing the boat around to a heading of ninety degrees, we'll wind up back where we started."

"You're sure?"

"No. In an airplane you'd have to take wind direction into account, so I would assume in a boat you would have the same problem with the current."

"So what do we do?"

"Turn to a course of ninety degrees and pray." He swung the wheel around, shoving the throttle full forward.

"I'm going down to get some hot water. I'll be right back." She left the bridge, returning a few minutes later with a pan from the galley, a wet rag and the ship's first aid kit. Then she washed and bandaged his wounds. When she was finished she handed him Wolfe Stewart's flannel shirt and he put it on.

"Does the shoulder hurt much?" she asked.

"I'm trying not to think about it."

"I'm sorry."

"Don't be, it's not your fault.

"It's 11:30, we only have a half hour left."

"We'll make it?" he said.

"What if we don't?"

"We will."

"How do you stop it?"

"What?"

"The boat. When we get there, how do we stop it?"

"I suppose we slow down and throw it into reverse just before we dock, then shove it into neutral."

"Oh," then she said. "Is that what you're going to do?"

"I don't know."

They spent the next five minutes silently on the bridge, with their eyes reaching out ahead, then Judianne said, "I see it," and Rick saw it too, land dead ahead.

"We're about half a mile south of the pier," she said.

He continued on a straight course.

"You have to make a left if you want the pier."

"I don't want the pier."

"Why not."

"There's no time. If I have to slow down and try and park this damn thing, we'll never make it."

"So what are you going to do?"

"Run it onto the beach." He pulled the throttle back to a quarter. "When we get as close to the beach as we dare, I'll make a hard right and you can dive off and swim to shore. Then flag a car and save J.P."

"What about you?"

"I'll beach the boat and follow you up."

"I don't want to leave you."

"I'll slow you down, right now the important thing is to save J.P."

"You're right."

"You better get on deck."

"I love you," she said, leaving the bridge.

"I love you, too."

* * *

She climbed down the ladder, stood on the starboard side, waiting and watching as the beach closed out of the fog, and when it looked like the beach was impossibly close, Rick slid the boat into a left turn. She took her shoes off and dove into the surf, swimming for shore with long easy strokes. As Ann, she had been a mediocre swimmer, but as Judy, she was world class and in excellent shape.

She caught a six foot wave as she closed on the beach and body surfed into three feet of water, where she stood and sloshed her way to the sand. Then, without looking back, she broke into a dead run for the road, waving and screaming at a black Toyota that sped up as she approached, its driver ignoring her.

In frustration she turned and watched as Rick took the *Seawolf* into a wide circle under full power. When he had completed the first half of the circumference he straightened it out and headed for the beach.

The *Seawolf* ended its last voyage with a loud scraping crash as she scratched along the bottom, but Judianne couldn't wait and see what happened to Rick, because a green Porsche was coming down the road.

This one wasn't going to ignore her. She staggered like she was hurt and fell on the road. The Porsche stopped and a leggy, young blond in a low cut sailor shirt and skimpy white shorts, scrambled out of the car.

When she heard the car stop and the door open

Judianne jumped up, saying, "Sorry, but I need the car."

"What," the blonde said, startled.

"Life and death—Sorry." Judianne pushed the girl aside, jumped behind the wheel and sped away.

* * *

Rick braced himself, but when the boat hit ground, he was thrown against the wheel and knocked onto his back. Painfully, he got up and when he was sure the boat was beached, he climbed down from the bridge. He stumbled along the deck and thought he saw someone approaching as he leaned over the side and dropped into the water. He hoped he could touch, because he was too worn out to fight the waves.

He slid into the sea, holding his breath and his heart cried in dismay when his feet didn't hit bottom. He opened his eyes and saw only black. He held his breath and pushed toward the surface. Flapping his arms, he grabbed a great gulp of air, flopped onto his back, trying to do the back stroke, but only one arm wanted to obey and he went under again.

He came up, gasping for air, fighting a wave.

"Don't panic, I've got you." It was the voice of an angel.

He tried hard not to panic.

"Relax, let me do the work and everything will be all right." Not an angel, a living, breathing human being. A woman.

He lay back and obeyed as she circled his chest with a strong arm, then kicked with her long legs, pulling him safely and surely toward shore.

Rick leaned on her as she helped him out of the water and, once they were safely on the sand, he told her, through panting breath, that he needed to get up the hill, could she flag down a car, "It's a matter of life and death."

"I've heard that before," she said as she went up to the road to stop a passing car.

* * *

Judianne slammed on the brakes and jumped out of the car. She fumbled with her keys on the front porch, opened the door and dashed up the stairs. Out of breath, she flung the bathroom door open and sank to her knees in anger and frustration. The bathroom was empty.

She looked at her watch. 11:59. Dammit, she'd made it on time. He should be here. The man said he would be here. She stared at her watch and watched as the digital seconds ticked away to 12:00 and she cried.

At 12:05 she heard a car drive up and she went outside and met Rick and the woman whose car she'd hijacked. She saw a green van drive away, its driver apparently wanting nothing more to do with a situation he was beyond understanding.

"Your keys are in the car," she said to the woman.

"You said it was a matter of life and death," the young woman said, "did it end up life?"

"No."

"I'm sorry." She slid behind the wheel of the Porsche and slowly drove down the hill.

"Is he dead?" Rick asked.

"He wasn't there. He was never there."

"Maybe he meant my bathroom."

Judianne ran across the clearing to the other house with Rick on her heels. They flew through the kitchen, dining and living rooms and up the steps to the second floor. She pushed the door open and saw J.P., tied by the neck to the water faucet, naked, with his hands covering his private parts and a sheepish grin on his face.

"It was easy," he said, "once I figured it out. I pulled the plug."

"I'll get a knife, honey." Judianne dashed from the bathroom to the kitchen below.

She was back in an instant, handing Rick the knife and Rick sliced through the noose that bound J.P. to the tub, and then he handed him a large bath towel, which the boy wrapped around himself.

"Where's the Ragged Man?" J.P. asked.

"Dead."

"Did you kill him?"

"I hurt him, but your mother finished him off."

"He killed my birds."

"I know."

"Did he kill 'em all?"

"Yeah."

"Dancer, too?"

"I'm afraid so."

"He was a bad man. He killed my dad."

"He killed a lot of people."

Judianne couldn't take it anymore. She held her arms out for a hug, but before he could fall into her embrace, she heard the meow of a small kitten from behind.

* * *

"Oh, look!" J.P. darted past his mother. For a second he could have sworn the kitten's dark eyes flashed red, but he paid it no mind as he scooped it up and snuggled it to his face.

He turned and smiled at Rick and Judianne and asked, "Can I keep him?"

THE BOOTLEG PRESS CATALOG

RAGGED MAN, by Jack Priest
ISBN: 0974524603
Unknown to Rick Gordon, he brought an ancient aboriginal horror home from the Australian desert. Now his friends are dying and Rick is getting the blame.

DESPERATION MOON, by Ken Douglas
ISBN: 0974524611
Sara Hackett must save two little girls from dangerous kidnappers, but she doesn't have the money to pay the ransom.

SCORPION, by Jack Stewart
ISBN: 097452462X
DEA agent Bill Broxton must protect the Prime Minister of Trinidad from an assassin, but he doesn't know the killer is his fiancée.

DEAD RINGER, by Ken Douglas
ISBN: 0974524638
Maggie Nesbitt steps out of her dull life and into her dead twin's, and now the man that killed her sister is after Maggie.

GECKO, by Jack Priest
ISBN: 0974524646
Jim Monday must rescue his wife from an evil worse than death before the Gecko horror of Maori legend kills them both.

RUNNING SCARED, by Ken Douglas
ISBN: 0974524654
Joey Sapphire's husband blackmailed and now is out to kill the president's daughter and only Joey can save the young woman.

NIGHT WITCH, by Jack Priest

ISBN: 0974524662

A vampire like creature followed Carolina's father back from the Caribbean and now it is terrorizing her. She and her friend Arty are only children, but they must fight this creature themselves or die.

HURRICANE, by Jack Stewart

ISBN: 0974524670

Julie Tanaka flees Trinidad on her sailboat after the death of her husband, but the boat has a drug lord's money aboard and DEA agent Bill Broxton must get to her first or she is dead.

TANGERINE DREAM, by Ken Douglas and Jack Stewart

ISBN: 0974524689

Seagoing writer and gourmet chef Captain Katie Osborne said of this book, "Incest, death, tragedy, betrayal and teenage homosexual love, I don't know how, but somehow it all works. I was up all night reading."

DIAMOND SKY, by Ken Douglas and Jack Stewart

ISBN: 0974524697

The Russian Mafia is after Beth Shannon. Their diamonds have been stolen and they think she knows where they are. She does, only she doesn't know it.

TAHITIAN AFFAIR: A ROMANCE, by Dee Lighton

ISBN: 0976277905

In Tahiti on vacation Angie meets Luke, a single-handed sailor, who is trying to forget Suzi, the love of his life. He is the perfect man, dashing, good looking, caring and kind. She is in love and it looks like her story will have a fairytale ending. Then Suzi shows up and she wants her man back.

BOOKS ARE BETTER THAN T.V.

THE BOOTLEG PRESS STORY

We at Bootleg Press are a small group of writers who were brought together by pen and sea. We have all been members of either the St. Martin or Trinidad Cruising Writer's Groups in the Caribbean.

We share our thoughts, plot ideas, villains and heroes. That's why you'll see some borrowed characters, both minor and major, cross from one author's book to another's.

Also, you'll see a few similar scenes that seem to jump from one author's pages to another's. That's because both authors have collaborated on the scene and—both liking how it worked out—both decided to use it.

At what point does an author's idea truly become his own? That's a good question, but rest assured in the rare occasions where you may discover similar scenes in Bootleg Press Books, that it is not stealing. Writing is a solitary art, but sometimes it is possible to share the load.

Book writing is hard, but book selling is harder. We think our books are as good as any you'll find out there, but breaking into the New York publishing market is tough, especially if you live far away from the Big Apple.

So, we've all either sold or put our boats on the hard, pooled our money and started our own company. We bought cars and loaded our trunks with books. We call on small independent bookstores ourselves, as we are our own distributors. But the few of us cannot possibly reach the whole world, however we are trying, so if you don't see our books in your local bookstore yet, remember you can always order them from the big guys online.

Thank you from everyone at Bootleg Books for reading and please remember, Books are better than T.V.

JACK PRIEST
TORTOLA, 2000